# THE CALLER

'Why?' Julia whispered. 'What are you doing this for? I never saw you before in my life . . .'

'Sitting in that car,' he said, 'waiting for him. I knew then, he'd always take you from me.'

*He's crazy*, Julia thought, *absolutely crazy. But Fox will get me out of this; Fox won't let him hurt me.* She felt a great numbing unreality, a conviction that this was not really happening – to her.

'I'd sure like to stop and play with you right now,' he said with regret, 'but we'd better push on. But there'll be plenty of time. I'm going to play with you real good. Not like you played with me . . .'

MARY-ROSE HAYES

# The Caller

FONTANA/Collins

First published in the United States in 1979 by
Pinnacle Books Inc.
First published in Great Britain by Fontana Books 1979

© 1979 by Mary-Rose Hayes

Made and printed in Great Britain by
William Collins Sons & Co Ltd, Glasgow

For Juliette

## JOE

Joe Capelli followed the woman into King Henry's Tavern at 10.30 p.m., after the movie let out. He had watched her go into the movie at 8.45, then had gone for a couple of drinks and a steak sandwich, arriving in plenty of time before it ended.

Of course, he could have followed her into the theatre; sat near her – but there was always the risk that she would notice him. Women going to movies alone in the evening were sensitive. *No*, thought Joe, *play it safe. Wait for her outside. See where she goes* . . .

So he watched her walk through the brightly lit foyer, thick gold-brown hair swinging with the lustrous heaviness he remembered so well. Had she enjoyed the movie? It was impossible to tell. Her face was an empty mask.

He moved silently into step behind her, allowing half a block between them, cursing the numerous slow moving pedestrians – it was a soft, warm night and the whole city appeared to be out there on Union Street, wandering meaninglessly between bars, peering into the brightly lit boutiques, clotting the sidewalk in mirthful, inane groups. He quickened his pace, afraid to lose her, and a swirl of youthful figures erupted from a discotheque, surrounding him momentarily, a dense, fleshy, moving fence which blocked his view of her totally.

Joe cursed and shouldered his way through them.

But it was too late. She was gone.

For an instant he stood quite still, hollow inside with anger and frustration. But then noticed King Henry's Tavern right there beside him, warm light glowing invitingly through mullioned windows, moving shadows inside, a buzz of laughter and talk reaching out to him. *She would have gone in there for a drink before going home. What could be more natural? And there was nowhere else*, Joe told himself sensibly, *where she could have gone.*

Inside it was somewhat dark, and hard to see. Vaguely aware of a heavily Tudor motif, of oak panelling, pewter beer mugs hanging from hooks above the bar, dark portraits of sinister-looking, bearded men, all wearing neck ruffs, Joe moved purposefully through the crowd towards the bar, behind which hung a huge reproduction of Holbein's Henry VIII.

Joe knew he was looking good. He had dressed carefully for her. He wore his new suede jacket, the leather as soft as a second skin, and narrow-cut pants of natural-coloured sailcloth, belted over his narrow hips with a wide leather belt and chased gold buckle. He moved between the crowded tables and chairs with grace, knowing the women were watching him, assessing him as one of the best looking men in the room. But the knowledge meant nothing to him.

He was only interested in one woman.

Lisa . . .

She had to be here. Had she gone to the ladies' room? Possibly. Joe peered through a doorway, down a short reddish-lit passage, at the end of which he could see a cigarette machine, a public telephone, and a dimly lit sign saying RESTROOMS. He considered checking it out back there; pretending to make a phone call; buying a pack of cigarettes which he would not smoke. But although it was only a Wednesday night, the crowds were too thick. He might still miss her; here, at least, he commanded a strategic view of the door and if she left he would notice.

He ordered a Scotch and water. There was a girl on his right who was not at all bad if he were somebody else; she had short blonde curling hair and a big nose, but her body was terrific. She wore burstingly tight white jeans, and a bright pink T-shirt with some kind of inscription undulating across her lavish breasts.

She turned to him and said, 'Hi. My name's Lou.'

Joe answered absently, 'How you doing?'

'Better now,' Lou said archly. 'Tell me yours.'

'Mine? My what?'

'You turkey – your name. What else?'

'Joe,' he replied, watching the room, the door, the approaches from the ladies' room.

'Ah,' said Lou, drinking, watching him over the top of her glass, wondering whether he would buy her the next one. 'Never seen you in here before, did I?'

'I guess not. I don't come here much.'

'And tonight's the night! How's that for timing; wow! Live around here?'

'No.' *She had to be finished in the john by now, for Christ's sake. What the hell was keeping her? Had she guessed he was following her, and left by a back entrance? Was there a back entrance?* He felt suddenly nauseated, tightness clutching at his stomach, prickling down his spine. *Let her not have left. Please, God...*

Lou was telling him all about herself, with determination. She came from San Pedro – 'My Dad's a yacht broker' – but now lived up here, in San Francisco, where she shared a Victorian cottage with three other people, two male, one female. 'It's really neat – we all take care of each other; it's just never lonely or boring –' *So what are you doing in here then, alone,* wondered Joe vaguely, hearing Lou's rather nasal, high-pitched voice as though through a bad connection on a long-distance wire. *Did Lisa have a room-mate? Was she living with some man? What did she call herself these days?* For Lisa led many different lives . . .

'. . . like most, there's no pollution,' Lou said loudly in his left ear. 'Like, I'm really into conservation, you know? Neat, up here. Of course, I . . .'

And there she was.

Suddenly materialized, right in front of him, as though plucked from mid air by a magician.

'Lisa,' Joe said tightly, but she did not even turn.

She was looking for a seat; she did not want to join a group of strangers at a table. There were no empty stools; no place for her to sit.

Joe said, 'Here, take mine.'

Lisa looked at him, and a flicker of something – recognition? – crossed her eyes, then was gone. She had always been so cool. 'No. That's all right. Thanks. No, please don't get up.'

'I've been sitting all day,' Joe said. 'No problem.'

'So have I.'

'Hey, take it, for God's sake.'

'All right then,' Lisa said blandly. 'Thanks. I won't fight you over it.' Acting now like she had never seen him before in her life. Contained. Cracking just a small smile. Taking him for granted. Poised. Such a lady. But Joe knew better.

Lou said plaintively. 'You should've told me – said you were meeting someone.'

Joe did not hear her. He never even turned his head.

Lou sighed and pouted at the wasted effort, and the man on her left with the thinning blond hair who had been trying to catch her attention for the past hour, said, 'I got a hot tub back home. You ever tried a hot tub?'

'Who hasn't,' Lou said wearily, but then smiled at him. *No sense spending the evening here for nothing . . .* and her glass was still empty.

Lisa said, 'Bartender.' Her voice was low and carrying; it implied an expectation of instant service. Joe noticed without surprise that the bartender came to her at once. She ordered a glass of white wine, drank it down, looking around the crowded room – paying no attention to Joe at all.

He said, 'Let me get you another.'

She looked at him coolly, and smiled slightly, very very slightly, the corners of her mouth lifting a fraction. 'Thanks anyway,' she said, 'but I guess I'll just settle for a stool.'

'I'm Joe,' he said. *Don't you remember?*

Her second drink came. 'I'm Julia.'

*Julia. So she was calling herself Julia now.* He repeated it silently, deciding he quite liked it. The time before, she'd been Janice. Before that some crazy cutesy little diminutive – Itsy Bitsy Betsy. Before that, Gloria. Now, Julia. Not bad. And she'd gone to a lot of trouble, too, being Julia. He could see inside her purse as she removed her wallet to pay for her wine. There was a cheque-book in there, with her name – Julia Naughton – engraved in the corner in gold. So much trouble. He sighed. When would she learn that all this running was useless? That despite the different identities – the names, faces, cities and backgrounds – he would always find her in the end.

But thinking like that did not help him now. Joe could find nothing to say. Now that he was beside her again, not much more than a foot away from her, he found himself as tongue-tied and sticky-palmed as a sixteen year old. As though he had never seen her before in his life and was starting over. Finally he said:

'The wine OK?'

She shrugged. 'Not too bad. For house wine.'

'You know a lot about wine?'

'Not really. I just know what I like. Like people say about art.'

'That's fair enough; that's what it's supposed to be about, after all,' Joe said, desperate to prolong the conversation.

There was a silence.

Then: 'One of the good things about California,' Julia said, sounding as though she found these to be few and far between, 'is the wine.'

As though she had never been in California before.

Joe asked carefully, 'Have you been in San Francisco long?'

'A couple of months.'

'Where before that?'

'Back east.'

'Is that so? Where back east?'

'New York City.'

Last time, Portland, Oregon. The time before, somewhere tiny in the San Joaquin Valley – 'like Nowheresville. You'd never have heard of it.' The time before, from Fresno. Now she was from New York City. Sophisticated. Cool. Big city girl.

He needed to orient himself with this new Lisa. Find out what she did this time, how she lived . . . She shifted uncomfortably and resentfully on her stool – he was staring at her face fixedly – but still she did not appear to recognize him. This time, it seemed, she was in Public Relations, or had been in New York. 'But there's nothing here,' she sighed. 'Just nothing. I've been looking for a job – anything, really – for two months. There just aren't any jobs. I can't afford to stay much longer, the way things are going.'

'Will you go back?'

'No.' It was said firmly, with obvious discouragement for further questions. Then: 'Do you usually stare at people like that?'

Joe blinked. She was looking impatient. 'I'm sorry; I guess I . . . I thought you . . . I mean, you look just like . . .'

'Oh come on.' She laughed. Not kindly. 'You can do better, surely.'

*The bitch,*

'But you do,' Joe said. *Calm. Cool. As cool as Lisa herself.*

She looked at him dismissively, and drained her glass. She put some change on the counter. She was preparing to leave.

Joe said: 'Don't go.'

She stood up. He made a motion to stop her; she backed away from him. 'Oh but I must,' she said calmly. 'Tomorrow is a long day's work looking for work.'

'One more drink. Let me buy you a drink. One drink.'

Lisa never walked out on him. Not any more.

'Thanks,' she said, 'but not tonight. Thanks anyway.' And she was gone. Unbelievably, she was gone, hidden behind a momentary swell of bodies, out through the door while he stood staring after her like a dummy, absently touching her empty, still-warm bar stool.

Joe cursed himself for his slowness, and then suddenly re-activated as though someone had pulled a switch, he moved quickly after her, pushing his way through the thick crowd, oblivious of the crescendo of anger in his wake.

'Hey, what's the big hurry . . .'

'Listen man, watch it . . .'

'For God's sake, will you look at that? All over my new . . .'

She was walking quickly, a block down the street already, hair flying.

Going home alone.

After everything, after all this time, looking at him as though he were a stranger.

Joe stood there on the sidewalk outside the bar, pounding one fist softly against the palm of his other hand. It would be useless chasing after her; with this new, changed, aloof Lisa it would be both pointless and humiliating.

*No,* Joe told himself, eyes withdrawn and blank, *give her time. Wait for her.*

He reminded himself again that there was no panic, after all.

He knew where she lived . . .

## PART ONE

# FOX

He leaned his chin in his hands and waited with brooding trepidation for the model to take her bathrobe off. Last week there had been an attenuated ballerina, all eyes and long silky limbs. She had been physical perfection. 'And who needs *that*?' Fox had demanded, irritated. But this one, to-day, was quite different, with a chunky peasant body, round face and crinkled beige hair tied at each side of her head in a bulky braid. Fox sighed with relief and pleased antici-pation. She would be good to draw.

He rummaged quickly through his satchel; arranged his things on the table in front of him. A large sketch book of newsprint – cheap paper on which to capture the model's warm-up one-minute poses, after which he would switch to his pad of better paper for the longer poses, some of which he might think were good enough to go into his portfolio, to be worked up later. But then – perhaps he would work with brown and white crayon on the butcher paper today – there was wonderful texture in those Rubensian hips and treetrunk thighs.

Ms Mendoza said, 'Good morning, Fox,' and angled him a nervous smile. Ms Mendoza was the instructor. Fox al-ways upset her by being a much better artist than she was, although personally she did not care for his style. Ms Men-doza was 45. She had frizzy grey hair which she lashed tightly behind her head in a tortured-looking bun, a thin olive face where heavy black brows met on the bridge of her nose in accordion pleats of worry, and where the small mouth was always pursed – 'like a hen's behind,' Mrs Pospicil, Fox's table partner, had once said so rudely.

*Surprisingly, or perhaps not so surprisingly, really*, Fox thought, *Mendoza's drawings and paintings were wildly un-disciplined.* Now she was saying, 'Please Fox, today, be more free. Open up more. Let it flow.' Ms Mendoza whirled her arms in a curious windmill gesture. '*Release*, Fox. Free up your work. Draw huge!' Thinking wearily how she was wasting her breath; how he never listened to her. Never.

Fox raised his head, narrowed his terra-cotta-coloured eyes and gave her a brilliant smile. He had beautiful teeth. And Ms Mendoza ducked her head at once. It was very hard for her to look him in the eye; she found his overt young masculinity embarrassing in her class, where all the other men were comfortably ancient. She never gave up, though, forcing herself to try with Fox, always, even though he had said gently during his first morning, 'Don't worry about me. I'm really just here for the models.'

'I know what I'm doing,' he had finally complained as she leaned yet again over his shoulder, insisting, 'Larger, larger yet, Fox. *Do* loosen up.' He knew she would never quite forgive him for that.

But he turned away and at once forgot her, for the model flexed hefty shoulder muscles and leaned over with her hands caught between her knees, presenting a curve of spine with beautiful ridges, bulges and shadows, massive buttocks.

Fox sighed with pleasure. He began to draw.

The next ten minutes passed in tense, concentrated silence while the model changed poses every minute and a roomful of amateur artists chased pencil over paper in desperation. Ms Mendoza passed between the bent-over figures, solicitous, murmuring things like, 'Don't try for detail,' and 'Aim for the flow.'

At the end of ten minutes there was an audible sigh of relief and relaxation as the model took a short break before starting the longer poses. There was a hum of chatter; people started to move towards the coffee pot in the corner. Mrs Pospicil, to Fox's left, reached into the paper sack at her feet and dragged out a bag of doughnuts. 'Fresh from the bakery, Foxy. See, still warm.'

'You bet,' Fox said. 'Thanks a bunch.'

Mrs Pospicil – 'that's pronounced Poss-pee-shull' – was small and wiry, had hair like steel wool, with a thick accent from some eastern European country which had long ago ceased to exist. Mrs Pospicil was probably in her middle sixties, the median age of most of the students in the class – Figure Drawing II, Wednesday a.m., 9-12, Mendoza. She always arrived with a paper sack crammed with food and sat munching and gossiping throughout the morning. 'So what else does an old woman get to do with her time; you tell me.' Or, 'Foxy, you're one damn good artist. Better believe it.'

It was an adult education class run by the City of San Francisco. Adult, thought Fox, most certainly, for most of the students were senior citizens, like Mrs Pospicil, and like Mr Brucker and Mr Bottarini, both over eighty, who sat together in silence to one side of the room working on the same still life which had held them engrossed for the past three weeks – a blue bottle into which were thrust a few plastic flowers, with three wax apples artfully arranged about its base. At first Ms Mendoza had worried about them, had whispered to Mrs Pospicil, 'They come to stare at the girls. Don't you think? They come to stare at the girls.'

But although Brucker and Bottarini, a laconic and distant duo, would indeed gaze absently at the models from time to time, their interest was obviously fixed obsessively in their bottle, fruit, and flowers. They would have to dismantle it each time and set it up again the following Wednesday; there would be much impassioned argument while they checked back over the past week's work, like the continuity department on a movie set checking yesterday's rushes, and it would take them on average 30 minutes to achieve perfection. Now, 'More to the right,' Giuseppe Bottarini snarled. He was tall and angular, with the heavy pouched eyes of a bloodhound. 'To the right, I'm telling you, you old fool.' And inevitably, 'Who are you calling an old fool?' Karl Brucker was short, fat, and quite bald. 'You're older than I am, for Chrissakes,' he snapped. 'Put your goddamn glasses on; your eyes are going.'

'To the right,' rumbled Bottarini ominously. And again – 'Old fool.'

There were three or four middle-aged women with sons and daughters grown and gone, using their time constructively; but today, Fox noticed with interest, there was somebody new – young and good looking too, quite a change. She sat across the cluttered semicircle of drawing boards, a tall, slender girl with thick dark blonde hair. She chewed the end of her pencil and frowned hideously at her drawings. As he headed for the coffee pot Fox looked over her shoulder. They were not very good.

Her name was Julia. The first words she said to Fox were: 'Do we have to drink out of those? Aren't there any paper cups?'

'People bring their own mugs,' Fox said. 'I guess they don't wash them out too well afterwards.'

'I guess not,' said Julia.

'Here,' said Fox generously, 'use mine. I can always use Mrs Pospicil's Thermos top.'

Julia said: 'Are you sure? I mean, if I don't have some coffee right now I'll just die.'

'Sure, no problem.' Fox spooned instant coffee into the mug, and held it under the coffee pot where the water was kept at a boil. 'There you go; help yourself to cream and sugar. People put a dime into the saucer usually . . . to go towards buying stuff.' He returned to his seat.

Mrs Pospicil gave him a cup of her own personal coffee, which was thick, black, and well spiked with slivovitz. She leered at him. 'Pretty, hey?'

'Sure,' said Fox. 'Hell of an improvement.'

The old woman nodded, small black eyes beady with interest. 'Healthy young guy like you, needs a nice girl.'

'Sure,' said Fox. 'Don't we all.'

'That'll fix all your problems.'

'Who says I've got problems?'

'Got no devil in your eye. Mr Pospicil used to say, "Your girl takes care of you good, then the devil looks out of your eye." '

'No kidding,' said Fox.

'So there you are,' Mrs Pospicil said triumphantly. 'No devil.'

'Oh, I get along.'

Mrs Pospicil shot him a crafty look from eyes like polished jets. 'Don't fool around with boys, do you?'

'Only on birthdays and holidays.'

Mrs Pospicil gave a witchlike cackle and punched him in the upper arm. 'Hah! Foxy, you're wicked.'

'And you're a dirty-minded old woman.'

Fox sighed and went back to work.

# JULÍA

Julia packed her things away slowly. 'Bring newsprint next time,' Ms Mendoza said. 'It'll save you money. You don't want to waste good paper on . . . uh . . . you don't want to waste good paper.'

Julia smiled wryly. She said, 'Yes, thanks. I'll certainly do that,' thinking: *Ah well, what the hell. She doesn't need to tell me I'm a rotten artist.* But it was something to do with her Wednesday mornings . . . *And I'll meet some new people; some of them might be nice, although God knows all of them are about a thousand years old except for the kid with the coffee mug.*

The class was held in an unused army barracks beside the San Francisco Bay, where no amount of artistic endeavour, no thudding of potters' wheels or chemical stench from the silk screen printing room could entirely drive the military aura from the long gloomy corridors, iron railings, and flights of narrow concrete steps. She crossed the parking lot, wishing she had brought her car, for unless the buses ran right for her she would be late for her downtown job interview and she had to go home and change first. It had been a beautiful morning though, and not such a long walk, but Vallejo and Baker Street seemed a long way now and such an awkward journey with at least one bus transfer.

Julia began to hurry down Laguna Street, gaining on the backviews of Mr Brucker and Mr Bottarini, also headed for the bus stop, arguing furiously. Her bus, the westbound No. 30, pulled in two blocks ahead of her and she began to run knowing that hampered as she was by her awkwardly large sketch book and packages, she would never catch it, and there would not be another one at this time of day for at least another 10 or 15 minutes.

The doors opened with a breathy sigh and a mother and a small child climbed out on their way to the playground. 'Hey,' cried Julia, 'hey, wait!' dropping her sketch book which slid backwards from under her arm, cursing, stopping to pick it up, seeing the young mother turn and pound on the glass of the already closed door as the bus pulled away.

And then it was gone, leaving behind a thin blue cloud of exhaust fume.

'Oh shit,' muttered Julia, picking up her things and moving on slowly, breathing heavily, furious, barely noticing the sleek car that had pulled alongside her, creeping gently along in pace with her footsteps, until a voice said: 'Hey! Don't you *want* a ride?'

Julia turned sharply, chin raised, about to deliver a quelling look. But it was the young man in the art class, driving an old-model Jaguar – a beautiful machine, dark blue with a yellow racing stripe. *Custom paint job*, Julia thought automatically, and saw beside him, sunk deep into the bucket seat, the odd-looking old foreign lady with the wild grey hair, clutching bags, paper sacks, and sketch books in her lap.

Fox parked in the bus stop, opened the passenger door, and Mrs Pospicil swivelled in the bucket seat, planted both solidly tubular old-lady legs on the sidewalk, and heaved herself up. She looked from Fox to Julia, eyes gleaming, and said, 'Remember about the devil, Foxy.'

'Thanks,' Julia said. 'Thanks a lot. I should have left early . . . I'd never have made it on the bus.' She leaned back comfortably against the plush seat as the Jaguar roared across Lombard Street and began its steep climb into Pacific Heights – Mr Brucker, Mr Bottarini, and Mrs Pospicil left standing in a curiously posed and balanced trio, as though for a photograph, staring after them with the lively curiosity and malicious relish of the old. 'Are you sure I'm not taking you out of your way?' Julia asked anxiously.

'No problem,' said Fox, thinking about Mrs Pospicil and the devil, 'no problem at all.' *The timing was perfect; perhaps the old bat was right.* He would stop at his house and pick up his wallet, then take Julia out to lunch. After that . . .

He swung right on to Pacific Avenue, and half a block later turned right again, into a long courtyard which ran the length of a red brick, L-shaped mansion, the short arm of the L being formed by a two-storey garage block, ivy covered, at the end of the courtyard.

There was another car parked in the driveway – large, expensive, European looking. *Probably a Mercedes*, Julia thought, uncertain as the traditional three-pointed emblem was missing from the hood. Fox pulled up alongside it.

She said: 'You live here?' hoping she did not sound too surprised. If she had pictured Fox as living anywhere at all, it was certainly not in a mansion, and the Jaguar had been unexpected too.

'My mother's house,' Fox said. 'I live in the garage. Wait right there. I'll be back.' He charged in through one of the garage doors, leaving it gaping open behind him. Julia saw the rear end of a Cadillac inside, or perhaps a Lincoln. But then another man came out of a side entrance of the main house, and Julia forgot about cars. He was striking to look at – very tall, and elegantly dressed in a three-piece, light grey suit, blue shirt and navy tie with a narrow, pale blue stripe. His hair was blond, of a true, rich gold, and he wore heavy-rimmed glasses which he took off immediately when he saw her sitting in Fox's car.

He stood still a moment, looking at her pensively, then strolled across the courtyard, car keys and glasses dangling from his hand.

He said: 'It's a great day to have the top down.'

Julia smiled up at him, agreeing, thinking privately that it was far too nice a day, also, to be going for a dreary interview for a job which, even if she was lucky enough to get, she would probably dislike. She wondered who this man was. Fox's older brother? She was about to introduce herself, to say, 'I'm Julia Naughton,' and somehow (shamefully) to indicate that she was not a close friend of Fox's; that he had only been kind enough to give her a ride home. But abruptly, reminding her of a Swiss clock she had once seen where a male and female figure simultaneously emerged on the stroke of the hour from separate doorways, Fox came out of the garage tossing something in one hand, and an elderly woman appeared in the side entrance.

*And for an instant*, Julia was to remember later, *there we all stood, the four of us, quite still, staring at each other*; although at the time she was only aware of the expression on the face of the older woman – *staring at me as though . . . as though she knows me*, Julia thought, confused – *with*

*her hands going up like that . . . pushing out . . . as though
she's pushing something, or someone . . . me? . . . away.*

Then Fox said laconically, 'Hi, Elliott. You leaving?'

And the blond man, after a final quick smile to Julia,
turned abruptly, swung himself into the Mercedes, and was
gone.

With his departure, something charged left the air. Fox,
relaxed, said, 'Julia, I want you to meet Miss Doyle. She takes
care of Mother.' And Julia turned obediently to where Miss
Doyle still stood, arms fallen to her sides, face empty and
confused.

'Doyly,' Fox began. 'Hey, Doyly. What's up?'

'Julia,' said Miss Doyle. 'Of course.' And regaining a
degree of poise, 'Nice to meet you, dear.'

Fox said again: 'Doyly? Are you OK? Did something
. . .'

'Yes.' Miss Doyle exhaled sharply. 'But it's gone. I don't
know. I . . .' And to Julia's concern, her eyes filled with tears,
she hooked her fingers sharply into the long grey cardigan
she wore, and turned clumsily to run back into the house.
Julia started after her. 'Fox, she must be ill. Can't we do
something?' But he caught her by the arm, drawing her
back.

'No,' Fox said. 'Leave her. There's nothing you can do.
She likes to be left alone after she's had a message.'

'After she's had a . . . a what?'

'A message. She calls them messages. She's superstitious,
you know . . . Irish, going way, way back. They're simply
tiny little seizures. She gets them more often, now that she's
getting on.'

'Oh,' said Julia, slightly reassured by a scientific explanation. 'You mean like epilepsy?'

'I suppose,' agreed Fox.

'But a doctor . . . I mean, shouldn't she see a doctor for
it?'

But Fox just shook his head. 'No way. She hates doctors.
She tells her beads.'

Miss Doyle crouched in the downstairs bathroom, hearing
the ringing in her ears recede, feeling the roaring emptiness
inside her heave and tilt as she emptied her guts into the

toilet. A bad one, this. She felt instantly better after she had vomited, but she could still see Julia's face looking up at her through the car window.

A pretty face. Actually, a beautiful face, but not the way Miss Doyle had seen her. Not with her eyes like that, and her pretty green dress all torn, and with the blood on her hands.

Miss Doyle wiped her mouth on her handkerchief. The room looked normal now. She flushed the toilet, closed the lid, and sat on it for a moment, still shaken.

She fumbled for the rosary in the pocket of her cardigan, sought in her mind and heart to begin the comforting little ritual. 'Hail Mary . . .' Miss Doyle started, haltingly, but she could not go on.

The messages were always so much stronger . . .

# ELLIOTT

It had been three months now since Fox came back.

His return to San Francisco after five years of global wanderings in strange places had been greeted with mixed feelings. With delight by Miss Doyle, who loved him; resigned annoyance on the part of his mother and his sister, Nancy; with anticipation by hopeful mothers of the right-aged daughters, for when he was 25 Fox would inherit 10 million dollars outright.

Elliott felt dread.

During the past five years he had gradually begun to forget about Fox. He had almost managed to persuade himself that his young brother-in-law had never existed, save in nightmares. Until: 'Hey, guess what?' Nancy had said so casually that evening while she dressed to go out. 'I forgot to tell you. Foxy's back. Doyly called to tell me this afternoon. She was so thrilled she could hardly speak. Poor old thing.'

Elliott froze inside, but his hands continued to do small mundane things. Knot his tie. Choose a co-ordinated handkerchief for the pocket. Check his wallet and car keys. He said: 'Back, huh.'

'Zip me, please Ell . . . there's a dear.' Nancy drew a deep breath while Elliott fought with the zipper. 'Yes. Back. Do you know, Cousin Whitney saw him in Paris last fall. Selling dirty pictures in the cafés. That he'd *drawn*. Can you imagine? Poor Mother.'

Elliott could, but said nothing, and Nancy soon lost interest in Fox, thinking with pleased anticipation of the evening ahead of her – who would be there, what they would be wearing, what would be served for dinner.

Although the delicious hors d'oeuvres were followed by shrimp mousse, hearts of romaine salad, beef Wellington, and baked Alaska, Elliott might as well have been eating stewed rubber and ashes. He weathered the evening well, however; he had become accustomed, by now, to spending such evenings chatting about nothing at all with people he saw almost every week. He smiled, held his lighter for cigarettes, flirted dutifully with old Mrs Roach, his dinner partner, who was fat and stinking rich and always wore fuschia-coloured lipstick, and with Helena Winthrop Wendell on his other side, 45 years old, divorced again, just back from the clinic with another tuck job, who smiled at him warily with unfocused eyes from a face like a taut sheet. Yes, Elliott said of a play just arrived from London on a United States tour, Nancy and he had seen it, of course. Loved it . . . terrific production. All the while, his soul was trembling at the thought of seeing Fox again.

He did not have to wait long.

The very next day Elliott walked into his mother-in-law's boudoir for one of his three-times-a-week visits, and Fox was there. He was perched uncomfortably on a striped love seat looking as though he longed to be somewhere else. Anywhere else . . .

Elliott stood quite still in the doorway, feeling a shock as though someone had punched him heavily in the stomach.

Fox looked up at him quickly, his tawny brown, animal eyes, which Elliott had once seen flash almost scarlet, registering only relief that he no longer had to be alone with his mother.

He said: 'Hi, Ell.' *He might have been gone five days,*

thought Elliott, *and not five years.*

'Welcome back,' Elliott replied. 'Quite a surprise.'

'Thanks. It's good to be back.' Fox was standing, politely, but did not offer to shake hands. Elliott did not expect him to.

So here he was, back again.

Wesley Bishop Fox III. With the same mane of red brown hair, deep freckles, and lean mobile face. The same heavy-lidded, thickly lashed eyes with their expression of simultaneous innocence and cynicism. Never called Wesley or Bishop, except by his mother. Always Fox. But the boy's slender body Elliott remembered was now a man's body, taller and sturdier, although no doubt still housing that same nervous energy and uncanny assurance. There was no doubt, Elliott thought wanly, that Fox, now mature, was more of a threat than ever before . . .

Now, Elliott stood outside his mother-in-law's house seeing Fox, dressed in dirty corduroy pants and a paint-stained work shirt, leap from his car and rush headlong into the garage. He lived in the garage; or rather, in a small apartment above it which had first belonged to the coachman, later to the chauffeur, and, more recently, to Wong the houseboy.

There was a girl sitting in Fox's car – a strikingly beautiful girl in an outstandingly elegant car. And in Elliott's mind, the girl, the XK-140, and Fox all belonged together. They fitted perfectly in this world of money and careless elegance in which he also lived now but did not belong, and the familiar rush of jealousy made him feel physically queasy.

Life was filled with these small sour vignettes in which he envied or feared Fox.

For Fox was the only person Elliott had ever known who had seemed to understand him at once and to know, without ever being told, just what that long-ago failed misfit, Egon Milhausen, might have had to do in order to become Elliott Millner.

Nobody else knew or cared. Not his mother-in-law, not his wife, nor their circle of friends. For Elliott had admitted once to coming from the Midwest, and the Midwest, as every San Franciscan knew, was a featureless three-hour stretch between the Rockies and the Hudson River when one ate, drank, napped, or watched the in-flight movie.

But Fox knew all right.

At 17, young Fox had stared at Elliott with those odd, rust-coloured eyes, and had looked right through him to his hate-filled, striving core. And worse. Coupled with his intuitive realization of Elliott's outsider's need to be 'one of us', was a complete dismissal of the very heritage which Elliott craved so desperately, which he had been told for so long was essential for his well-being and ultimate happiness. Fox was a walking denial of the very fabric of Elliott's life. It angered him, and hurt bitterly.

*After all, what did Fox know? About anything?* Elliott cried silently.

Fox had been born Wesley Bishop Fox III in a mansion, not Egon Milhausen in a squalid little house in Milwaukee.

Fox's father had spent his days juggling multinational corporations, not driving a forklift in the loading dock of a brewery; while Fox's mother was Hope Hartley, one-time movie star, and not, like Egon's mother, a washed-out, whining, retired teacher, continually reminding his father of how far she had married beneath her.

Fox had been born into a golden world but did not need it. Elliott hated him for that.

The girl in the Jaguar was staring at him. He knew it must look odd, him just standing there like a dummy, staring back. He took his glasses off and walked over to say hello. He had to do something. He smiled at her, and she smiled back.

Just once, he had made the mistake of trying to impress Fox.

Elliott's election to the Northern Pacific Club, when he had secretly dreaded being blackballed, came as a heaven-sent gift; almost as the ultimate assurance that at last, despite everything, he could forget Egon Milhausen, could lock him up in some murky hidden room in the back of his mind forever, and throw away the key. The Northern Pacific Club occupied a vast, drab, red brick building at the top of Nob Hill. Before the tall apartment houses and hotels had been built around it, the view must have been spectacular. Now, one could only glimpse narrow strips of the Bay waters and the Marin County hills through gaps between the buildings. But one did not come to the Northern Pacific Club for the view.

One came for the atmosphere of wealth and solidarity. For the reassurance that one belonged with the elite, even though the other members were hardly companionable and their average age probably over 60. One came, if one was Elliott, for the rich dark panelling; for the thick maroon carpeting showing the worn trails made by the feet of multi-millionaires; for the famous dining-room (Fox thought it looked like an English Victorian railroad station and about as clean) with the stained glass cupola; for the library with its floor-to-ceiling leatherbound unread books. And for the dark brown cracked leather chairs, whose hollows and contours had been moulded by some of the richest bottoms in the country.

The Northern Pacific Club was all of this.

Egon Milhausen did not, could not, exist here; this was Elliott Millner country. And so he had invited his young brother-in-law to lunch.

'Have lunch at the N.P. Club?' asked 17-year-old Fox, plainly mystified. 'Why *there*?'

Something in Elliott had shrivelled then.

And later, entering through massive oak portals into the dim, echoing lobby, he had shrivelled further. For Fox did not act impressed at all. Worse, it seemed as though their roles had somehow reversed, for all the staff at the club seemed to know exactly who Fox was, treated him with deference, called him *Mister* Fox. And Fox himself, like a shaggy-haired hippie even though wearing his Thayer Academy suit which had been nicely pressed and brushed by Miss Doyle, behaved with the casual grace and easy manners of one who lunched at the Northern Pacific Club every day.

During the meal, however, Fox had been very constrained, preoccupied almost, continuously shooting overt glances up at the cupola over their heads which served to make their arid conversation even more disjointed than it should have been. And the food was terrible. (Not that that mattered, Elliott hastened to remind himself; one did not come to the N.P. Club for gourmet cooking.) Of course, the wine was magnificent; by the time they reached the over-cooked steak in the watery sauce, Elliott had ordered a second bottle. He felt he needed it.

Afterwards, he took Fox on a tour of the Club, from top to bottom, Fox trailing after him dutifully, through a succession of dim brown leather rooms – the trophy room with its cases of tarnished siver cups, the billiards room, the card room, the writing room, the library – his only display of animation when they braved the nether regions, down in the basement, where there was a steam room, a sauna, and a swimming pool.

'Hey,' said Fox, 'that's neat. There's a pool. I'd forgotten. Hey, Elliott, let's have a swim.'

So Elliott obediently found the attendant, an ageing gnome with iron fingers, busily massaging one of the members who lay face down, grunting gently, on the massage table outside the steam room. He arranged for suits, although the idea of swimming after the heavy meal and the better part of two bottles of wine nauseated him.

And then . . .

The pool was very cold and over-chlorinated. He shivered getting in, his stomach cramping, but determinedly swam some laps, not wishing Fox to think him soft. Fox did not seem to mind the cold at all. He swam enthusiastically, long red hair streaming behind him in the water like a banner. And afterwards, while Elliott dried himself in a changing booth, Fox pranced around the room naked as a jaybird, haphazardly towelling himself with the ridiculously small towel provided, humming cheerfully, the water pearling on his young white body, his hair hanging, a wild tangled mane down his back, drying in soft tendrils around his face.

He had looked wonderful, Elliott thought, caught in a rare emotion of quite genuine tenderness. Seeing in Fox a young, spirited animal moving with the leggy grace of a yearling stallion . . . until . . . he could not help but notice . . .

*Oh my God*, Elliott thought in despairing rage, abstract tenderness vanishing like smoke, *he's hung like a stallion too*; then cringed under the recurring tidal waves of disgust which engulfed him.

'*Shame on you*,' cried Erna, *slapping away his small, pudgy hand*. '*Shame on you for touching little Peter. You touch little Peter one more time*,' she told him with a face tight with revulsion, '*and it'll turn black and drop off . . .*' And little Egon, six years old, stared up at his mother, his round face flushed with guilt and humiliation, eyes wide with fear.

Fox was silent, standing still, holding the towel defensively in front of himself, watching Elliott. His eyes flashed once, then were guarded, and with a stab of shock, Elliott realized where he was still looking. He thought: *Christ, now he'll tell everyone I'm gay.*

But Fox never said anything; he merely made sure that he and Elliott did not meet often; and soon after that, mercifully, he went off on the boat anyway.

'It's a great day to have the top down,' Elliott inanely told the girl in the Jaguar, involuntarily comparing her, to her great advantage, with his wife Nancy, thinking this was the kind of wife he should have. Long-limbed, slender, elegantly casual, delicate-boned face – not like Nancy, who was squat, heavier by the day, and no one's image of an aristocrat.

But this girl was not for him, for Nancy had more essential and lasting attributes than mere beauty. Only if he had been born a Wesley Bishop Fox III could he have indulged himself with a girl like this one. Almost grinding his teeth with anger, Elliott forced himself to make a casual gesture of farewell, the mandatory, 'Take care, see you later', for Miss Doyle had come out, was standing right there behind him, and Fox himself clattered down the wooden stairs inside the garage and slammed out through the door.

Elliott climbed into his car, and buckled the seat belt. He thought: If only . . .

But then he reminded himself that to have arrived at the point where he now stood, a miracle had been required – a miracle of guts and tenacity. He had wrought the miracle himself; had travelled an immense distance since Egon Milhausen. Why should he fear Fox? What possible threat was

Fox, an itinerant bum who drew trashy pictures?

*No,* decided Elliott, fair brows drawing together in resolution, *even now, with Fox back, things aren't going to change. How can they? And there is nothing to worry about . . . Is there?*

## JULIA

One life was over, and she stood at the beginning of nothing, her present one of strange suspension.

These days she felt burdened with inertia and aimlessness. She had to force herself into any form of activity, as she had done tonight. There was a movie playing she had wanted to see for weeks. *So go and see it . . . what's the big deal? And afterwards, since it was only half past ten, for God's sake, go into a nice warm cozy-looking bar and have a glass of wine. Everybody does that. The only problem,* she thought with apathy, *is in trying to make myself want to do anything.*

Her apartment was charming – a small one-bedroom, newly decorated, in an old mellow building near the park, on a very steep hill, surrounded by elegant one-family homes. There were seven other apartments in Julia's building, which was a mansion converted some time in the forties without, she suspected, the help of an architect. Her living-room had at one time been a back hall; one wall sloped very strangely. The first few nights she heard footsteps in her room, moving above her head, which had been bizarre and frightening until she realized that the sloping wall was under a staircase originating in some other part of the house. There was also a curious little blind balcony halfway up the opposite wall; the balcony was there for no apparent purpose, but she guessed at one time it had been on a half-landing overlooking the hall which had been boarded over. She kept plants in it now; they looked delightful, dangling through the white-painted wrought iron.

There were other good things about the building, too. She had a garage – very important for a woman living alone, having a garage – so she did not have to park her second-hand yellow Volkswagen blocks away when returning home late at night. *Not,* thought Julia, putting a kettle on to boil to make instant coffee, for she was still not ready to go to bed, *that that happens very often.*

And the other tenants were very quiet. They all went to work in the morning before she was up; arrived home around six o'clock, and stayed home. They did not appear to drink, throw raucous parties, or play the stereo loudly. On the rare instances when she did meet other tenants, they were always polite, smiled, and went swiftly away about their business. Until now, she had been grateful; now she was not so sure. Nobody had ever asked her name, what she did, how she felt beyond a perfunctory, 'Hi, how are you?' To which she'd say, 'Fine, thanks, how are you?' And they'd say, 'Fine. 'Bye now.' *One of these days,* Julia thought, unaccountably savage, *I'll tell them I've got syphilis, bubonic plague, and leprosy. And they'll say, 'Fine, fine. Take care now.'*

She had been alone for six months, her aloneness beginning that night before Christmas in New York when Gerry had gone.

She drank her coffee slowly, trying not to remember, trying to push back the slow-creeping tide of hurt. And the now sour memories of that first encounter back at CBS on the news documentary.

Gerry Naughton, brilliant young director. Actually, he had not been so young; 38 years old, and his body starting to thicken. On the set he always wore a narrow-brimmed straw hat with a striped band. Julia had thought that was because he was going bald, but she saw him take his hat off on the third day and thoughtfully scratch at his hair and it was thick and curly, healthy looking, chestnut brown mottled with grey. Apart from the hat, he generally wore jeans and scuffed loafers, a gingham shirt – blue or red – under a V-necked Shetland sweater, styled long to hide the slight mid-sectional bulge.

The video crews would do anything for Gerry. He was quiet, authoritative, utterly professional. He treated the lowliest gofer – at one time, Julia – with the same courtesy accorded to the show's producer and sponsor. Gerry's shows began shooting on time and finished on time. There were seldom histrionics. People were relaxed; they laughed and made jokes. And for Julia Naughton, 22 years old, newest production assistant fresh from film school, scampering about the set with furious energy, clipboard, stop watch, and dangling reels of tape, Gerry Naughton was God.

And then . . . and then . . . the night Julia, exhausted and confused from a hard day with too many new things crowding her mind at once, forgot to pass on a message to Gerry's secretary.

She had wakened in panic at 2.00 a.m. Why, oh why, had she been the only one near the phone? Why had Gerry and his secretary both been out to lunch? How *could* she have forgotten? Thinking about the cancelled dinner meeting; that Gerry must have wasted hours sitting vainly in Le Buc for companions who never showed. She did not go back to sleep but lay on her back watching the rhythmically flashing red neon stripes on her bedroom ceiling. She would be fired. She would never get another job. She would never see Gerry again. She was through.

Heroically she forced herself to go to work in the morning, although common sense said 'Why bother? You'll be crucified.' And when she arrived the first person she saw was Gerry.

She was abject. She said: 'Gerry, I feel *terrible* about last night. It was all my fault. I don't know what to say . . .'

And Gerry, amused, noticing her for the first time, seeing the earnest grey-green eyes turned up to his in anxiety and worship, the long dark-gold hair, the young peach bloom of skin, said solemnly, with a slight hint of a chuckle: 'Whatever is it you did?'

And when she told him, he smiled at her and said that it didn't matter, he'd had a great dinner anyway. Julia thought that showed total class, and fell in love.

And later, Gerry called Wendy in Westport, told her he would be tied up in town again that night, infuriating, so sorry, but sometimes there was no pleasing a sponsor, to please kiss the kids for him.

And took Julia out to dinner.

And to bed.

A year later, with Wendy and the children in Connecticut reduced to a fading memory and a monthly bank deduction,

Gerry Naughton married his starry-eyed, devoted young production assistant with just one proviso – that she leave television; or at any rate, his network.

Julia, who had envisaged them the production team of the century, was disappointed, but slipped with ease into the wonderful job Gerry arranged for her with Sherbrooke and Associates, Public Relations, where soon she alone was handling the prestigious Arlo Allen account, publicizing their elegant accessories in the glossy magazines, attending fashion shows featuring Arlo Allen silk scarves and costume jewellery, holding press receptions, taking Arlo Allen himself to lunch; loving it all while she and Gerry in their Upper East Side co-operative (no banishment to Connecticut for her – she knew better) became known as one of the city's most brilliant and successful young couples.

Until one night she came home to find the apartment different.

It did not strike her all at once why it was different; but after she had wandered from room to room in growing confusion, she knew.

All Gerry's personal things were gone.

She sat down in the living-room, knees together like a little girl, hands clasped in her lap, staring at the place where Gerry's favourite painting, a small watercolour of a harbour scene in soft blues and browns, used to hang, and where there was now only a darker, ghostlike rectangle against the faded paint of the wall.

Gerry had gone.

She hurtled through the apartment then in a rising, suffocating panic, searching. But it was all gone – his clothes, his straw hats (which he still always wore on the set), his books, the portable colour Sony in his den where he watched the weekend football games which bored her, the framed photographs of Gerry drinking, laughing, handshaking with the famous, the Emmy he had won for the documentary on birth control among the urban poor. Even the copper-bottomed Revereware saucepans and skillets, and the set of butcher knives which Gerry had originally contributed to their marriage. They had come with him from Westport, remained with him through his time with her on 84th Street, and were now who knew where? He had even taken the wooden rack from which they had hung. The cheap bastard had even taken the screws out of the wall.

Julia stared round her kitchen, which now looked suddenly bleak and cold, wondering whose kitchen they were in now.

Of course, there had been a letter; Gerry had always been neat. It was propped on the living-room mantel, typed professionally on an IBM executive typewriter. Obviously not by Gerry himself.

And the letter told her he was gone for good.

With Sarah Sturgis, the production assistant on the show. Everybody Gerry worked with must have known all about it for a long time. Julia crimsoned with humiliation. No wonder Gerry had never wanted her on the set; how many other eager young girls had there been, so worshipful of the virile director with his crooked dimpled grin, his apparent humanity, his goddamn straw hat? . . .

What hurt most was not having a chance. Not being able, not once, to fight back against this unknown Sarah Sturgis, so young, trusting, fresh faced, naïve—so deadly. Just as she herself had been once, five long years ago.

Occasionally Julia pondered with sour satisfaction over the probable fate of Sarah Sturgis, who undoubtedly in her turn, once the freshness and the dewy-eyed worship had gone, would be left alone to stare blankly at the kitchen wall, at the screw holes in the plaster where the Revereware saucepans no longer hung.

Of course, everybody had been incredibly kind. She had been invited everywhere, for a while. She had tossed her head with defiance, saying things like: 'Of course, it just couldn't have gone on,' and 'Gerry and I haven't had much to say to each other for months.' But she did not think she fooled anybody for long, for she could not entirely hide the hurt in her eyes or always sound convincing in her airy denunciation of Gerry, their marriage, and how deeply on the rocks it had been.

She began to avoid her friends, who naturally did not call her so often. And soon she began to hear of other evenings, and other parties, where Gerry and the adoring Sarah were invited and she was not. She was hurt and unsurprised; Gerry had always been far more fun than she at parties.

Her parents called almost every day, begging her to come home.

She began to work longer and longer hours at Sherbrooke and Associates.

She had a short defiant affair – the first since her marriage to Gerry – with Humberto Perez, the very young Puerto Rican boy who worked in the cafeteria downstairs and brought coffee, soft drinks, and pastries up to the 14th floor in the afternoons.

Life became empty and hateful, and she began to dread 3.00 p.m., when Humberto Perez would shoulder open her office door to push in his goodies cart, smoulderingly desirous of finding her alone.

For the first time, New York was ugly, cold, and cruel.

So she left, and came as far west as she could, and now she lived in San Francisco, where she went to movies and drank in bars alone, had no job and no friends.

*Oh boy*, Julia thought dispassionately, *what do I do now?* She was lonely – *but how do I start all over again, build up a whole new life, from less than nothing?* For instance, that nice young boy in the art class who had invited her to lunch. She had been glad for the ride, and had liked him, but when he had asked her out she had been suddenly unaccountably panicked and half resentful. She remembered being brusque to the point of rudeness. He would never ask her out again.

And the man tonight in the bar who had stared at her. He had been much better looking than Gerry – tall and macho, with dark brown curling hair and good features – and certainly much better dressed. He had also seemed interested, but she had looked at him and frozen inside with the sure foreknowledge of failure. Her faith in herself had been shaken too badly; *I can't do anything gracefully any more*, Julia thought wryly. *I can't even refuse a lunch invitation without hurting people's feelings. And I just can't go out there and meet people. I don't know how any more. I don't know how to start. I don't know what to say. All I know is it won't work out.*

She switched out her light and prepared to try to sleep.

And the phone rang abruptly, sounding incredibly loud

in the midnight darkness.

Julia's heart pounded; it was 3.00 a.m. in New York.

Dry mouthed, she said: 'Hello?'

And listened to silence. Then to a click as someone replaced the receiver.

'Hello?' Julia said again, into emptiness.

After that, it was even harder to sleep.

## JOE

Joe Capelli replaced the receiver cautiously. Hearing her say just two or three words had been enough; he knew where she was. She was at home, in bed, and probably alone. He was satisfied.

He slept.

And dreamed the same dream again – the same one he dreamed so often these days. Sometimes there were very small variations, but the end was always the same and he never woke up in time.

He was standing on the rug – it was a cheap imitation Turkish rug – quite naked except for his shoes and thick black wool socks. Lisa sat on the sofa in front of him, looking up at him, smiling her open mouthed smile, her arms up over her head to show how the round hardness of her perfect breasts pushed out her sweater, the nipples stiff under the fabric pointing at him like little thumbs.

'Let me look at you,' said Lisa. 'Let me just look at you. Oh, lover, are you ever ready. Let me just get this junk off . . .'

*Oh Lisa, I love you . . . love you . . . love you . . .* His voice coming back to him down time, mocking, as though through an echo chamber.

And a blinding explosion of light, glaring heat, a wild crescendo of noise, Lisca's body a black outline against agonizing incandescence except for the red lips which drew wide, wider, laughing, screaming at him with that terrible laughter.

Joe woke up at last, moaning and sweating, his body

writhing, too late as usual. He had to see it all through to the end, always.

He curled himself into a ball, his hands between his legs, holding himself protectively. He whimpered softly.

But nobody heard him. He had moved from his wife's bedroom months ago in case she heard him cry for Lisa in the night.


# FOX


Fox supposed his car was pure indulgence; nobody needed to have a car like that. But seeing it the second day of his return, unloved and battered on the windy street yet, with its classic lines, standing out from all the other cars like a race horse among a herd of cattle, Fox had known he must have it. And as if he had been meant to have it all along, the Jaguar wore a FOR SALE sign.

All it took after that was money, which was easy.

And after less than a week in a British garage where Fox spent most of each day, agitated, harassing the mechanics to the point where they would have done anything just to be rid of him, the car emerged, dark blue and gleaming, tuned to perfection, and it was the consummation of a love affair.

Besides drawing, Fox's only other obsession was driving fast cars. He drove brilliantly, as part of the machine, and possessed an instinct for the lurking presence of the Highway Patrol which bordered on the eerie. He had never had a ticket for anything save parking offences in his entire life. And it was largely the possession of the car, and the relief it brought him, which carried him through those first barren months back home.

'Mother,' he had cried over the phone, thinking it wise to give her some warning before going to see her in case the shock of joy might be too much, 'Mother, I'm back. I'm home, Mother.'

For he had been gone so long; she *must* have missed him. Must have realized how much she loved him. Everything would be different now; she would say, 'Wesley, darling,

T.C. – B

how wonderful!' And clasp him to her and perhaps even
cry a little.

Instead, Hope demanded testily: 'Who *is* this?' And
when, shaken, he told her, 'It's me, Wesley – your son,
Mother,' she said vaguely, 'That's nice, Wesley. Do drop by
and tell me what you've been up to. But not tonight; Mother's
much *much* too tired tonight.'

Fox had said: 'All right, Mother. Th – thanks. I'll d-do
that.' And hung up, desolate, feeling the old panicked con-
striction clutch at his breath, for nothing had changed at
all.

But now, of course, at least there was the car. The anger,
frustration, and disappointment which coiled poisonously
in his body after the visits to his mother were dissipated
slowly but certainly by driving somewhere – very fast – in
the Jaguar. It did not matter where. Once he had driven
all the way up to North Lake Tahoe and back, 400 miles
on Interstate 80, stopping only once for gas. It had taken
him less than six hours, and in the mountains he had opened
up to 100 m.p.h., watching the quivering instruments, feeling
the power under his body, allowing the heavy growling
vibration of the engine to take him, sink through him, bring
him peace.

That had been a very bad time. Other times it was usually
enough to drive up Highway 1 along the coast road, north
to Stinson Beach, driving the hairpin bends as though he
drove a race circuit, pushing the car to its limits.

He and Nancy had jointly inherited a beach house there,
willed to them three years before when Uncle Bishop died. It
had been the only good surprise of his homecoming. And
since Nancy was not interested in the beach house other
than for throwing the occasional al fresco summer party, it
had become virtually his alone. 'Elliott likes it,' Miss Doyle
said. 'He used to go over quite a lot and walk on the beach.'
But since Fox came back Elliott never seemed to go any
more. Only once – arriving late one afternoon around sunset,
Fox had seen, to his surprise, Elliott's Mercedes parked outside but no visible sign of any Millners in the house. Walking
out on to the beach he found Elliott sitting on the sand, still
dressed formally, straight from the office, in his dark grey

business suit and black shoes, his hair brilliant in the dying sunlight.

Fox had begun to say, 'Elliott? Hey, Ell . . .' but stopped himself, for Elliott turned his head and looked straight through him, he told Miss Doyle. Elliott's face was empty . . . 'like nobody lived inside,' Fox said. Miss Doyle had nodded, as though in agreement. Fox had left at once, quietly, eaten dinner at a small restaurant down the street, and returned after dark. But Elliott had been gone.

Today, the day after his art class, Fox visited his mother. He did so doggedly twice a week, not relinquishing the hope that perhaps some day she might . . . *I mean, odder things have happened*, Fox told himself stubbornly, not quite daring to say the word 'love' aloud.

And as usual, she greeted him coolly, wearing a floor-length chiffon garment which Fox thought was called a peignoir but did not like to ask for fear of seeming ignorant. She extended him a limp white hand, palm down, as though he were expected to kiss it, a queen greeting a lowly vassal, never forgetting, even when extremely drunk, that she had once been one of the most beautiful and sought-after women in the world.

STAR WEDS TYCOON, the headlines had screamed in 1940, when Fox's father, Wesley Bishop Fox, Jr., President of Cordex Business Machines Inc. (which was now Cordex International), had romantically swept Hope Hartley away from her fans and into nominal domesticity at the very peak of her career.

Fox had killed his father.

His mother was fond of telling him that when she had had too much to drink, which was nearly always. She had been telling him this all his life, even when he was very little. Fox supposed she had never forgiven him for it, although of course killing his father had hardly been his fault.

Wesley Bishop Fox, Jr., had died as a direct result of too much sun on the golf course at Pebble Beach, too much excitement over winning the tournament, too much Scotch in celebration, with the final exuberant sexual demand on Fox's mother providing the last straw for a heart labouring far beyond its capabilities already.

Immediately following his final plunging spasm, Fox's father had rolled off his mother and expired dramatically on the floor. It had been instantaneous, the doctor said. Here one minute, gone the next. *One hell of a way to go*, Fox privately thought, but Hope would say, voice quivering reproachfully, 'You killed him. You might as well have plunged a dagger into his heart.'

'Oh Mother, come on.' Then, 'I'm sorry,' he would say for the thousandth time. 'I'm sorry, I'm really sorry. I'm sorry for being born, Mother.'

Fox was born nine months to the day following his father's massive coronary. 'A hideous baby,' Hope said, correctly; Fox had been undersized, crushed looking, jaundiced, and quite bald, his eyes swollen slits in his battered face. 'My God,' Hope had added with a shudder, 'he looks like a goddamn coolie.' And Miss Doyle had silently wrapped him up again in his shawl and taken him away.

Now Hope said faintly, 'Wesley, how nice,' and Fox felt, as always, like an agent presenting a slightly dubious contract. 'Did you have an amusing morning?' she asked languidly, not really interested. As well as killing his father, Fox had compounded his sin by not demonstrating a single one of his father's talents. He had been expected to follow his father as a Captain of Industry, but he had no aptitude for business and no ambition. 'He's a bum,' Hope had snarled at Miss Doyle late one afternoon, when three empty bottles of Pinot Noir stood among the bric-à-brac on the little Louis XV table beside her bed. 'Nothing but a goddamn bum, drawing dirty pictures.'

Fox had run away from Thayer Academy, the expensive boarding school in Southern California, although, he contradicted gently: 'I wasn't running away. I told them I was going.'

He had idled through one year at Berkeley, then one windy winter morning had sailed away on a wide-beamed ketch on its way to Australia, his first communication, received five months after his departure, being a grubby postcard mailed from the Galapagos Islands to Miss Doyle. He had not come back for five years, and never once had he asked for money. Nobody knew how he lived after leaving the boat, and Fox never said. Rumour was that he was living with a religious commune in Northern India. Positively he had driven a ramshackle tourist bus filled with English students from Bombay to Istanbul, where he had disappeared again for the better part of a year, before surfacing in Europe, where he had been seen in Paris by one of Hope's relatives, peddling whimsically obscene drawings in the cafés.

No, Fox would never be a captain of industry. Nor, Hope suspected, would he ever be a good artist either. A good artist, she knew, attended an accredited art school, and then had openings at the most expensive galleries in New York, San Francisco, and Los Angeles. Fox, however, learned his trade, 'On the *streets*,' Hope had once said, shrinking, 'and *worse*.' Once she looked at his sketchbook and cringed with horror, disgusted by what she saw there, for Fox was not interested in drawing beautiful things she could relate to – wasn't that, after all, an artist's business, to make pretty pictures? Fox enjoyed drawing derelicts and drunks, the helpless faces of the old people who lived in cheap hotels, and the tenderloin hookers lounging dispiritedly in doorways.

'Thank you, Mother,' Fox said. 'Yes, it was quite an amusing morning. How about you?' He decided that this afternoon he would go to the beach. It would be a good day for the beach. It was unusually windless, but clear. It would be warm on the sand, the water blue and friendly, and there would only be light traffic on Highway 1, going over. The Jag would really be able to move.

'. . . about an hour ago. Now it just pounds and *pounds*.'

'Oh boy,' Fox said automatically, 'that sounds awful.' And perhaps on the way back, he would stop in Sausalito, say hello to the Professor, his old skipper, back once again in the Bay area with the *Avrion*. For an instant he allowed himself to dream of sailing with the *Avrion* again – to the Marquesas, Tuamotus, Papeete – for the Professor was putting together his next charter, an oceanographic survey of . . .

'. . . think I'm going to just *die*.'

Fox said: 'What?'

'My head, Wesley. I have this *terrible* headache, and . . . you're not even *listening*, Wesley,' Hope said, voice tremulous with reproach.

Fox said: 'That's bad, Mother. I'm sorry you're not feeling – '

'Well, you don't *sound* sorry,' she snapped.

Miss Doyle said: 'I'll get you your aspirins, dear.'

Hope inclined her head, lips pursed with impatience. 'I do think you could have thought of it earlier, Doyly.' And perhaps for the thousandth time, Fox wondered: 'Why *does* Doyly put up with this?' shivering with indignation for Miss Doyle, his eyes hot and angry as he stared at his mother.

He had always loved Miss Doyle.

And she had never let him down. Not once. Not like Hope.

He had vague memories, far back but still painful, of dreadful nights waking in strange beds, of not being able to breathe, of hearing distant sounds of laughter and music, and whimpering in panic until Doyly came. Miss Doyle had been the only person who seemed to like him. He had been such an unattractive small boy (and of course he had killed his father), and until he was 10 he had asthma attacks always at the most difficult moments. There had been the time on the *Queen Elizabeth*, in the early sixties, sailing for Southampton out of New York, when he had been really bad. He remembered his mother bending over him, resentful at having been recalled from the Captain's cocktail party, tinkling with jewellery, smelling powerfully of 'Jolie Madame' and gin. And Nancy. The long ago 16-year-old Nancy in the black sheath cocktail dress, dark hair lacquered and twisted into a towering structure fashionable then, eyelids extended with black eye-liner almost to her ears, saying: 'Mother, I told you we shouldn't have brought Foxy. He always spoils *everything*!' While he gasped and whooped and clung to Doyly who held him tight and worked his aspirator for him. 'He'll be all right, won't he, Doctor?' Hope had demanded, as though daring him to say 'no'. And after reassurance that little Wesley would probably live through the night, she had returned thankfully to the party.

That summer, spent in the Ritz in London, the Hotel Georges V in Paris, and somebody's villa at Antibes, had been a long grinding hell. Fox had been ill the whole time, and Hope had never taken him with her again on her summer travels, for which he had been tremendously thankful.

Now, Hope yawned delicately behind her hand and tried to think of something to say. To bridge an awkward pause, she sipped a little wine as a chaser for the aspirins, trying to remember whether Fox was here for a purpose, or was just passing the time of day with her. She found it hard to remember things these days; facts seemed to slip away from her as soon as they came into her head. 'You drink far too much,' Dr McBride told her sternly. 'But I don't drink,' Hope protested again and again. 'Not liquor. Just a little wine, now and again.' But now and again came around very often, and in fact she sipped all day, beginning early. Finally she said: 'Was there something you wanted to talk with me about, Wesley?'

'Just stopped by to see how you were doing, Mother. And I'm really sorry to hear about your headache.'

Miss Doyle filled his wine glass, and Fox drank carefully. She told Hope: 'Foxy . . . uh . . . Wesley's going to art class now.'

'Indeed?' Hope raised thin eyebrows.

'I go Wednesdays,' Fox said.

'How . . . how nice,' said Hope. 'I'm sure it's about time.'

'Yeah,' Fox said, finishing his wine, refusing any more partly as a small gesture of reproach to his mother, partly because he never drank very much anyway. He knew he could never tell her about the class, the great model, and the new beautiful girl he had driven home who wouldn't go out with him. He added lamely: 'It was OK.'

He could never tell her about anything, for she simply did not care. And, as Hope was plainly beginning to fidget, he said: 'Well, Mother, I guess I'd better be going. I guess you're . . . uh . . . probably pretty busy.'

Hope's smile was brittle, but genuine now because he was going. 'Well, one does one's best.'

He set his glass on the tray and stood up gratefully. Miss Doyle said: 'Did you eat lunch yet, Foxy? I could make you a sandwich.'

Her voice pleaded. Fox, who was feeling sick to his stomach, said, 'OK, Doyly, thanks. That'd be nice. I'd like that.'

Hope said: 'Would it be too much to ask for a little bouillon? If you could spare the time, Doyly?' She pressed the tips of her long white fingers against her forehead, and gave a small moan, eyes tightly closed now against the pain. Fox's eyes met Miss Doyle's over the top of the thinning, strawberry blonde hair.

'I'll see you later, Mother,' Fox said tautly. 'Goodbye, now. Hope the headache gets better,' and dutifully kissed the air somewhere near her overpowdered, sweet-smelling cheek.

Her perfume, as always, reminded him of the scent of funeral flowers.

## JULIA

Julia Naughton heard her telephone singing as she crossed the hall, began to run, fumbling for her inside door key, dropping her grocery bags, trying to fit the wrong key in the lock, changing it for the right one, while all the time the phone continued ringing inside the apartment with perhaps a job offer, or . . . or perhaps even Gerry calling to say it had all been a terrible mistake, please, please, would she come back to him, in which case what should she do, whatever should she do? . . .

She flung herself in through the door, leaving groceries strewn outside, small items spilling out of her opened purse, dangling lopsided from her wrist.

She picked up the phone, breathless. 'Hello?'

But nobody answered.

'Hello?' said Julia. 'Who is this?'

Nothing.

She said crossly: 'Is there anybody *there*?'

Click.

Oh Christ, Julia thought, not again. All that rush and all that emotion just for a breather, or a burglar checking if she was in, or a wrong number. She collected her scattered groceries and set them out on the kitchen counter without much enthusiasm, thinking about the calls she had received during the past weeks. The Salvation Army, in need of the old clothes and discarded furniture she did not have. A life insurance salesman. A very deaf, elderly woman who had called twice wanting Marvin. And now, twice, a burglar or whatever.

Why ever should she delude herself, thinking it was Gerry.

## FOX

Miss Doyle followed him out of his mother's boudoir, carrying the small silver tray with the empty wine bottle and glasses. A telephone rang somewhere in the depths of the house – once . . . twice, and was answered, presumably in the kitchen by Wong the houseboy.

'Wong can't be a houseboy,' Fox had said, puzzled, so long ago. 'Wong's *old*.' In fact, Wong had been 40 years old, and Fox had added critically, 'It's not *right*.' But the designation of houseboy did not bother Wong. Nothing ever bothered Wong. And at this moment, having successfully cleared up a small matter with Hope's wine merchant, he was cleaning silver, his mind far away, waiting for the evening and the moment when he could begin to live again, when he could re-treat into his little room behind the kitchen with the colour television Hope had given him ('Thinking he'd watch her old movies,' Nancy had said spitefully) and steep himself in violence. Wong's evenings were spent in vicarious blood baths of police drama and war, followed in due course by giant spiders, mutations, witches, ghouls, and monsters from outer space, until 3.30 a.m., when he would switch off, yawning with tired pleasure. And none of these movies ever starred Hope.

Fox followed Miss Doyle through the oak-panelled hallway, where the light never penetrated beyond a murmurous red- and green-shot gloom when the last rays of sunshine fell on the stained glass fanlight above the massive, carved front door.

He had never liked the house. His mother's room stifled him; the rest of it had always oppressed him, crushing him under years of wealth and expensive clutter. *No wonder I*

*had asthma*, Fox thought, *for no child could breathe here.*
The furniture was mostly of heavy mahogany; the rugs from
the east, in shades of maroon and crimson. The staircase,
with the intricately carved oak handrail, curved up above
his head, leading to darkness. It was not a young person's
house although once . . . impossible to imagine . . . his
parents had been young here.

*Now in my house*, Fox thought yearningly, sitting down
at the kitchen counter while Miss Doyle sliced roast beef
delightfully thinly, using an old iron kitchen knife sharp as a
razor which was honed every day, *there'll be all the light in
the world. It'll be something like the beach house, but high
up . . . on the top of a hill, overlooking the ocean. And it'll
be all windows, floor to ceiling, with no drapes. There'll be
great rough beams, an enormous fireplace, and leather chairs
and pillows. And there'll be a lady in it, wearing a nice flow-
ing dress, all bright colours, with . . . with . . .* But here,
mysteriously, for the first time his familiar fantasy failed
him. There should have been a billowing yellow-haired smiling
girl, with the motherly breasts he had never known. Instead,
the face was lean and haunted, the eyes long, tilted at the
corners, greenish grey . . .

'Mayonnaise or mustard, dear?' asked Miss Doyle.

'Uh, thanks,' Fox mumbled, thinking about the green-
eyed girl, pushing his hands down into his lap to conceal
the sudden swelling erection. *That* had never happened before; the voluptuous blonde had never aroused him like
that. 'Both.'

And to divert his attention, for the moment anyway,
until he could be by himself to think about it, he concentrated
on the roast beef, which was huge – a charred dark brown on
the outside, red and juicy in the middle. His mouth filled
suddenly with saliva, and his stomach rumbled. He was
hungry after all; and food, he told himself firmly, is just as
important as sex.

Miss Doyle cut until a small mountain of beef lay on the
cutting board. Then she tucked it all between two slices of
rye bread, one spread with horseradish mustard, the other
with mayonnaise, and cut the thick sandwich in two delect-
able diagonals. Fox ate as though starved, and she watched
him with satisfaction. *He's too thin*, thought Miss Doyle.

*Too pale and stretched looking.* Although, of course, he always looked horribly peaked after visiting Hope. It was too bad, Miss Doyle thought angrily. Terrible of Hope. Couldn't she see what she was doing to the boy? Couldn't she either behave like a mother, or let him go? *One day soon,* Miss Doyle promised herself, *I'm going to have a talk with Foxy. A serious talk . . .*

'Doyly, why do you stay with Mother?'

She started so sharply she almost cut herself. His timing was so exact, and he had never asked her that before.

'I don't want to pry, Doyly. But – ' *But she's always so rude,* he wanted to say. *So unfeeling. She treats you like dirt,* he would like to say. But couldn't. *She treats you like she treats me.* Fox thought, *but you can't seem to get away from her. Not like I can. Like I thought I could . . .*

'Your mother and I have been together forty years, give or take a few,' Miss Doyle said. 'Too long to change now.'

Wong marched through the kitchen carrying a load of silver objects of unguessable purpose piled haphazardly on a metal tray. Wong, of course, was quite impervious to any ill nature or capricious whim of Hope's. Wearing his usual expression of bland patience, Wong would carry out almost any unreasonable demand with the calm placidity of one who, although his body might be at Hope's beck and call, his mind dwelt safely out of reach on a different planet.

'I just don't like it,' Fox persisted. 'How she talks to you sometimes.'

'Doesn't bother me none,' said Miss Doyle.

'If you say so,' Fox said dubiously, confronted again with the sad realization that he really did not like his mother at all, although he tried so hard, and certain that Miss Doyle's life was really miserable. No matter what she said.

'We go back a long way, you see,' Miss Doyle said evasively, cursing herself for missing the chance Fox had given her. 'It'd be too hard, leaving her now.'

And she went to put the water on for Hope's bouillon.

# JOE

He sat quite still behind the heavy oak and leather desk in his office, staring at the silver-framed photograph of his wife holding the children in her arms, only seeing Lisa. Behind the closed office door voices called and spoke to one another; telephones rang; footsteps hurried down hallways. He heard none of it.

His stomach was churned into a tight fist inside his body which clenched at each tight breath.

Lisa. What was she doing now? Where was she?

It was 9.30 in the morning, and he should be in a meeting. Already his secretary had buzzed him twice; they were all in there, waiting; the last time he had said he would be right in.

He stretched out his hand for his private phone and dialled Lisa's number without lifting the receiver.

All he needed to do was lift the receiver and dial again. She would be in or she would be out. If out, she might of course be anywhere. She might have a job interview. Be shopping. Be with a lover . . . Joe's forehead suddenly filmed with sweat.

He dialled.

She answered.

Joe said: 'Lisa?'

She said, sounding slightly annoyed and out of breath (had she been in the shower?), 'Sorry. You have the wrong number.'

'No Lisa,' Joe said. 'No, I don't.'

She said: 'What? Who is this? Who *are* you?'

Joe hung up. He left his office, feeling better, to join the meeting.

## PART TWO

## JULIA

Julia sat down on her unmade bed, bath towel held tight around her damp body, staring at the telephone, puzzled. *Lisa?* She shrugged , , . Some idiot . . . and began to unpin her hair.

The phone rang again: Miss Preston from Macy's. So sorry; they had decided to fill the opening in the publicity department internally. They wouldn't be needing her to come in after all.

*Wonderful.*

So what to do today, instead? It was sunny, cool, and windy. A walk? Why not? What else did she have going?

While she dressed, Julia was deciding she did not like San Francisco. She was considering moving on, although that would be an admission of failure, *and once you start to run*, she thought, *where do you stop?*

That was morbid. Definitely a walk would do her good.

She wandered all the way down Union Street, peering unseeing into small boutiques, bookstores, at the people sipping coffee or drinks in sidewalk cafés, thinking about how badly she had wanted to leave New York and be entirely on her own, but how frightening it was to live somewhere where there was not one person – not one – who gave a damn about her. *I'm lonely*, thought Julia, watching the other people walking in couples; the mothers with small children; a line of old Italian ladies, perched like migrating birds in the sun on the long window ledge outside the Wells Fargo Bank. *I'm lonely, but I don't know what to do about it.*

It was hard nowadays not to take a pill to help her sleep; not to finish the half bottle of wine she allowed herself with dinner. That would be disastrous, she knew. The beginning of something dangerous.

*How does one meet real people?* she wondered gloomily, turning down Laguna Street towards the marina, answering her own question with ironic resignation: through the job she did not have. Through the family contacts who did not live here. Through the church she did not believe in any more. And then, perhaps, through chance conversations in public places, drinking in warm dimness beside all the other people who were there because nobody wanted them to be somewhere else.

*No*, decided Julia, *I absolutely, quite definitely, am not going into another bar by myself.* She had felt lost. Customs changed so fast. She had been with Gerry for a total of six years, exclusively Gerry's; before that, four years in school. And now, adrift, she was out of phase. People talked and acted differently. She no longer knew what to expect except that on chance meetings in bars one was apparently expected automatically to go to bed; she thought wanly: *Whether you remember his name or not. Or he remembers yours.*

She marched across the Safeway parking lot, past the art centre where she had met Fox, until she arrived at the marina, where she stood still, hands thrust deep into her pockets, staring at the boats, reflecting that she had better not walk so fast. She was halfway home already.

And once she got home, then what?

She walked on more slowly, past the Harbour Master's office. Past phalanxes of pleasure craft and sailboats tied up at finger piers. The farther down the marina she walked, the larger and more opulent grew the boats. At the very end there was a small, tacky-looking beach, where the tide was very low, and if she walked in the muddy part, which would normally be underwater alongside the concrete abutment of the breakwater, she could pass within yards of the 60-foot berths containing the biggest and most beautiful yachts of all.

There was one coming in as she watched; it had graceful, lean lines, a raked bow, and two masts. *You could sail around the world in that*, Julia thought, longing to be somewhere . . . anywhere . . . far away. She could see three men on board, one up front, holding bowlines as the boat nosed slowly and precisely into its berth. He jumped ashore – a young man with golden hair and beard. *A young viking*, thought Julia, admiring, *as handsome as the boat*. Another man, shorter and dark, worked astern, and a third, presumably the owner, stood at the wheel. Julia watched them work, interested, until the viking turned and saw her, grinned and waved and called out something to her which she could not hear. The dark man grinned too and beckoned, and the man at the wheel let it go and made wild scooping motions, as if to pick her up and toss her across the water and into the cockpit.

The wind blew from behind her. It was impossible to hear what they called to her, but the invitation was unmistakable. For a wild moment, Julia wondered: *Should I go on to that boat and meet those men?* They were healthy, nice, athletic and wholesome. But they were strangers. She could not do it. She waved, smiled, but shook her head.

The viking glowered at her, then clasped his hands in front of his body in supplication. Julia waved again, and turned away to walk across the beach to the other side of the yacht basin before turning back.

Back to what? Her apartment? Her TV?

She turned again, irresolute. The viking still stood there, the rope in his hands, watching her.

Was this the crucial turning point, wondered Julia, when she would step back into life? Certainly she could imagine no more suitable people with whom to do it. And after all, how could it hurt? She thought ahead, to an afternoon spent regretting the decision not to kill a harmless hour on a boat, chatting with three attractive men.

They all watched her as she walked down the wooden pier towards them. *Oh my God*, thought Julia, *I'm doing it; I'm really doing it.* Feeling reckless and giddy. *What am I doing? This is crazy. What am I thinking of? What the hell am I doing?* But the, triumphant: *Something. I'm doing something. At last* . . .

The owner, who looked slightly older than the other two, said: 'We were wondering who'd get the prize.'

Julia said: 'You were, huh? Really.' Thinking as she spoke how unbearably old-maidish she sounded. 'And who won?'

The viking said: 'Would you believe, all of us?'

Julia climbed carefully aboard; the viking holding her arm. His name was Jim. The dark man was Tom. The older man was called Herb. He led the way down below, to a luxuriously fitted cabin. He said: 'What can I get you?' The perfect host. 'We have everything your little heart could fancy – Scotch, brandy, wine, beer . . .'

She settled for a beer. She was also given a tour of the boat. There was a nice little cabin up forward, with its own hot shower and head; the main cabin was huge, so Herb assured her, comfortable accommodation for four at least: 'These both turn into double bunks, see . . . at the flick of a switch.' And astern there was another stateroom with its own bathroom.

'We have some good parties here,' the viking said. (Was it Jim or Tom?)

Tom or Jim agreed. 'Yeah.'

'I'll . . . uh . . . bet,' Julia said weakly, sitting down gingerly on a seat upholstered in a tasteful wool plaid which would become a double bunk at the flick of a switch.

They had returned that morning from escorting to the Golden Gate Bridge a friend who was about to sail to Japan single handed.

'Single handed?' Julia said, awed. 'You mean alone? All the way across the ocean?'

'Sure,' said the viking. 'Some idiots do it all the time.'

Herb said: 'Only idiots.'

And the dark man said: 'They go pretty nutty pretty quick.'

The viking said: 'Can you imagine, getting up in the morning, meeting yourself in the cockpit, saying "Well, hi, pal, what'll we do today?" '

Herb said: 'I like to take a woman along. Who wants to go anywhere without a woman?'

The viking said: 'Hey, Herb, see if they've got us on news. It's about time for the news. All the networks had boats out there with TV cameras,' he told Julia. 'We'll be stars.'

'Great idea,' said Herb. 'Let's get us some news.'

He pressed a switch, and a 17-inch colour TV slid from a recessed panel in the bulkhead. Most impressed, Julia could see that there was also a tape deck, stereo equipment, ship-to-shore radio, telephone – in fact every electronic device to make seagoing life more enjoyable.

Her glass was filled.

The screen lit up. Herb flicked channels from a remote control device held negligently in one hand while pouring Chivas Regal into his own glass with the other.

'What do we need?' asked the viking. 'Channel Five?'
'Gotcha,' said Herb.

A woman sat sobbing in front of a shiny walnut desk, while a smooth-faced, white-coated figure told her: 'I'm sorry, Mrs Hall, but the tests were absolutely positive. I'm afraid there's no doubt that when the baby's born it will be mongoloid.'

'But Dr Armstrong . . .'

'No doubt at all, Mrs Hall. Of course . . . abortion . . .'

'Never, Dr Armstrong. I'd rather die myself than murder a . . .'

The three men sat watching the screen expectantly, talking now among themselves about people Julia did not know. Strangely, having invited her aboard and given her a drink, they appeared to have lost interest in her. *Perhaps*, she thought, *I look better from a distance than close up. I think I must have become a very boring person.*

The organ music swelled on the television, to give way to a coy little song about deodorant tampons – 'Now you can be a real woman, every inch . . .'

Tom, Jim, and Herb gossiped around her about the party that had been thrown the night before for the departing Harry, Larry, or whoever, on his transpacific odyssey without a woman, and Mr Hall told Mrs Hall that if she persisted in her pregnancy and did not abort the mongoloid fetus he would leave her.

The organ music swelled again.

Julia sighed and decided to leave the moment she had finished her beer, which was mysteriously refilled, and for the sake of anything better to do, glanced again at the drama of the Halls.

'I reckon ten more minutes till news time,' said Herb.

Mrs Hall was now naked on a bed with another woman. Julia watched them writhe together, glistening with sweat, their legs twisted about each other like snakes, while the dark one said, 'What's the matter? Never fucked with a woman before?'

Mrs Hall gasped: 'No . . . it's so new . . . so exciting . . . Oh God!' And screamed: 'I'm coming. Oh God; Oh *God* –'

*Good heavens*, thought Julia, *daytime programming is certainly more racy out on the Coast.* She stared hypnotized at the screen, where a jeep drove at mad speed up a dirt road to park with a flurry of dust and gravel outside a woodsy-looking cabin, where, back in the bedroom, Mrs Hall screamed, 'It's Frank! Oh God, it's my husband!'; where the husband, who was certainly not Mr Hall, leaped out of the jeep, unbuckling his jeans in mid air . . .

Which was when Julia realized that she was not watching Channel 5 at all but a video cassette. That Mrs Hall was not Mrs Hall either, but just happened to have long blonde hair, two eyes, and a nose.

'Like it?' asked Herb. 'It's called "Foxy Chicks".'

## ELLIOTT

'There's an awful big bill from Saks this month, Nance.'

Nancy said, 'There is?' She peered nearsightedly across the lunch table. 'Oh yes,' she agreed absently, 'that was the Norell. You remember, Ell? The pink chiffon with the pleats . . . the one I wore to the May Festival Ball.'

'Oh,' said Elliott, cringing in memory, 'that one,' thinking *Jesus Christ what a mistake that one had been. Perhaps on somebody else it would be a nice dress, but it makes Nancy look like a strawberry float.* He wondered how Nancy, with a mother like Hope, had never known, and would obviously never learn, how to dress. But all he had to do was sign his name to these extravagant disasters; he did not have to pay for them. Or wear them himself.

'I think it's cute, the way you do the bills,' Nancy cooed, for the fifteenth time. 'Just darling. So homey.'

Other people in their circle had business managers and banks to organize their spending, but Elliott had always liked doing it himself. It brought him an almost orgasmic pleasure, still, to see how much money they spent, and how much there always was, coming in, all the time.

Before, there had never been any money.

There was never any money. Never, never, never.

'So where does it go?' Herman Milhausen roared at Erna, the other side of the thin wall.

Egon strained to hear his mother's answer.

Her voice reached him, very faint. 'Things go up. More expensive every day. I'm telling you, the stores charge robber's prices.' And more. A light, whining drone.

'But I gotta raise. Last month. Up to near a hunnerd a week. You tell me we can't have meat on a hunnerd a week?'

Egon smiled faintly in his small bed, his face knowing.

'You don't even give the kid a buck for a movie and a shake, Saturdays,' growled Herman through the wall. 'The kid don't get no fun. Not ever.'

'Doesn't have any fun,' his mother corrected automatically.

'Ah *shit*,' snarled Herman. 'Doesn't have no fun. And what about me? I ain't got no –'

'Don't have any –'

'Jesus Christ on a raft, will you quit it?'

'You'll never have to worry, Egon,' his mother had told him proudly months and months ago. 'You're going to go to college, no matter what. And a good one, too. Trust your mother.'

She never mentioned it again.

But Egon remembered. It made life more bearable, thinking about college. And going to college, after all, was his right, for he was Somebody.

'Never forget,' Erna told him at least three times a day, 'that you're *Somebody*,' although it was hard to remember sometimes, when in the monotony of daily reality, he was so patently Nobody.

Egon Milhausen was too tall, too skinny, too shy, with every available area of his face sprouting a rich crop of zits. He hated his appearance, his washed out pale Nordic eyes, his light, lifeless hair. He wanted to be dark and dashing, with black curls like Jack Miller, who could grow a moustache already. Who possessed a magnificent wardrobe of tight, greasy jeans, T-shirts, and leather jackets. Who had screwed his first girl (so he claimed, and who would dare disbelieve Jack Miller?) when he was 13.

Egon wore secondhand blue suits of excellent fabric and outdated cut, bought by Erna, whose motives were the best and whose imagination was short. She also sent him to dancing school, where he was supposed to wear white gloves. The other kids called him 'The Freak'.

Egon was probably the unhappiest teenager in Milwaukee; his home life an arid desert of meagre gentility, his school life sheer torture.

But at the end of it all, there was always college, and beyond college the future was bright; for – 'Never forget,' Erna reminded him, 'that you're Somebody . . .'

'More coffee, Ell?' Nancy asked, ready with the heavy silver pot. They sat in the dining-room, at one end of the overlong, highly polished oak refectory table. Elliott's chair, at the head of the table, was an original wine master's chair from the Napa Valley which had cost $3500. Using it was even more enjoyable, thinking, $3500 *for just one chair.*

Nancy was enjoying this lunch with her husband. It was cosy, so unusually domestic, just the two of them, having a cocktail together, then a quiche with sourdough French bread and a salad, with a delicious cheesecake from the bakery to follow. Then, while she sipped her coffee, Elliott sorted the bills prior to taking them downtown with him to the office.

Watching her husband's handsome profile, as he studied her various extravagances, she almost wished there was time for a quick trip up to bed, but then, Elliott had never been exactly the world's wildest lover, and recently seemed less interested than usual. Of course, she knew this to be partly her fault; she was putting on a pound or two. But the main reason for Elliott's increased sexual apathy, obviously, was Fox's return from wherever the hell he'd been. Fox had never liked Elliott, had always somehow made him feel uncomfortable. Once, like a fool, she had asked Fox the reason. It had been a long time ago, before she even married, and Fox was only in his mid-teens. But he had looked at her with those odd, reddish eyes – cynical even then – and said: 'He's using you.'

'Watch your mouth,' she had said indignantly, furious. 'How would you know, anyway?'

'I just know,' said Fox.

'Elliott wants to marry me. He loves me.'

'Elliott only loves himself,' Fox had said, maddening in his self-possession, adding cruelly: 'And money, of course.'

She would never forgive him that; never. She wished with all her heart that Fox would go away again and never return, would take his shifty animal's eyes and poisonous tongue out of her life for good. She could shriek with laughter at the very idea of poor Elliott being a fortune hunter. Why, Elliott was the perfect husband. He had never so much as looked at another woman since they had been married. He never gave her one minute's anxiety. And smugly, she thought of her friends' husbands, compared with whom Elliott was the very model of perfection.

Linda had a private detective follow Bradley, certain he was cheating on her, and found that he was indeed, with a dreadful little crew-cut man who wore leather jumpsuits and bunches of keys, who whipped him in a basement apartment three times a week after work. Janet's husband was a lush, and Angie's husband, only 36 years old, was bald and weighed 300 pounds. Then there was Freddie, Naomi Peterson's husband, who worked until midnight every night and slept with the *Wall Street Journal*. It was endless. She could go on and on.

*No*, thought Nancy complacently, *I guess I don't have a single complaint. Things are pretty much perfect. Elliott loves me, doesn't drink much, takes care of himself, and comes home every night on time unless he's working late. And as for marrying me for my money, my brother is just a vicious little creep with an evil mind. Who cares what he says? Things are just peachy dandy*, thought Nancy, finishing her coffee.

Elliott stood up, stretching his tall frame. He yawned slightly, and ran his fingers through his yellow hair. 'Guess I'd better be getting on back downtown.'

'Too bad you can't stay.'

'I know. But duty calls. I'll check on Hope on the way home.'

'Great. She'll like that.'

'Good lunch, honey. I'll see you later.'

'Take care. Love you.'

And Elliott smiled down at her, his eyes tender. 'Love you too, Nancy,' thinking: *Liar.*

# JOE

Joe did not go back to the office right after lunch. Instead he walked in the park. The sprinklers arced rainbow streams of water across the sloping lawns; ahead of him a knot of cypresses leaned drunkenly into the wind. He closed his eyes. Spray dashed against his face, and he was back at the lake again, 16 years old sitting on the small, driftwood-strewn beach, feeling the rain while the wind drove the water in rhythmic wavelets across the pebbles, just like at the ocean.

Joe had never been to the ocean. On bad days like this, however, he could sit on the beach at the lake, unable to see the opposite shore for the rain and mist, and pretend it was England over there, and Ireland and France . . .

He did not like to share his beach. It was *his* beach, his alone, where he would swim despite the acrid taste of the water and faint unpleasant smell. He was a good strong swimmer. And he would lie on the sand under the hot sun sometimes, flat on his stomach, thinking how nobody else knew about it. No one at all. One day, though, he would bring Lisa here. Lisa would love the beach too. He thought of Lisa in a bathing suit, and his body ached. They would bring a picnic; he imagined her carrying a wicker basket covered with a red and white checked cloth. There would be cold cuts, crusty bread, apples and . . . daringly . . . perhaps a bottle of wine. And after the picnic they would spread their blanket in the shade under the skimpy little trees, and then . . .

The afternoon wind gusted hard across the lawns, moist fog tendrils mingling with the water drops from the sprinklers. A mother passed him, followed by two small children wearing warm jackets and knitted ski caps. In the middle of the lawn to his right, a man wearing a sweatshirt and running shorts, bare footed, was poised motionless on his head, toes pointed to the sky. Some dog owners stood on the path, leashes in their hands, chatting desultorily, watching a dalmation, an afghan, and a large, matted sheepdog gallop in circles after each other. One of the dogs bounded exuberantly towards the man standing on his head, and began to lick his face. The man did not move.

Joe Capelli, still at the lake, paid no attention to any of it.

Right in front of him was a public telephone. It was placed there as though by magic, or by divine ordination, at the precise moment of his most urgent need. A clear plastic bubble, with a telephone inside, and even a directory hanging on a chain. Apparently unvandalized.

Joe reached inside his pocket for a dime.


## JULIA


She did not remember going home. She must have walked all the way, her mind a confused blur of Mrs Hall and her foetus, Foxy Chicks, and outrage. Remembering horribly clearly the grins on the faces of Herb, Jim, or Tom, or who-ever; the invitations to go sailing on Sunday – 'It'll be a blast. Hey, what was your name again?'

The perfect people to help her start refocusing her life.

And herself, trying not to react, to finish her drink calmly, like a lady, to preserve her dignity and not rush too pre-cipitately for the companionway, while the black-haired girl told the husband: 'Hey, gorgeous, I just gave your wife some-thing to remember; now it's your turn . . .'

Julia staggered into the bathroom and threw up.

The telephone rang while she was rinsing her mouth; shakily, she answered it.

A man said: 'I thought we'd go to the beach, Lisa. Just you and me. How about that?'

'Darling, how nice. You've come to visit. And just in time, it's been a *boring* afternoon. Just *endless*, darling.'

Elliott stood in the doorway in his favourite pose, hands resting against the lintel of the door, his body displayed. His best smile was directed full at Hope like the beam from a lighthouse. She thought: *What radiance. What perfect teeth. What gorgeous hair.*

Elliott said: 'It's been a whole three days since I saw you. How could we have let that happen? We mustn't ever let the days slip by us again.'

'Oh naughty,' said Hope, and extended her hand – the sultry movie queen again. 'Come, darling boy. Sit down beside me and tell me *everything* you've been doing.'

Elliott said archly: 'Everything?'

'But we've no secrets, darling, have we? None at all.'

'Certainly not,' Elliott said gallantly, kissing Hope's hand the way he assumed it was done by European noblemen, deciding it felt like a bunch of dried sticks in a loose leather bag. He smiled at her, bored, thinking: *Doesn't she realize what a mess she looks? Doesn't she have any kind of a clue?*

Hope lounged in her boudoir, her make-up applied with poor aim after most of a bottle of Chablis, artfully lit by several pink-shaded lamps which provided her kindest light. An ageing, rather stupid woman who had once been beautiful. *Who still thinks she's beautiful*, Elliott thought, disgusted. *She really believes people can't see all those lines and pouches and liver spots. She's revolting. She makes me feel sick.*

Hope was thinking: *He really is the most beautiful animal; why could I never meet anybody like that after Wesley died?* Deciding he was wasted on Nancy; thinking suddenly: *If I had another face lift, and a chin tuck and a bottom job, I'd look far lovelier and much younger than Nancy . . .* She imagined herself, in a cloud of pale gold chiffon, her hair a burnished shield, sweeping into the box at the opera on Elliott's arm. Elliott looked so distinguished in a black tie.

*Sure she looked good once*, Elliott admitted silently, *but that was nearly half a century ago, for God's sake*. But he had bought into the game; he had to play out the hand. He said: 'God, Hope, you look younger every day. You really look terrific tonight.'

'Don't tease me, darling,' Hope said, sipping wine, peeping demurely up at him through lumpy, beaded lashes. 'I'm just an old woman. Your mother-in-law, for God's sake. Imagine *me* a mother-in-law . . .'

'I *never* think of you as my mother-in-law,' Elliott said bravely. 'I still think of you more as . . . as Nancy's sister. Or even . . .'

'Yes?' said Hope. 'Or even?'

'No,' Elliott said bashfully, 'that would be too much. That really would make you conceited.'

'Oh, Elliott. Now come on. You have to tell. You can't torture me, you wretched boy.'

*I really make myself sick sometimes*, thought Elliott, and said manfully: 'If you tell a wish, it won't come true. You know that.'

Hope blushed. With the misplaced rouge she looked like an old hooker. She giggled, saying coyly: 'Now, Elliott Millner, how you do run on.'

Elliott knelt beside her, took her hands back into his, and obligingly indulged her favourite fantasy, the one where she beat Vivien Leigh out of the Scarlett O'Hara role.

He said: 'Just call me Rhett, Miss Scarlett.'

## JULIA

The man had called her twice in the morning, and again as she ate the solitary lunch she did not really want.

He said: 'Baker and Vallejo, Lisa. Right?'

'Wrong,' Julia snapped. 'I am not Lisa. You have the wrong number.'

The man laughed at her gently.

Julia hung up with a crash, leaned her face into her hands, fingers clutching at her cheekbones. *He knows where I live,* she thought shivering. *Oh my God, he knows where I live. It was not a wrong number after all.*

She was very frightened, suddenly.

She had to get out. Quickly she changed into more respectable clothes, drove downtown.

She spent the whole afternoon shopping at Macy's and I. Magnin, and bought nothing.

She ate an early supper at David's Delicatessen, which was friendly, noisy, Jewish, and reminded her, achingly, of New York. Suddenly she felt desperate nostalgia for New York.

Immediately after supper she bought a theatre ticket, and watched a play which she remembered nothing about afterwards, but to be lost in the city, among crowds of people, was protection from whoever it was out there who knew where she lived.

Who wanted Lisa.

### JOE

Joe Capelli sat alone in the bar on Clement Street, looking at the girls, thinking about all those wasted years without Lisa. How long had it been, from the beginning, since the first day? Twenty years? She was wearing pretty well, he had to admit. She was the same age as he was – 37 – but sometimes she could look barely out of her teens.

*Oh Jesus Christ,* thought Joe. *Oh Lisa* – his soul yearning. *Lisa, where are you? Why did you leave me again?* He had stopped by her place tonight to find her, but her window was dark and her car gone. Her garage door leaned open; inside there was no yellow Volkswagen.

He had sat outside her house for a long time, waiting. It must have been an hour, thought Joe, an hour at least, until, almost of its own volition, his car had begun to move and had carried him here to the Shady Lane Café. Joe had come, over the years, to believe fiercely in fate. He told himself that somehow, on some hidden level of his mind, he had known where Lisa was, and this secret knowledge had been transmitted unwittingly to his car. So who was he to buck Fate? He had been brought here for a purpose; the only conceivable purpose could be to meet Lisa. And if she wasn't here yet, then she would be very soon.

But he had waited a long time; he did not want to wait much longer.

Following a current trend, the bar was so filled with Tiffany lamps, ferns, and overstuffed sofas it was difficult to move about. The cocktail waitress brought him another beer. She was tall, her blonde hair long and straight, but she was not Lisa. She wore a long denim skirt with an appliquéd pattern of rhinestone stars. Frustrated, Joe watched her as she twisted with graceful hip movements between the furniture, for Lisa was after all not here, and his patience wore unexpectedly thin.

There must be a hundred girls here, thought Joe, and not one of them was Lisa. There was a dumpy girl at the bar, her hair a bushy red natural, wearing a long Indian cotton skirt and hiking boots. Over there, a medium-sized one in red velour gaucho pants and an embroidered vest. And there, a very scrubbed, clean-looking one who, Joe decided, was either a nurse or a dental assistant. And just then a woman came up to his table, right up to him, cool as anything, wearing dirty jeans and a white tank top with no bra with her breasts hanging halfway down to her stomach and her nipples showing through the fabric clear as anything. Joe was disgusted. Her hair was short and messy; she had large pores, blackheads on her nose (she stood that close to him) and a sour smell. She told him her name was Clancy and she was an artist. Then, 'Do you want to fuck now or later?' she asked, looking him straight in the eye.

Joe was outraged and wanted to hit her. He only just controlled himself in time. How dare this dikey-looking tramp interrupt his search for Lisa. He stared at her, lips thin over his teeth, eyes rabid, and Clancy backed away, saying, 'Uh, excuse me.'

And then he saw her. She wore a scoop-necked beige sweater wih a blue bandana tied around the throat. She looked unbelievably fresh and healthy, straight from the farm. Joe could imagine her riding horses, feeding chickens, growing her own vegetables. How could he have missed seeing her earlier? She was sitting at a table with a friend. The friend had blonde hair frizzed up in the front in a forties pompadour. There was an empty chair at their table.

Joe moved over at once. 'Anyone planning on using this chair?'

They both looked up at him. Frizz said: 'Help yourself.'

Joe said: 'Can I join you? It looks like my date's not going to show. My name's Joe.'

Lisa smiled: 'Of course.' Then, 'Hi, Joe.' Her smile was lovely, soft pink lips parting on a double row of toothpaste commercial teeth. She was far more friendly tonight.

Joe said: 'How are you, Lisa?'

But the girl laughed. 'I'm not Lisa. Maybe you're thinking of someone else.'

She was Marian. She worked downtown, a book-keeper in an import-export office. Her friend's name was Marcia; she was a key punch operator for an insurance company in the same building. But Joe was not interested in Marcia.

Only in Lisa. Or, for tonight, Marian.

He wondered: *When will she give up on all this stupid stuff?* He was tired of playing games. But tonight he supposed that he would go along with it. One more time.

He bought both girls another drink, after which Marcia left them alone together, making for the bar in search of prey, since Joe was obviously zeroing in on Marian. He had gone after Marian right from the beginning; it was too bad. The best looking man in the bar, and she was wearing her new outfit, too. *Ah well*, Marcia thought philosophically, *you can't always be lucky.*

By now, Lisa had had quite a lot of wine. She was giggling a little, becoming garrulous, filling him in on her new life and regaling him with boring tales of Mother, Daddy, her sister Susan and Brother Benjy; about going to Sacramento State; how this was her first time really away from home ever.

Joe said: 'How about it, Lisa? One for the road?'

Marian started to protest, 'But I'm not . . . oh well, I

guess it doesn't really . . . oh, sure. Why not? OK, thanks.'

Soon, Joe said: 'Well, shall we?'

'Uh, sure,' Marian agreed, flustered, not quite sure what to do now. It was the first night she had met him, after all, and he was, however she might try to rationalize things, a pick-up in a bar. She tried to imagine explaining it to Mother and Daddy: 'Marcia and I – that's a girl in the same building I work . . . she lives near me, too – we went out for a drink, you see, and there was this really neat guy whose date hadn't shown up. He was so nice, bought us drinks and everything . . . and then he took me home. . .'

And when he took her home, what then? Should she ask him in? She probably should, him having bought all the drinks – although she had only been drinking wine and not liquor, which would have cost more.

She looked around for Marcia, needing guidance, but Marcia had left.

And if she *let* him, would that mean he would not respect her, and would not ask her out again? She had not had many dates since coming to San Francisco, even though she had been here two months. It was fun being with a man, especially this one. She wanted to see him again. But she had *never* gone with a man she had only just met in a bar. She wished Marcia were still there . . . But then the wine spoke. The wine told her Joe was the most attractive man she had met in a long time, and she was a young, healthy woman after all. The wine reminded her that she was no inexperienced virgin, she had practically been living with Hugo Hempel for three years. The wine further reminded her that she and Hugo had broken up after New Year's, which was one reason she had come to the city.

The wine suggested she let nature take its course.

Joe took her arm on the way out, holding her close against him. He said: 'I'd make it a habit getting stood up if I thought I'd meet somebody like you every time.'

Marian felt her insides melt with pleasure. She allowed him to walk her to his car. Impressed, she said, 'What kind of car's this? It's terrific.'

'I know,' agreed Joe. 'I like it.' Then, 'OK. So where do we go?'

\*

'Would you like to come up for a minute?' she asked.

He sat in the darkness beside her, not touching her. A perfect gentleman, Marian thought, reassured. He seemed to consider her invitation, then reached a decision and switched off the engine. 'I'd really like to. But just for a minute. I have a real early start tomorrow, but if it means seeing you for another few minutes . . .'

*So there*, Marian told herself. *Of course he respects me.*

She lived in an old-fashioned, single-family home, now converted into four small units. Her studio was on the second floor, facing front. Joe followed her up the worn stairs. 'It's not too bad,' Marian said, unlocking her door. 'I look straight into the trees. It's like living in the country, except for the traffic of course.'

Joe stood for a moment in the doorway, looking at the room. A bow window faced the park across busy Fulton Street. He walked across and pulled down the shades.

'Uh . . . coffee?' Marian asked.

He made an inventory of the furniture. A sofa bed, with small throw pillows on it. A vinyl and Formica dinette set against one wall. A matched pair of Danish-style armchairs upholstered in brown tweed. Plants. French Impressionist reproductions pinned to the walls.

A teak-veneer coffee table, four or five feet long, which looked solid.

He leaned his weight on it, experimentally. It was solid.

From behind him, Marian said: 'Joe, can I get you something?' She opened up a folding door to reveal a shoddy little kitchenette. There was a small refrigerator, a three-burner stove, a tiny sink and drainboard. 'What'll you have, Joe?' She turned to face him.

And knew at once what a terrible mistake she had made.

She would never be able to describe the actual change, but Joe Capelli was suddenly a different person. The way he stood. The way his face looked, the musculature altered subtly, his very pores effusing hatred.

She could not know that he stood, once more, in that other tacky little room long ago, eyes half blinded, narrowed against the glare, but that this time, unlike the nightmare, it was Lisa who cringed, who backed away in helpless despair, and that this time there were no others. It was just Lisa and him . . .

He moved towards her. 'It's been a long time, Lisa.'

She shrank away. 'Joe, please . . . listen, you've got the wrong person, Joe . . . I'm not Lisa . . .'

He moved slowly towards her, face triumphant. 'You shouldn't have done it, Lisa. You should have known that one day . . .'

'Joe. I'm not *Lisa*.'

'OK, if you insist. You're not Lisa. Come here, Lisa.'

One more step and he was standing against her, rubbing his body the length of hers, smiling at her. She did not know what made it the nastiest smile she had ever seen. It made her feel dirty. He reached for her breasts and squeezed them in his hands. It hurt. He backed her up against the wall and leaned his weight on her, pressing her against her Van Gogh reproduction of sunflowers. His hands crawled up her body, until they rested lightly on her neck.

Marian said, with thumping heart and quivering knees: 'Joe. Please, please go.'

'Go?' said Joe. 'Now, why should I want to go anywhere?'

'Joe, *please*.'

'Come here, babe. Come to Joe . . .'

'Leave me alone. Please, oh please . . .' Marian moved suddenly, her body loose with fear, hands moving up in front of her breasts in vain protection, her mouth opening to scream.

Joe's fingers barely moved on Marian's neck, but her scream was cut off in her throat. She stared up at him foolishly for a second, not even feeling the press of his fingertips under her ears, just watching the colours drain from his face and the room around her to leave a grey nauseous monotone. Then nothing.

She did not feel her hands fall limply to her sides, her knees buckle, or Joe pick her up lightly, carry her across the room to the sofa bed and undress her.

Marian awoke some unguessable period of time later. It could have been hours or seconds. It was, in fact, less than five minutes.

She found herself gagged with her own bandana, quite

naked. She was also . . . oh God . . . bound face down on her own coffee table. In panic, she jerked at her wrists, which were tied together with white nylon cord which had been passed under the table to secure her knees to the legs at the other end. She could move her legs from the knees down, but that did not help much. She struggled desperately, but Joe had done a good job.

'It won't work,' he said chattily. 'I'm great with knots. Something I picked up in the Service. Along with other things . . .' He was sitting, relaxed, in one of her Danish chairs, which he had pulled around to face her. He was smiling. In his hands, lying across his lap, he held her broom which he must have found in the little closet in the kitchenette.

She knew he was going to beat her to death with it. She stared up at him, neck arching, bright hair sweat-darkened, face blotched with tears. *Please God*, prayed Marian hopelessly, *don't let him hurt me; please, please God don't*, and to her utter humiliation felt warm wetness on her legs.

'Well now, look at that,' said Joe. 'Poor baby's gone and wet herself. Gone wee wee on her nice table. Never would've known you for such a chicken, Lisa.'

Marion moaned. It emerged through the gag as a useless, muffled squeak.

Joe said: 'I'll bet you're wondering what I'm going to be doing with this broom here.' He stood up, moved over to her, and straddled the broom. It stuck out between his legs like a monstrous orange penis. He laughed softly, staring down at her where she lay so helplessly, shamefully exposed, with buttocks spread.

Then he moved out of her vision, behind her.

It had been beautiful. The best ever.

Joe Capelli sighed with pleasure as he drove decorously along Park-Presidio Drive. He had certainly taught Lisa a good lesson this time. She had never peed with fright before; that had been great. And so crushed and humiliated. Of course, it must have hurt like hell, but he had been careful, as always, not to damage her.

And there was nothing, absolutely nothing whatever she could do about it.

'His name was Joe, Officer.'

'Last name?'

'I don't know.'

'Yes, Ma'am. And where did you meet him?'

'In . . . uh . . . the Shady Lane.'

'That's a bar, right?'

'Yes. Yes, a bar. On Clement Street.'

'Uhuh. Then what?'

'He . . . he took me home.'

'What kind of car?'

'I'm not sure. It was a nice car though . . . expensive.'

'What colour?'

'Dark blue . . . green . . . maybe maroon. It was a dark colour.'

'Know where he works?'

'I don't. No.'

'Anyone see you leave with him?'

'Maybe. I . . . I'm not sure.'

'What about your girl-friend?'

'She'd left already.'

'Then you got home. You asked him in?'

'Y – yes.'

'And you say he tied you to your coffee table and shoved a broom handle up you –'

'Oh God, yes.'

'What did he tie you with?'

'White ropes. Well . . . cord. Like you can buy at the hardware store.'

'Got them?'

'No. He . . . he untied me when he had . . . had finished. And then he took them with him.'

Joe smiled happily, imagining the scene as he turned right on to California Street. He could read the officer's mind like an open book. 'Oh lady,' he would be thinking, 'you pick up a stranger in a bar and take him home, you're fucking lucky you're still alive. One hell of a lot worse could have happened.'

No, Joe decided, she'd never call the police. Not in a thousand years.

T.C. – C

# JULIA

Julia wriggled uncomfortably on her stool, her awkwardly sized newsprint pad open on the table, and let her eyes rove slowly around the room, considering each bent head. There was the usual background of small sounds: uneasy creaking of aged furniture, a dozen pencils moving fast over paper, Ms Mendoza's heavy breathing, the ticking of the kitchen timer the model used to time his poses. The two crazy old men worked again on their still life, the tall one, one eye closed, holding a paint brush in front of his face, tightly between forefinger and thumb, to measure proportion, the short fat bald one working with obsessive concentration, tongue clenched between widely spaced yellowish teeth.

'It's wrong,' snapped Mr Bottarini. 'You got it wrong again. You moved the goddamn apple. And if you don't believe me, look at that.'

He held his painting up for Mr Brucker's inspection. Brucker glowered at it, thrusting out his lower lip.

'See? Ain't right,' Mr Bottarini said in triumph. 'You moved it again. Every week the same. Crazy old man.'

Mr Brucker said crossly: 'Go see an op – opertho ، ، ، go see an eye doctor.'

Mr Bottarini moved one of the apples a millimetre to the right. They glared at one another.

Julia heard Ms Mendoza say: 'That's better, Fox. Much much better,' with a grunt of exasperation from Fox in reply.

Of course, one was forced to work big with this particular model. He was about six-foot-five, weighing in at about 150 lbs. He had lank black hair bound in a braid by a piece of tired looking cloth. Julia could not get all his limbs on to the same sheet of paper.

At the moment he sat on the platform with one incredibly long skinny leg stretched out in front of him, chin resting on one hand in somewhat the same pose as 'The Thinker', although his expression, as he gazed across the room towards the window, was blank to the point of imbecility.

Meditating, thought Julia, or stoned to the eyeballs.

Mrs Pospicil sat beside her, chewing something. She had remarked cheerily to Fox, 'Not often they get us a man. At my age you gotta make the most of it, better believe it.'

Fox had grinned absently; the housewife on Julia's other side flushed rosily on each cheekbone and ducked her head.

But Julia was not thinking much about Mrs Pospicil. She was too busy wondering whether one of the people in this room could be the man on the telephone.

The calls had begun last Wednesday.

Hang-ups only until Friday morning – two days of hang-ups, and then this Lisa business.

'*I thought we'd go to the beach, Lisa.*' Crazy. '*Baker and Vallejo, Lisa. Right?*'

The Telephone Beast, as she had begun to think of him, had not been exactly threatening, but enough of a threat was implied, him wanting her to know he knew where she lived.

Then the calls stopped. Two days later she had begun to allow herself to believe that her caller had realized his mistake. Was not after all a sick person. Had even found the real Lisa . . .

Until today. This morning, 8.00 a.m., she had answered her phone with confidence. At that hour, it could be a job interview, her parents calling, anybody.

But there was nothing; just a faint click as whoever it was at the other end replaced the receiver. *It's starting again . . . all over again*, Julia thought, shaken. Telling herself it was a genuine mistake; someone realizing too late they had misdialled . . . anything. But deep inside knowing better.

So . . . could the Telephone Beast be right here in this room? Could it be Mr Brucker? Mr Bottarini? She doubted it. Both spoke with quite heavy accents.

But Fox spoke with no accent. And he knew where she lived, too.

Of course there were other men in the room, and she had filled out a registration form on joining the class, which had lain around for most of the first morning. Anybody could have picked it up and seen her name, address, and telephone number. But then, why would somebody in her class insist she was Lisa when they would know her; know she was not Lisa but Julia? Only one explanation for that. He was nuts.

*Oh God.*

*One more day*, decided Julia, placing one of the model's eyes much higher than the other one, staring down at the paper for nearly a minute, wondering why her drawing looked so strange. *One more day, and if he calls up for Lisa again, I'm calling the police.*

But what could the police do?

Realistically, she had to admit, very little.

Undoubtedly they would recommend she get an unlisted number, and that, for someone looking desperately for a job, would be disastrous. Maybe, Julia wondered, just maybe this Lisa had my number before I did, and this guy has been out of town for a while, and thinks it's still Lisa's number. Perhaps my voice is like hers, too.

But that would not work, unless by insane coincidence Lisa lived on the same corner she did.

Who was Lisa? And where was she? Was she somewhere in the city, blithely going about her business, quite unaware that Julia was taking the rap for something Lisa had apparently done?

She glanced surreptitiously around the room again, thinking about last Wednesday, when Fox had taken her home. All he needed to do was call Information to find out her phone number. She did not want it to be Fox, but he did seem to be the most likely candidate. Although, thought Julia, I met other men that day. There had been the blond-haired brother-in-law; Fox had called him Elliott. But Elliott did not know her name. She could almost swear she had not told him. He could have asked Fox later, however. And then there had been Adrian Robens, who had interviewed her for the winery job, dutiful and bored. But very gay. Most unlikely. And the man . . . Joe . . . she had met in the bar, who did not know her last name either. No way of finding out her phone number.

But then – Julia winced as another thought crossed her mind – she had of course had very slight personal dealings with a great many people since arriving in San Francisco. Had she somehow offended or unwittingly turned on a sick mind at the Department of Motor Vehicles, Pacific Gas and

Electric, the Pacific Telephone Company, the *San Francisco Chronicle*? She remembered the secondhand car dealer, the department stores where she had credit cards, all the companies she had applied to for jobs. The list was potentially endless, all with her name, address, and phone number. Could somebody at any of these places be bearing a grudge against her? Taking revenge by frightening her and calling her Lisa as cover? Oh surely not. But you could never tell; there were some extremely weird people in this world.

The face that stared up at her from the paper out of his crooked eyes looked like something Picasso might have done in a drunken moment in the dark. *God*, thought Julia, *I'm wasting my time in this class; I can't draw. Certainly not like* –

Fox.

Still the prime suspect because of her complete inability to classify him, and thus make him predictable and easy to understand. Fox seemed a human contradiction; even his presence in this class of mediocre amateurs, when even she could recognize his ability, was absurd. Particularly when he seemed to have a lot of money – *'Julia, I want you to meet Miss Doyle. She takes care of Mother* –' which appeared to place Miss Doyle in the position of old family retainer – a dying breed, found only among the remnants of the very rich old families.

There came a ping from the model's timer. Instantly he rotated his body halfway to the right to expose a different aspect of himself to the room, crouching on his haunches, a huge hairy spider, all bent elbows and sharp knees. Julia, Mrs Pospicil, and the nervous housewife were now confronted with an endless length of hip and skinny flank. Mrs Pospicil, defeated at last, sighed, got creakily to her feet, and headed for the bathroom.

Julia decided she should try and find out some more about Fox. She would talk with him at mid-morning break.

Fox, bored with the model, began to draw Julia.

# FOX

By the time Mrs Pospicil had trudged back again to her place through all the drawing boards and the thicket of stools, the portrait was going well, the tied-back hair revealing the high forehead, straight nose, well-shaped ears, and good bones, uncluttered. *It's a shame*, Fox thought, *that she looks so worried and unhappy.* He had not really noticed before he began to draw, but with the development of the portrait it all became so plain: the puckers of strain at the corners of her lips, the hollowed cheeks, the shadows under the eyes telling of anxious nights. Once or twice, while he worked, she looked at him, eyes strange, almost furtive. Fox wondered whether she could be embarrassed, remembering their last parting, when she had been so abrupt. Surely not. He had been a bit hurt, true, but had got over it. He was not so sensitive as that, for God's sake. Still, having given her a ride home and all, she could have been nicer.

At the end of the 15-minute period, when Fox had completed his drawing as far as possible, Mrs Pospicil had done nothing at all, and Julia had struggled to contain her drawing on the page and given up, Ms Mendoza called for a coffee break. The model stood at once, flexed his joints, stretched his arms impossibly high above his head and released a sudden gust of body odour into the overheated air, before pulling on an old grey wool bathrobe, lying down flat on his back, head and long bony feet dangling over the end of the platform.

Julia filled the mug she had remembered to bring this morning.

Fox stood immediately behind her.

She said: 'Listen, I wanted to talk with you. I mean, last week, I didn't mean to be rude.'

'That's OK.'

'I had a job interview and I was nervous. It was really nice of you to give me a ride; I'd never have made it otherwise.'

'Don't worry about it,' Fox said, pleased she had taken the trouble to explain. 'Did you get the job?'

'No,' Julia said flatly. She added: 'I don't suppose I'll ever get a job.' She moved towards the window. 'Why were you staring at me so much?'

'Staring at you?'

'Through the last pose.'

'Oh.' Fox grinned. 'I was drawing you.'

'Drawing *me*?'

'It was either you or Spiderman. You're much more interesting.'

'Oh. Thanks – I guess.'

Fox poured himself some coffee. 'You're welcome.'

'Could I see it?'

Mrs Pospicil proffered a greasy bag. 'You kids want a snail?'

Fox took one. 'Thanks.'

'And what about you, girl?' Mrs Pospicil sniffed. 'You're a toothpick already. Men like to feel some meat on the bones.'

Julia shook her head. 'Not hungry. Thanks anyway.' She studied Fox's drawing of herself. 'It's very good. Awfully good. But I didn't know I looked so old. And sad.'

'It helps with the devil,' added Mrs Pospicil.

Fox grimaced. 'It must be worrying for you, not having a job.' She stood beside him, tense as a runner poised on starting blocks. She was very pale. The thick, dark gold hair was tied back in a blue bandana, and he could see the dark tracing of vein and artery in her neck, at the corner of her jaw. He wanted to touch, very gently, where it pulsed. She was wearing a bright blue cotton shirt and orange slacks, but the colourful clothes only served to accentuate the impression of muted distress. He thought how strange it was, that he should not have noticed this before, that it was not until he had drawn her face that the suffering inside emerged. She seemed such a calm, aloof person, while all the time, underneath . . .

She moved away from him, across the room to her seat, apparently quite composed. He followed her, leaned his hip against her table, looking down at her while they both drank their coffee.

Suddenly confiding, she said: 'I guess this is just a bad time for me. It's not just the job. It's been a bad year. No wonder I look like that.'

Fox thought she looked beautiful, even if sadder and older. He said: 'That's rough. What happened?'

'What didn't.' Julia sighed. 'I don't . . . well, I guess you might as well know. It's no secret.'

'Only if you want to tell me,' said Fox.

She stared down, unseeing, at her bad drawing of the elongated model. She said nothing for several minutes. Fox waited, quietly.

'My husband went off with someone else, for starters,' Julia said flatly. 'And . . . I guess I just feel somehow ashamed. It's odd, isn't it? To feel as though it was somehow my fault. Of course, it happens all the time,' she said, forcedly bright. 'I mean, people are always getting divorced. Every day. But never me before. So I left New York and came here, which was probably a bad mistake. I mean, to leave my job . . . just walk out . . . and run away. And now . . . now there's a . . .'

Fox said encouragingly: 'Now there's a what?'

She looked up at him, eyes huge. 'Now some freak keeps calling me on the phone. He started by just hanging up on me. Now he says things, like: "I know where you live, Lisa." He calls me "Lisa".'

'Wrong number. Must be.'

'It's not.' She was watching him under her lashes. 'And he knows where I *live*.'

'Sounds like a nut. I hate phones; they take advantage of people,' Fox said, endowing the telephone with an independently malignant personality. 'And they could have been designed with nuts in mind. The perfect untraceable device.'

'When things start going wrong, they all go wrong at once. Together. It's just too *much*.'

Fox nodded. 'A rough year. But can't you at least change your number? Get an unlisted number?'

'I've thought of that. But it's on my résumé, and I've sent that out to a hundred places. I don't dare. I mean, then I'd miss out all round.'

'Oh,' said Fox, who had never applied for a job, 'I never thought of that.'

'It'll work out, though,' Julia said determinedly. 'Of course it will. And anyway, not having a job's my own fault. Nobody *forced* me to leave New York.'

Fox looked down on the top of her head, seeing the whiteness of skin under her parting, the individual honey-coloured hairs, strong and shining, and felt a sudden surge of tenderness he had never known before. He wanted to enfold her, to beg her to believe him, that everything would be all right. That he would *make* everything be all right. But he made no move to touch her – not yet. He munched the rest of his snail, pondering what to say to comfort her, russet brows knitted.

There was a small silence then, while Fox understood for the first time how worrying about someone else's problems, especially the problems of somebody he cared about, made his own shrink into insignificance, while Julia regretted pouring out her troubles to a stranger. Particularly to Fox, who still might be the Telephone Beast.

*So much for finding out about him,* she told herself crossly. *All I've done is talk about myself.*

She asked: 'Is Fox your real name, or just what people call you? Because of your hair?'

'My last name. I'm Wesley Bishop Fox.' He held out his hand to her, formally, 'The Third. I guess we've never been introduced properly.'

His hand was square, practical, short-fingered. The kind of hand, popular myth to the contrary, most common among artists, surgeons, and concert pianists. It was warm and strong. 'Doesn't anybody call you Wesley? Or Wes?' she asked.

'Only my mother. She calls me Wesley. I always think she's talking to somebody else.'

'And your father?'

'Died before I was born,' Fox said, matter-of-fact.

'Oh,' said Julia. 'I'm sorry.' Then, struggling with a shred of memory: 'Your father was Wesley Bishop Fox. I know I've heard of him. Didn't he . . . didn't he marry an actress? A movie star? I think I remember reading in the papers . . . some time . . .'

'My mother's Hope Hartley.'

'Hope Hartley!' Julia's face cleared. 'Of course. And I've

seen her. Actually, I saw her on late-night TV a few weeks ago. She doesn't still act, does she?'

Fox laughed. 'Not for about thirty years. She made her last movie in about 1941. I reckon my father got her out of it just in time. She finished out her contract, and that was it. There was all that stuff when they got married, how she was giving up her career for love, how she was leaving her public, her fans . . . all that garbage.'

'She must have been . . . I mean she was . . . gorgeous,' said Julia. 'Really lovely.'

'Oh yes,' Fox agreed. 'She was stunning. But acting? Forget it. Of course she always thought she was fantastic as an actress.'

'Hope Hartley's a beautiful name, too.'

'Better believe it,' said Fox. 'A hell of a lot better than Hilda Katz.'

'Hilda . . . for heaven's sake!' Julia began to laugh.

'Hey, terrific,' said Fox. 'You look good, laughing.'

'And she never tried for a comeback? After your father died?'

'How should I know? I was a baby. I wasn't even *born*,' Fox corrected himself. 'She might have tried . . . probably did, but nothing ever happened, thank God. Doyly would have talked her out of it. Doyly knew the score, all right.'

'Doyly? You mean Miss Doyle? The woman who had the . . . the blackout, or whatever?'

'Right. She lives with Mother. She's been with her since forever – her dresser, then secretary, companion, housekeeper, nanny for Nancy and me . . . you name it.'

'A tower of strength.'

'You bet. The Fox family would never have made it without Miss Doyle. Father was so fond of her, and grateful, he even left her some money, and the will was made years before he died. Maybe he knew his heart was bad.'

Fox's voice, cold and cynical when speaking of his mother, mellowed to strong warmth when he talked about Miss Doyle.

'She must be very fond of your mother,' Julia said, 'to stay with her all these years if she doesn't have to.'

'Maybe she is,' said Fox. 'Maybe. Though I sure don't

know why,' he confided, precipitously. 'My mother's a bitch.
Doyly's life must be godawful.'

He sounded angry. Julia stared at him without speaking.

Across the room Mr Bottarini complained loudly to everyone in general that there was a different shadow on his vase
and a highlight on one of the apples which had not been
there before. 'You moved it,' he accused Mr Brucker. 'You
moved it while I was drinking my coffee.'

'Sure I moved it,' said Mr Brucker. 'I had to dust the
goddamn thing; nobody has cleaned it in weeks. I polish it on
my sleeve.'

Mr Bottarini grumbled: 'It's too shiny.'

Ms Mendoza said: 'Now, now, boys. You two must
keep it down.'

They glared at her, united for once in their disgust.


The mood was broken.

The model shed his bathrobe again and coiled his long
limbs into the next pose. The second half of the morning had
begun. An element of briskness charged the room as paper
rustled, the electric pencil sharpener buzzed and spat coils
of shavings, and chairs were squeaked along the linoleum
while the class settled back down to work.

'Oh well,' said Fox, 'enough of that. You don't need to
hear about Mother.'

'Your family's interesting.'

'If you say so. Hey listen,' said Fox, leaning across her
table, lowering his voice. 'Are you doing anything special
tonight?'

Her head jerked upwards. For an instant her eyes met his,
startled. 'Tonight?' echoed Julia, and as he watched he seemed
to see metal shutters fall in place, on guard. *Against what?*
wondered Fox. *Against me?*

He said: 'Yeah. Like could you have dinner with me?
Maybe we could see a movie.'

He knew she would say no, now. And didn't know why.

'Thank you,' Julia said, voice taut. 'That would be nice.
But I guess I . . . I'm kind of busy. Maybe some other
time?'

Fox looked at her, searchingly. He had been so certain of her. *But you should never be certain,* he told himself wryly, *of anything.*

The steel shutter never wavered.

He shrugged. 'Sure,' Fox said lightly, hurting. 'Some other time. That'd be fine . . .'


ELLIOTT


Hoping he sounded convincing, Elliott said: 'Looking mighty terrific today, as usual, m'dear,' and lowered his elegant, well-tailored figure on to the boudoir love seat.

He was finding it harder, each week, to really put his heart into these little sessions with his mother-in-law.

But Hope bridled as usual, and pushed at her hair. 'Elliott darling! How divine of you to say so. Why, Ah declare, Mr Butler, how you do run on!'

*Games with Rhett and Scarlett,* Elliott thought derisively, plying her with Cabernet. *Fun with Dick and Jane. Where Dick, the dashing ersatz aristocrat from Milwaukee has to win and keep right on winning his Jane (aka Hilda Katz) who otherwise, being notably capricious where men and money are concerned, is quite capable of leaving her whole big bundle of loot to the latest muscular gardener/painter/plumber/mailman to catch her lascivious, wine-sodden eye.*

He studied Hope dispassionately while playing his semi-automatic stale charade, able to gain some cold comfort from the sure knowledge that Hope was drinking herself to death as sure as God made little green apples, and that he was helping her along as best he could.

*Give her a year or two,* Elliott thought hopefully, pouring wine, *and if I still have the decaying old wreck eating out of my hand the way she's doing now I'm in like Flynn.* But holy Christ it was hard sometimes. Once again he allowed himself a glimpse of reward, just to keep himself going: a glimpse of Nancy and himself living in this house. He would neither let Nancy sell it, nor (God forbid) Fox – the unknown quantity, the 'x' in the equation, who would unfortunately have to have his say in such matters – for Elliot loved the house, every gloomy fusty inch of it. And by God he deserved it, had earned the right to enjoy it.

As Fox never had.

Although, Elliott reminded himself comfortably, Hope had never been able to stand Fox. And don't forget about the Children. In this connection the Children, the trumps in his hand, were always dignified with an uppercase C. Fox could not hope to compete, there.

But unfortunately, between now and Hope's ultimate demise, too much could happen despite Hope's dislike for Fox, and his own uppercase Children.

Which was why he must continue to be very nice to Hope.

One of Elliott's favourite dream images was a long series of doors, one behind the other in diminishing perspective. They were all slightly ajar, and Egon Milhausen stood behind the last door. As time passed and Elliott's station in life prospered, door after door slammed shut in sequence, with Egon retreating farther into the shadows each time. And when Hope died, the ultimate door would close in his face, trapping Egon Milhausen where he belonged, in the far distant past forever.

Then Elliott really would be Somebody, living like a lord in a mansion.

His father and mother would never know about it, though. In a way it was a shame . . .

His father, Herman Milhausen, had a squat, hairy body, a thick beer-drinker's belly as hard as a watermelon, a bald head with a fringe of coarse black hair around the back and sides, and wore his underwear to bed. Erna, his mother, had very pale blue eyes, like his own, and colourless hair, pulled back so cruelly tight the hairs dragged up from her skin. She wore her hair in a braid around the crown of her head. She never wore lipstick, nice clothes, or tried to look attractive like other women, for 'Vanity is sinful,' Erna announced with flat assurance, compressing thin lips.

His parents seemed to hate each other. His father often called his mother a bloodless bitch, while Erna herself spent years and years, ever since Egon was small, telling him how gross his father was, how she had married beneath her and paid the price, ever since, for forgetting that she was Somebody. (Apparently, thought Egon later on, pride was not a sin.) Egon's price for being a Somebody of the future was loneliness. Erna hated him to mix with the neighbourhood kids although, as the years went by, she had little if anything to worry about for the neighbourhood kids would have nothing to do with Egon except as an object for derision.

With his shyness, pimples, tacky blue suits, and disastrous ability to always say and do exactly the wrong things, Egon was a natural-born loser to be shunned at all costs.

He was the Freak.

While his own attitude to his peers was compounded of contempt, envy, and fear – the fear relating most particularly to the girls, shrill and gaudy in their matador pants, crimson lipstick, and ballet slippers, taunting and cruel as hell.

He never asked a girl for a date, for what girl would ever go out with him?

And if by some extraordinary chance a girl did, what would he do with her? How would they get through the evening? He couldn't afford a movie ('No, Egon, that's to save for college'), and no kids went ballroom dancing. They gyrated and shook their bodies to Bill Haley and the Comets, or Presley, while the only dances he knew were the foxtrot, quickstep, and waltz, learned so painfully at Thelma Krause's Dancing Academy. With white gloves on.

And then there was sex. He would be expected to neck with her, at least. Perhaps to French kiss her. To touch her *there*. Of course he would, because as Jack Miller said, and he should know, most girls secretly were insatiable nymphomaniacs. Even thinking about it made Egon break out in a cold sweat.

For sex was fearful, not to mention foul.

Sex was waking that morning to find his pyjamas and lower sheet stiff and warm from his first night-time emissions, and in horror – how could this happen to *him* – bundling the telltale sheet and pyjama pants into the laundry hamper before leaving for school and making up his bed carefully, wondering how to take a clean sheet from the linen closet when he came home without his mother knowing what he had done.

Of course, it had all been futile.

For Erna greeted him when he came home in the afternoon with a tight disgusted face and accused him of unnatural acts with little Peter in the darkness. She reminded him how revolting his act had been for fully a week after the sheets and pyjamas had been laundered in carbolic and Clorox. 'Filthy,' Erna said, brooking no argument. 'No better than the animals.' And resignedly, 'You're your father all over again.'

His coarse, ignorant, beer-swilling father.

No.

He rejected that idea totally.

For being Elliott Millner was about the furthest he could expect to come from Herman Milhausen, and he would never go back. Not if he had to go on pampering this dreadful sick old woman for the rest of his life. Who just happened to be Nancy's mother. Who controlled a vast sum of money and whose good regard he had always, so far, managed to keep alive through his skilful manipulation of her mild boozy lust for his body.

*Two years*, Elliott thought longingly; *two years at the most, of making sure Hope goes on singing my song.*

He vowed: *I won't make one mistake, I won't set a foot wrong, no matter what Fox might say or do.*

'Hopey darling,' he murmured gently, 'your little glass is empty. Let Elliott pour you another little drinky-poo.'

'Darling,' Hope purred, 'you take care of me so well. What would I do without you?'


## JULIA


Julia prepared for another evening alone at home. While changing her interview clothes for jeans, she paused suddenly, grimacing at herself in the mirror, calling: 'Well, hi there, pal. What are you and I going to do together tonight?' Thinking that there was not a great deal of difference between herself and Harry (or Larry?) halfway across the Pacific on his solo voyage. Except it would be better on the ocean; there was no telephone.

On the kitchen table lay a letter from McKenzie and French, Advertising, which began: 'Dear Ms Naughton: It was good talking with you the other day, and we have read your résumé with great interest. However . . .' This was a blow, since McKenzie and French had seemed the only people so far who had appeared to have genuine interest in her. It had been waiting on her return from class. She had fixed herself a vodka and tonic in her disappointment, then walked over to Polk Street, to a movie house which had a double bill of good second-run movies with a Wednesday afternoon matinee at budget prices. She had spent nearly four hours there for $1.50, not getting home until six o'clock.

Now, she prepared herself another drink, deciding, after she had finished it, to cook an omelette. She spent several almost pleasurable minutes deciding what to put in it, settling for cheddar cheese and parsley, and a half bottle of Charles Krug Gray Riesling to go with it. She had taken to buying rather expensive wine to drink with her dinners, sipping slowly from a Waterford goblet (a wedding present from one of *her* friends), and making it last, for there was a certain comfort in twirling the wine gently, in watching the refracted splinters of light shine through the diamond facets of the beautiful crystal. One derived a lot of pleasure from small things. And in little routines.

*This is how old-maidism really begins*, Julia decided. *Fussing over my omelette, and drinking my wine – just so much and just so – at the same minute every evening.* Thinking that she did not have to be alone at all. She could be out right now with someone who, although younger, was both attractive and sympathetic. But who just might also be a psychopath.

*So what do I do instead*, she wondered. *Talk to my plants? Get a pet? A cat would be company. Quite good company, really. It could sleep on my bed, and –*

The telephone rang.

Her head snapped up. 7.00 p.m. Not about a job.

Ten o'clock in New York. Perhaps . . . but no. It would never be Gerry. She told herself sternly: *Forget it; it's over. Gerry's gone forever . . .* knowing all the time who it was.

'You won't get away this time, Lisa.'

Julia's hand began to tremble violently. 'Listen, I don't know who you are, or who you think I am. But you're making a mistake. *I am not Lisa.* Will you *stop* this!'

The man laughed gently. He said: 'Lisa, you kill me, you really do, you know it? Playing these dumb games.'

'If you call me one more time –'

'You see, I'm through with games. It's gone on for too long. Now, you know I want you, Lisa, and I can come and get you any time. You can't do anything about it, can you?'

'All right,' Julia said, her whole body shaking, 'all right. I'm calling the police. Right now. I'm calling the police, you hear me?'

The echo of her screaming voice hung in the air after she hung up. She found she was still gripping her glass of vodka and tonic, holding it at a tilt so it trickled in a thin stream down her leg.

She set the glass down, willed her hand to hold steady, and dialled the San Francisco Police Department.

'Please,' Julia said, voice all awry, 'I've got to get some help. Please . . . I need *help*. Somebody *help* me . . .'


JOE


Across the city, Joe Capelli continued to talk into the now dead mouthpiece. He talked for several minutes, telling Lisa just what he planned to do with her when they got together again. 'After all, Lisa, what did you *expect*?'

He stood with his back pressed against the door of the booth. He was wearing a light tan raincoat. The left-hand pocket was slit inside, so he could reach in, unzip his fly, and touch himself with nobody any the wiser. He had slit that pocket with a razor blade a week ago; it had never occurred to him in all the years before to do such a thing. But knowing that Lisa was there, frightened, at the other end of a piece of wire excited him unbearably, and now, standing in the booth outside the Washeteria on Eddy and Divisadero, he could knead himself to relief knowing that not even the large black woman standing so impatiently not three feet away the other side of the glass, bundle of wash in a pillow case at her feet, dime in her hand, could see what he was doing.

'Oh Lisa,' Joe breathed softly, sagging momentarily back against the door as he replaced the receiver. 'Oh Lisa, one of these days . . . one of these days *soon* . . .'

'Hey mister,' the woman yelled from outside. 'Hey, mister. Folks is waiting.'

Joe swept the phone booth with an analytical, wide-angled glance, making sure he had left nothing behind – no wallet, paper, letter – nothing which could in any way lead back to him. It was strange how quickly he had fallen into this habit of extreme caution, as though it were second nature and he had been born to a life of deception.

The woman was grumbling: 'That ain't no *private* phone, no way,' as he shouldered past her, unseeing, buttoning his raincoat around him to vanish on to Divisadero, blending with the swirling fog.

# FOX

The apartment over the garage had changed a great deal since the days of Wong.

The walls were now stark white throughout. The many layers of squalid linoleum had been ripped up and the old pine boards underneath sanded and waxed. Fox had set up his drafting table near the much-enlarged, north-facing window in the living-room; had built shelving and racks for his drawings, and installed batteries of spotlights across the ceilings. As soon as the day threatened to grow dark, he switched all of them on. There were no chairs; instead, a pile of fat, brilliantly coloured pillows were heaped in a corner.

This evening Miss Doyle sat among them sipping a mug of tea, legs drawn up uncomfortably, squinting at Fox through the customary harsh glare. Her eyes found the adjustment painful after the rosy, womb-like gloom of the boudoir, where she had left Hope drowsing cozily among her past glories.

Fox was working on a drawing. He was paying very little attention to her.

'I wanted to talk with you, Foxy.' She could feel the pillows slipping under her, and made an awkward rotative movement with her hips, trying to keep them in place. She wished Fox would get some chairs; *I'm too old to be sitting on the floor*, thought Miss Doyle. 'Foxy?'

'Yes. Sorry.' Fox stared down critically at Julia's face. Rubbed gently at the highlight on her cheekbone.

'You're not listening,' said Miss Doyle.

'Yes I am, Doyly.'

Miss Doyle sipped at her tea. 'What was I saying, then?' Fox raised his head and stared at her blankly.

'I was talking about Elliott.'

'Oh yes,' said Fox. 'Of course, Elliott.'

Miss Doyle sighed. 'I . . . I had another message. Today.'

'A message,' said Fox. 'I see.' Reminding himself that Miss Doyle's ancestors came from the gale-torn shores of Connemara; how, for her, the Celtic phantoms apparently still retained their powers even in California in the late 20th century, even though there was another explanation, scientifically rational, for the 'messages'. But Miss Doyle believed implicitly otherwise. *Oh really*, Fox thought impatiently. He said: 'A message, huh. What was it?'

'It was in Safeway,' Miss Doyle said. 'Today was one of Miss Hope's Safeway days. I only just got her settled down. It took me a good hour.'

She could never be hurried when imparting messages. Fox said: 'Poor Doyly.' He poured a shot of John Jamieson's Irish whiskey, which he kept just for her, into her tea. 'Try this. It'll settle your nerves,' for he knew trips with Hope were always traumatic. Approximately once every three months, driven by a peculiar compulsion to keep in touch with what she called 'the mainstream', and 'the little people', *as though they were elves or pixies*, thought Fox, Hope demanded to do the grocery shopping herself.

And each time, predictably, once out in the mainstream, she would almost drown, floundering between aisles, bewildered, coming to abrupt stops while exasperated shoppers crashed into each other all around her, while the little people, far from being wonderful, were downright rude. They said things like: 'Will you look where you're going?' 'Jesus, lady, you ran that cart right over my foot.' And, 'You clumsy fool, the baby had just got to sleep.'

They did not ask for her autograph any more, or take pictures. They no longer nudged one another: 'Hey, look Dad, Sis, Frank, Darlene, Thelma, there's Hope Hartley over there!' Nobody ever seemed to know who she was any more, but Hope tried again as soon as the memory of the last time had worn away.

'Foxy, this is strong,' Miss Doyle said.

'You need it,' he replied.

'Yes. Oh dear . . .'

'So tell me. What was the message?'

'You don't believe me,' Miss Doyle said bravely, 'do you?'

Fox said gently: 'Tell me anyway.'

She braced herself with another gulp of her laced tea. 'All right,' Miss Doyle said. 'It was in produce.'

'Produce. Yes.'

'I was looking at watermelons. Wong likes watermelons. Your mo – Miss Hope was looking at the avocados. The man had to tell her not to squeeze them so hard.'

'And?'

'I saw Elliott.'

'Well?' said Fox. 'There's no law says Elliott can't go into Safeway.'

'No, Foxy, no. You don't understand. Elliott wasn't *there* –'

'But you said – '

'I know what I said. I saw him in the watermelons.'

'Oh,' said Fox.

'Just his face, looking out. Dark green and dead looking. All dead inside, Foxy. He's all dead inside. All dark.'

'Gross,' said Fox.

And Miss Doyle said warningly: 'Foxy . . .'

Fox coughed and scrubbed at Julia's cheekbone again. 'Sorry.'

'He hates you, Foxy,' said Miss Doyle.

'Baloney,' said Fox.

'It's true.'

'Why should he hate me?'

'I don't know. Think.'

Despite himself he thought crossly, *It's a whole load of balls, and now I've gone and fucked up my drawing* – an image came seeping slowly into his mind. A long-ago image, poisonous as marsh gas – *which I'd quite forgotten*, thought Fox.

He and Elliott at the Northern Pacific Club.

'Doyly,' he said slowly, 'do you remember the N.P. Club? When Elliott took me to lunch there years ago?'

At Miss Doyle's age, time frames were different. Six years ago seemed like yesterday. She nodded.

'I always hated that place,' Fox said thoughtfully. 'I mean, if you want to go out to eat, there are so many really neat places to go.' He liked large, airy places with pretty waitresses and a lot of light. But the N.P. Club was important to Elliott. So he had gone, and even put his dreaded Thayer Academy suit on, and tried to be a good guest.

'There was this huge spider,' Fox went on with relish, 'crawling across the skylight right over our heads. It kept kind of slipping, you know, like it was going to drop in our soup. I reckoned it would hit the soup at about 100 m.p.h. That's one hell of a high ceiling, too – must be forty, fifty feet. It kind of got me through lunch, thinking about it.'

Miss Doyle said nothing; she watched him over the rim of her mug. He had stopped drawing; his face was tense and inward looking, remembering.

'After lunch he took me on this tour of the place, like I needed to see it all again or something, and then we had a swim. That was OK. That was the only good part of the lunch. Until . . .' They hadn't brought suits, he went on, but there was this wizened old guy down there in the massage room, and he had lent them suits, or rented them or something, for nothing came free at the N.P. Club.

'Yes?' Miss Doyle prompted.

'I . . . I don't know . . .' Fox stammered. How could he tell Miss Doyle that when they were dressing, he had seen Elliott staring at his cock like . . . *Jesus, I don't know.* 'I don't think I can tell you that, Doyly,' he said abruptly. Not about that, anyway. He remembered thinking, *Shit, he's gay*, but Fox had been approached by gays since he was nine years old, and this was different.

For a second his eyes had met Elliott's and Fox felt the naked cracking impact of what he realized now was hatred. Then it was gone, politely veiled. For whatever reason, Elliott hated him then, and presumably nothing had changed.

But why?

'And the girl too,' Miss Doyle said.

Fox looked up sharply, his fingers gripping the edge of the table, the knuckles white. 'What girl?'

'The girl you brought to the house that time. Julia.'

'Oh,' Fox said dismissively, 'her.'

'She was there too.'

'Where?' Fox asked with derision. 'In the watermelon?'

'Mock all you want,' Miss Doyle said doggedly, 'but you had better listen. The first message came when you brought her up to the house. When I saw her then, it was kind of . . . kind of like a warning . . .'

'Well you won't be seeing her again,' Fox said flatly. 'There's nothing to worry about. Not one thing. I won't be seeing her any more. She means nothing . . .'

'Why are you drawing her then?'

'Doyly, drop it. You don't understand. Just leave it alone.'

'But Foxy—'

'I said to *forget* it. Anyway, that's crazy. He only saw her that one time.'

'He hates anything of yours,' Miss Doyle said gently.

'Doyly,' Fox shouted, '*she is not mine.*' Then quietly: 'Maybe I ought to go away again. Get the hell out of everybody's hair.'

'Foxy! Please—'

'The Professor's going on another trip soon. He'd take me with him for sure. Maybe it'd be better for all of us— Elliott . . . Nancy . . . Julia . . . Mother . . .'

'But not for me!' It burst from Miss Doyle, uncontrollable, a wail of distress. 'Oh Foxy, no. I couldn't bear that. Not again, so soon—'

'Doyly!'

They stared at each other, Fox appalled, Miss Doyle defiant. Then: 'I'm sorry, dear.' She took a visible pull on herself. 'But I get so lonely, you know, with you gone so long.

Five years can seem like nothing, but sometimes it's forever.'

'Doyly,' Fox said, sounding very young, 'whatever I do, it seems wrong.'

She wished there was some way she could help him.


## JULIA


Officer Fein was young, portly, wore a sweeping black moustache. His patrol car was parked in Julia's driveway where his partner, Officer Gonsalves, sat munching from a bag of Fritos and reading the sports section of the paper.

Officer Fein said: 'Sorry to hear you've been having trouble, ma'am.' He thought admiringly: All *right*. Great shape; nice little ass. He was not particularly surprised to hear she was having trouble, sexy-looking chick like her. 'Been going on long?'

'A couple of weeks,' Julia said listlessly. Fear had given way now to an enormous apathy. She knew there was nothing anybody could do. Calling the police was a waste of everybody's time.

'So tell me,' said Officer Fein, 'do you live alone here? No husband, boy-friend, room-mate?'

'No. I'm alone.'

*But not for long*, thought the young policeman, *no way. Jesus, I'd sure like to get together with her*, then mentally shook himself, remembering Arlene and the kids in the little house in the Sunset District. Ah well, it did no harm . . dreaming. He smiled at Julia encouragingly. 'You're divorced?'

'Not yet. Separated.'

'Separated; yeah. Couldn't be your husband? I mean, your ex?'

'No. He still lives in New York.'

'He could still – '

'I'd know his voice.'

'Oh,' said Officer Fein. 'Let's hear it, then.'

So she told him. How it began with hang ups; how the hang ups had led to the Lisa business.

'Does he say anything dirty? Or is it just nasty stuff?'

'No,' Julia shook her head. 'He's never said anything like that. Nothing obscene.'

'How long does he talk?'

'A minute or two. Until I hang up.'

'You should of hung up on him right away. From the beginning.'

'But I thought it was just some guy with a wrong number. I mean, when somebody calls you by the wrong name . . Why do *you* think he's calling me Lisa?'

Officer Fein shrugged. 'Why not? He's a nut. So he calls you Lisa. He might as well call you Marge. Or . . . or Dorothy. Or . . .'

'You don't think it's important? About Lisa?'

'Doubt it very much.' He was making notes. 'Well, you just hang up on him right away from now on. For starters. And you should change your number. Get an unlisted number.'

'I can't do that.'

'Sure you can. Why not?'

She told him about her résumé. The policeman stood still, reflective. He said: 'Yeah. See what you mean.'

'So what can I do?'

'Get an answering service. One of those answering machines maybe – '

'I wish I could,' Julia said, 'but I can't afford one until I get a job.'

Officer Fein sighed. 'Well, just go on hanging up on him. That'll cool him off. These guys, they're all mouth. He'll give up, if you just don't give him a chance to talk any.'

'But he says he knows where I live. I mean. I *know* he knows where I live.'

At that moment, Joe Capelli cruised slowly down the block. He noticed the black and white patrol car at once, and drove slowly on. Officer Gonsalves finished his Fritos, crushed the empty bag into a little ball and put it in his garbage container. He was a very tidy man. He did not once look up from his newspaper but even if he had he would not have seen anything to worry about, not being possessed of second sight.

'Probably a neighbour,' Officer Fein said reasonably. 'Some

guy lives around here, sees you go in and out. Could even be watching you talk on the phone and jacking . . . uh . . yeah.'

'I doubt it,' said Julia. 'The phone's in the kitchen. He wouldn't be able to see.'

'Noticed anybody hanging around? Anyone at all? You probably wouldn't ever notice, but maybe some old guy out with his dog or something.'

'No.'

'Well, listen.' Officer Fein scratched at his moustache and put his notebook in his pocket. 'There's not a hell of a lot we can do, you know, if you can't change your number. Only thing, this is our car radio section. We can keep an eye on the house for you; make sure we cruise around here more often.'

'Well,' said Julia, 'thanks anyway.'

'I wouldn't worry,' said Officer Fein. 'I really wouldn't worry at all. Just remember what I said, and hang up on the jerk. Don't give him a chance to get talking with you. That's where he gets his jollies.

'And don't forget,' he added, removing his comforting portly authoritative presence from her doorway, 'it's just another crank. Don't encourage him and he'll give up. Honest. It happens all the time. They *never* do anything but talk.'


ELLIOTT


Elliott kissed the air above Nancy's head. 'See you in half an hour. I'm going to drop in on Hope while you dress.' Nancy, in pink satin slip, sat at her vanity surrounded by pots, pink powder, and lotions. Elliott was reminded of Miss Piggy in one of his childhood books.

She said: 'But you only just saw Mother. Didn't you see her yesterday?'

Elliott said: 'Ah, well, one more time won't hurt.'

Nancy warned: 'Don't be late. Don't let her keep you.'

Tonight, so far as he could remember, there was a gallery opening, or a book publishing party or some such, followed by a dinner party somewhere – who knew where? Normally he kept track of all these things since the social round both amused him by its vacuity and delighted him at the same time because of his inclusion in it. *Look at me, Egon Milhausen, chatting so familiarly with all these wealthy/aristocratic/famous etc. people, just as though I was one of them (Jesus Christ, Elliott, you are one of them; you are, goddamnit, don't forget it.)*

But tonight he was incapable of staying home, chatting to Nancy, and listening to Amparo feed the children (there would be crashes, whining, tears, and sullen Latin imprecations). He had to get out; he needed to move, to transport his restless body somewhere even if it was only the five blocks to Hope's house, where he did not want to go; but visiting Hope would certainly do no harm; would build up his credit even more.

And it was worth it. 'Elliott darling! Two days in a row! My, how you spoil me! And how clever of you to come tonight, darling. I'm just too bored for words!'

'It's my pleasure,' Elliott said, bowing over her wrinkled hand and kissing it. 'Just couldn't stay away.'

'Oh my, how naughty, darling!' Hope gurgled with pleasure. 'Now come and have a drinkie. I think somewhere . . . I just opened . . . I mean, dear Doyly just opened . . . ah, there it is. Sweet, pour us both a tot like a love.' She passed Elliott a half-empty bottle.

And then Fox walked in.

Hope said, with the raised eyebrows and tight voice which Elliott knew showed intense displeasure: 'Why Wesley, what a surprise. Shouldn't you have let me know you were coming, do you think?' She did not offer him her hand to kiss.

'Should I, Mother? I'm sorry. Am I interrupting?' Fox said placidly, and sank into an over-stuffed pink velvet armchair which appeared to enfold his body with the greedy avidity of a Venus's fly-trap. He opened the sketch book he was carrying. 'I felt like drawing you. Do you mind? Hi, Elliott.'

*Of course she won't mind, you cunning little bastard,* thought Elliott. *And if you're smart, you'll make Hope look gorgeous in the picture (somehow) and she'll eat out of your hand.* He said: 'Hopey, dear, your glass is empty. Well, how about that – so's mine.'

He poured. 'Fox? Want a drink?'

'No,' said Fox, busy. 'Thanks.'

Hope bridled, sipped at her wine, fluffed up her hair. 'Why, how nice, Wesley. I don't think you've ever done me before.'

'I haven't?' Fox said, surprised. 'I don't know why not. You've got a great face.'

'Wesley! Dear, how charming. And here I was, thinking . . .'

*Jesus Christ*, thought Elliott. *The little fucker's doing it. And he can really draw, too. He could make Godzilla look pretty good.* Now he had to stay until Fox left. He did not dare leave the two of them together, with Fox undoubtedly creating a likeness of Hope in her teens. He finished the remains of his wine and poured some more, his third glass in about five minutes. He saw that Fox noticed – one eyebrow quirked and his mouth twitched.

'Hopey, darling,' Elliott said desperately, 'I always wanted to tell you how much I love that portrait of you downstairs – the Ramon Diaz. (Fox was staring at him, unblinkingly.) Such a marvellous feeling; kind of simultaneous sensuality and innocence. Simply *you*. The dress is a Trigere, I think, isn't it?'

'Another droppie, Sweet,' Hope interrupted.

Fox went on drawing quietly. Hope appeared to have forgotten he was there, happily talking about sitting for Diaz, the Mexican sensation of the early fifties – 'Such a fiery little man. Christ, you wouldn't believe how passionate. My God! He used to kiss me, quite violently, too, before each sitting. He said it brought up the glow – and talking of a marvellous feel, the dirty little spic appeared to have ten hands.'

'You make me jealous,' Elliott said, aware that Fox was looking at him again, his expression unreadable.

Fifteen minutes passed. For Elliott it felt like a week. He found a bottle of burgundy and opened it, filled Hope's glass and his own several times.

Fox said suddenly: 'OK. I guess I've finished.'

'Darling Wesley,' Hope said, 'I'm just dying for a peep.'

'Sure,' Fox said, unconcerned.

*Jesus Christ*, Elliott thought, jubilant, looking over Hope's shoulder, *he's really fucked up this time*, as Hope said: 'Wesley, is this some kind of a cruel joke?'

And Elliott thought: *If there's any justice she'll die of a heart attack right now; two years to wait for alcoholic poisoning is too long, you stupid, ugly old bitch. And this time there won't be any Herman Milhausen to screw me up, either. Not if you die in time . .*

During his senior year in high school, where he would have no doubt been designated the boy least likely to succeed despite all Erna's exhortations, she suddenly began to leave him alone. His style of dress, dancing school (where she had hoped he would meet more suitable companions), even his moral standards, were suddenly greeted with apathy.

His mother was sick.

She started by getting tired more easily than usual, and letting things go just a little. The house became slightly less than immaculate.

And less so.

She began to lose weight, and her pallid hair and bleached skin turned a uniform grey until a yellowish tinge appeared, first in her eyes, and spread through her face. Mysterious pains in unmentionable places began.

She declared she was too pulled down for words, and bought some iron tonic from the drug store.

At last she went to the doctor, only to find it was far too late; she was very very sick indeed.

Against her will she went to hospital, where she agonized continuously about the mounting daily costs, where she suffered through seemingly endless radium treatments, which nauseated her, and blood transfusions which cost a fortune – all useless, for the cancer was devouring her entire body by then.

So she went home, and soon never left her bed again, surrounded by pills for the pain, and bottles, and disgusting little tubes and basins, with Herman changing the bed every day, silently carrying the brownish yellow, reeking sheets to the launderette.

The smell in her room got very bad, and all the time she was coughing up brownish phlegm. Herman stolidly changed the bedclothes, read to her, sat beside her, brushed the scanty iron-grey hair; Egon would not go into her room at all. Not under any circumstances. He couldn't stand the smells and the dreadful little heap of bones his mother had become, with the dry yellow skin stretched over them.

He wouldn't even go to her the day she died, whimpering for him from her stinking bed.

Herman never willingly spoke to him again after that, so perhaps he had loved her after all, in his way.

One had to admit, it was an ironic way for the immaculate Erna to die; Egon wondered occasionally which had been worse – the fear of death or the indignity.

Worst of all, in one of the bitterest moments of his life, he discovered that the insurance money had run out and that his father was paying for his mother's treatment with his own college money, so patiently and painfully accumulated over the years, at the cost of so much.

'That's my money,' Egon cried with horror, after Herman withdrew all the money from Erna's private savings account to continue the treatments.

'It's for Egon,' she cried, her voice rasping, determined the secret should not die with her. 'It's for Egon. For college,' pressing the passbook into Herman's hand with shaking, bony fingers. 'Promise me. For college.'

But regarding the money as a windfall from heaven rather than an advance payment on his son's college career, which at best he considered of dubious value, Herman used the money freely for extra time in the hospital, and the new nitrogen mustard treatments, which gave her a day or so of emaciated near-normality before gnawing away at her from inside faster than the natural course of the disease.

Herman stayed home from the brewery to take care of her the last couple of weeks. He took a leave of absence, unpaid.

Erna's savings frittered away pathetically fast.

'Dad, that's *my* money,' Egon screamed again, uselessly; and Herman, at last forced to admit the unthinkable, that Erna really was going to die, began to wear the remaining thousand dollars around his thick body in a money belt.

She should at least have a good, dignified funeral; it might make things up to her, somehow.

# JULIA

In the initial report, Julia's case was classified under 'Annoying Phone Calls' and assigned to Inspector House of the Sex Crimes Detail. At that time, however, there was a rapist at large in the Western Addition and Inspector House had a great deal to worry about, with several new cases reported each week. He had a huge investigation to control, with uniformed cops and plainclothesmen deployed in enormous numbers all over the area, all to be co-ordinated. Julia's 'Annoying Phone Calls' report accordingly received a very small part of his attention.

But he did call her, the day after Officer Fein's visit.

He tried to placate her during a three-minute gap between incoming phone calls.

He recommended she get an unlisted number. Or an answering service. 'And whatever you do, don't encourage him to talk to you,' begged Inspector House, watching his phones light up again. 'Listen, I've got to – '

'But Inspector,' Julia suggested, 'I've been thinking. Would it be possible to put a bug on my line? I mean, don't you think – '

*Oh Jesus*, thought Inspector House, *hell's breaking loose and I get some flaky broad talking about bugs.* But he said reasonably: 'It won't be necessary to go that far. Listen, now – we get twenty, maybe twenty-five cases like yours every month. And *nothing* ever happens. Believe me. Obscene calls, nuisance calls – they're all made by cranks who get turned on that way – just by making the calls. Now you do as I say, hang up on the guy, he'll stop. They always do. Don't worry.'

'But – '

'Don't worry,' said Inspector House firmly. 'Everything's going to be fine. And if he does go on bothering you, which he won't, then call me.'

He hung up, and forgot about Julia immediately.

# FOX

Mrs Pospicil asked: 'Sheesh, who's that? That's a movie star, maybe?'

Fox said absently, looking around for Julia, 'No. That's Elliott. My brother-in-law.'

Mrs Pospicil said admiringly, 'Then your sister's one lucky lady. Mr Pospicil should have looked like that.'

She studied the drawing while Fox said uneasily, thinking involuntarily of Elliott's face among the watermelons in Safeway, 'Oh, I don't know. Mr Pospicil must have been quite a guy.'

He had watched for Elliott's next visit to Hope, then steeled himself to join them, had listened to the nauseatingly coy banter between them, had drunk one glass of Chablis to their three (Elliott appeared to be matching Hope glass for glass), and sketched him from several angles. And Elliott was indeed a handsome man although, 'Handsome is as handsome does,' Mrs Pospicil said after a while, dismissively. 'Not got much of the devil in *his* eye.'

It was certainly hard to imagine that bland, complacent face leering, all green and evil, in the produce department. *Yet*, thought Fox, remembering one of Miss Doyle's favourite maxims, *'an empty room is the devil's work shop'. Here we are, back with the devil again. And although nothing shows up front, maybe something's going on in back, just the same. Maybe Doyly's right.* Although he did not like to admit she might be right; the whole thing got altogether too spooky then. And why should Elliott hate him, and just what the hell was Doyly about, bringing Julia into it – *'He hates anything of yours.'* Fox shook his head; *crazy.*

Mrs Pospicil turned a page. 'That your mother?'

'Her?' Fox laughed. 'That's Miss Doyle. She's been with my family since . . . I don't know. About forever.'

'You have the same eyes. What colour are her eyes?'

'I don't know . . . kind of brown? I guess kind of brown,' Fox said, trying to remember.

Mrs Pospicil shielded Miss Doyle's face from the nose down, took a pencil, and said: 'See? Make the eyebrows so, thicken up the hair into a doormat like yours, and who does that look like to you?'

'Jesus Christ,' said Fox, staring. 'But – ' he flipped a page – 'there's my mother.'

Mrs Pospicil gazed down at Hope Hartley, at the painted eyes staring from their nests of wrinkles, and the bleared, discontented mouth. 'That's too bad,' she said.

The ballerina was back posing. Fox looked at her body through critical, narrowed eyes, chewing on his pencil. He felt thoroughly disturbed now in three different ways. First, Julia was not here, and he had counted on seeing her, on having another chance. Second, it was alarming to be reminded that he was hated for no reason that he could understand. And third, this thing of Mrs Pospicil telling him he looked like Doyly. He felt unsettled and raw, as though a protective shield had been stripped from him to leave each nerve shiveringly exposed.

He took refuge in anger. *Why isn't Julia here?* He felt furious. *Why come to this dumb class if Julia isn't here?*

Quickly and spitefully he drew two caricatures of the ballerina, dripping moulting feathers, which he labelled 'Dying Swan' and 'Dead Duck'. And then Ms Mendoza, with disastrous timing, spoke from behind him, voice brittle with indignation: 'Fox, if you're going to fool around like this you'll just have to leave.'

'Oh go suck,' Fox muttered into a sudden total silence.

But as Ms Mendoza, face crimsoning, drew a deep and furious breath, there was a violent altercation across the room. Mr Brucker accidentally knocked Mr Bottarini's elbow, making his brush splatter vermilion drops across his picture.

'You clumsy, goddamn kraut,' Mr Bottarini screamed with wrath, Leonardo with his Mona Lisa defiled. He leaped to his feet. Brushes, paint pots, and pencils flew into the air around him, clattering to the floor, like hailstones. Mr Brucker hunched protectively across his own painting while Mr Bottarini gripped it by the two protruding corners, swept it from under his old enemy's elbows, tore it into shreds, and tossed the pieces wildly into the air. 'And this I do to your work –

to your stinking work. And *this*. And *this*.'

Balefully silent, Mr Brucker rose to his feet also, snatched Mr Bottarini's painting, ripped it across and across, hurled the fragments to the ground and stomped on them.

'Boys,' Ms Mendoza cried nervously, advancing, wringing her hands. 'Now, boys – '

Mr Bottarini picked up one of the shiny wax apples and threw it hard at Mr Brucker.

'Now boys, we can't *have* this. Now, please, boys – '

But Mrs Pospicil was there. Breasting through the clutter like a doublehulled ice-breaker through Arctic floes, she snatched a drawing board on the way from a broad-beamed blue-jeaned matron and brought it down in one sweeping skull-jarring movement on Mr Brucker's head while at the same instant jabbing Mr Bottarini sharply in the diaphragm with a backward stab of her elbow. Mr Bottarini folded back into his chair, whistling a sigh like a punctured balloon.

She cried with wrath: 'You act like kids, I treat you like kids. Now you get back to your silly damn pitcher and apples, and give no more of this crap. You hear me good, now.' She still clutched the drawing board fiercely in both hands. Mr Brucker frowned at her horribly, rubbed his sore bald head, but sheepishly bent to pick up the mess on the floor. Mr Bottarini wheezed and groaned.

Forgetting about Fox and his sudden startling profanity, Ms Mendoza began to worry about lawsuits.

The model yawned and checked her timer. Five more minutes to go.


JULIA


Julia did not get the job in the Public Relations Department of the art museum either. 'You really have a good résumé here,' she was told once again; 'it's too bad you're not more familiar with the area.'

She took the 47 bus down Van Ness, transferred to the 41 at Union Street, too depressed even to go downtown and shop for a while. Her savings were dwindling rapidly, and of course she would have nothing from Gerry until her divorce was final. To earn some money she had begun to accept secretarial jobs. 'I do suggest you learn a little shorthand, and brush up your typing skills a little,' she had been told at each agency. They all suggested she take a short refresher course at a business college, but Julia told herself rebelliously, *I can't, I simply could not stand it*, wondering whether she was finally beaten.

She decided to give San Francisco one more month.

She had spent two days filing for an insurance company. And a day filling out forms in a doctor's office. She was earning $3.00 per hour.

It was three o'clock in the afternoon, the fog starting to roll in under the Golden Gate Bridge, and the foghorns beginning to boom and whistle around the bay. She decided to make herself a cup of hot tea, thinking nobody would ever believe it was early June.

In fact the only good thing about her life right now was that, for whatever reason, her telephone caller appeared to have given up. *It must have been a neighbour all the time, just like the officer said, who saw it through the window and got scared off*. And of course, now that she was working on these silly jobs, she was out almost all the time anyway.

The telephone rang. She answered it with confidence; it had been several days since she had felt those tremors of fear at the ringing of a phone.

'Ms Naughton?' A woman's voice.

'This is she.'

'This is Hilda Mackintosh from the Frederick Meeker Agency. Can you work tomorrow?'

'I guess so. What —'

'The Bank of America. Filing clerk. Eight a.m. through four-thirty. You're to report to Mr Roblici in Personnel.'

Filing for Mr Roblici at the Bank of America would bring her, after deductions, around $20.00, Julia calculated quickly. And the day would seem longer than eternity. But what else did she have going? And money was money. It was incredible how fast the money disappeared.

She told Hilda Mackintosh she would do it, and hung up, more depressed than ever. The kettle began to whistle cheerily, and she scowled at it.

The telephone rang again.

The voice said: 'You really shouldn't have called the police, Lisa. I told you not to do that. And what can they do, anyway? They're – '

'Stop it,' said Julia. '*Stop it stop it stop it* – '

She hung up.

The phone rang again, instantly, in her hand.

'Listen to me,' Julia said all in one breath, trembling with fear and anger, forgetting all Inspector House's good advice. 'You fucking well leave me alone do you hear you can't do this . . .' she heard someone gasp.

Hilda Mackintosh said: 'Ms Naughton? Ms Naughton, are you there? Ms Naughton!'

Julia said: 'I'm sorry. Yes, I'm here.' She drew a long breath. 'I thought you were somebody else.'

'I see,' said Hilda Mackintosh, sounding strained. She was calling to say that Mr Roblici did not want Julia for tomorrow after all, but for the day after; for Friday. In the meantime, if she still wanted to work tomorrow, Great Western Canning needed somebody down on Brannan Street. 'Although you sound rather upset to me. Maybe you ought to take a rest?'

*Tired indeed*, thought Julia. *Try stark raving nuts.* 'No,' she lied to Hilda Mackintosh, 'I'm fine,' and went on lying. 'My ex-husband called right after you did. I thought it was him again. Listen, I'm really sorry. He's been b-bothering me, thought . . .' She thought dourly that between Great Western Canning and the Bank of America she would be away from her phone for another two whole days.

She considered calling Inspector House, but she would have to admit she talked back to the Telephone Beast. He would say she was encouraging him, that it was her fault.

She decided to leave her telephone off the hook at night.

And buy another lock for her door.

# FOX

Fox sat on the dunes, staring out to sea, where the leaden swells moved sluggishly under the clammy fog bank. Far, far out, he could see there was a line of dark blue, and dancing white caps. He closed his eyes for a moment, recalling the movement of a deck under his feet, glancing sunlight, the gentle sounds of rattling canvas, creaking winches, the swish of water past the bow.

He had broken his own speed record getting here this morning. After the battle between Brucker and Bottarini, which had been too good to miss, he had packed up his things without a word, watched beadily by Mrs Pospicil, who knew he would not be coming back, thrown his stuff in the Jag, and taken off.

He pushed deep furrows through the soft sand with his bare heels, thinking about the rest of the week with nothing, no plans, stretching into next week and into next year, and a horrible frustration at the aimlessness of it struck him in the pit of his stomach. *What am I doing?* Fox wondered dismally. *Where am I going? What do I matter? And . . . why did I come back? What was I hoping for? Did I really think that after all these nothing years, Mother and I might somehow . . .*

The wind was rising; he felt the chill of it; felt the stinging of sand particles blowing into his face. He must get up and walk. Or move into the sheltered patio. Or something.

But still he sat, chin in his hands, wanting a beer now, but lacking the energy to get up and look for one, wishing he was out there on that blue water, where life was simple and clean, remembering his time on the *Avrion* with feelings close to longing.

He knew, however, that it would do no good, retreading old pathways, following the old escape routes. This time it would not help; it made no sense, doing it all again.

Or did it? He had been so certain he should return to San Francisco, that it was necessary for him to go home.

That once home, he would find himself. That he would belong.

Instead, what had he found, and what achieved?

Nothing.

Fox grinned mirthlessly, thinking that the only positive thing he had done since coming back had been to buy the Jaguar.

So what was there to lose? What was he waiting for?

He decided to stick around at the beach for today and tomorrow; then on Friday go back to Sausalito and chat with the Professor again. It certainly couldn't hurt.

And there was usually something going on, Friday nights, in Sausalito.

That couldn't hurt either.

## JULIA

Julia wandered listlessly into Safeway. She felt desperately tired. For two solid days she had bent and stooped, filed, and carried heavy boxes. She had had a greasy hot dog at a counter for lunch with a garrulous woman called Alma Polaskie, and had made the mistake of ordering the potato salad too, which now sat on her stomach as though it had been made of cast iron.

Now, she stared at the meat counter with gloom. The prices seemed astronomical. But after her efforts this week – *Four of the worst days of my life*, thought Julia – she did at least have some more money. So she should celebrate. She chose some hamburger. A pair of small lamb chops. And some Dover sole, which was on special. She would have the fish tonight, and to go with it a whole bottle of wine and to hell with it, for tomorrow was Saturday and she would try to sleep late. The lettuce was cheap; so were the avacados. And broccoli and spinach. It was going to be a healthy weekend.

Julia reached the check-out clerk, a stout girl in a maternity smock who belched gently behind her hand, rolled her eyes to the rafters, and yawned. She wore a nametag which told the customers her name was Ceil and that she had a gold star from Safeway for unfailing cheerfulness and efficiency.

Today, however, Ceil was obviously reaching the end of her shift, was bored and truculent, and suffering from a severe case of heartburn.

'Those are three for a dollar,' said Julia.

'Thirty-nine cents each,' Ceil said firmly.

'No,' said Julia, determined not to be brow-beaten, 'three for a dollar. I checked.'

Ceil sighed heavily, flipped through the list of today's specials, and said: 'Well, parm me.' And as if granting Julia an immense favour: 'OK then. I'll take it off of the chops.'

She hefted Julia's one grocery bag into the cart with obvious resentment and a grunt of gas.

'When's the baby due?' Julia asked, trying to show she understood.

Ceil looked at her blankly. 'Baby? What baby?'

'I . . . I thought . . . aren't you pregnant?'

'Pregnant? Me?' Ceil stared at Julia with dreadful indignation.

'Oh,' said Julia. Why had she not just taken the groceries and gone? Why even try to be nice? Now she had really blown it. 'I just thought . . . I mean, wearing a smock and . . . never mind. Forget it. Sorry.'

'I should think,' cried Ceil, hands on hips, watching while Julia turned her cart with desperation. *If just one more thing goes wrong, if one more person is rude I'm going to jump off the Golden Gate Bridge.* She crashed into the back of a tall man pushing his own cart from the store.

He turned, angry. 'Look where you're going, lady.'

'I'm sorry,' said Julia. 'I hope I haven't hurt you.'

It was the viking. He began to tell her impatiently that that was OK, she hadn't really hurt him, just creamed the back of his ankles was all, when he recognized her. 'Well, hey, look who it is. Hey Tom!' he called, gesturing wildly with his arm. 'Look who we got here.'

Tom grinned with his lips; his eyes stayed blank. 'Well, hey, how are you doing? It's been quite a while. You know?'

Julia said: 'OK. How about you?'

'Pardon me,' a prim voice said behind them, 'but some of us want to go home. When you people are ready, of course.'

A bleach-haired man wearing an Indian muslin shirt open to the waist, a sharkstooth necklace, and jeans so tight they might have been painted on to his body.

'Well, certainly, ma'am,' said the viking, stepping back sharply and treading on Julia's foot.

'Oh *clever*,' said the man in jeans.

Tom snickered.

'I need to be getting home too,' Julia said. 'Nice seeing you again.'

'Hey, don't go,' cried the viking. He grabbed her cart, holding her hostage. 'Wait up a minute. Listen, what was your name – '

'Julia.'

'Julia. All *right*.' He told Tom, 'Julia.'

'Yeah,' said Tom. 'I remember.'

*Liar*, thought Julia.

'Listen,' said the viking, 'what're you doing, Julia?'

'Going home.'

'I mean tonight.'

Julia shrugged. 'I hadn't thought about it.'

'How about a party?'

'Are you *serious*?' She stared at him. 'What kind of party?'

'A party party. People. Fun. Booze. Music. Dope. Food.'

She had not been to a party in months. She thought about her recent life; about the Telephone Beast. Ms Mackintosh. Mr Roblici. Alma Polaskie. Inspector House. The art class and the invitation from Fox, seen across a grey chasm of boredom and fear, was a bright memory so remote as to be unreal.

Then she remembered the Foxy Chicks. 'I don't know,' Julia said. 'I guess not. Thanks anyway.'

'I'll pick you up at nine,' the viking said. 'Tell me your address.'

And then, for some extraordinary reason, she told him.

Never in her life had she done anything so stupid. She thought about it while trying on six different outfits and discarding them for one reason or another. These young men were terrible people. The party would be awful. 'It's at Herb's house,' the viking told her. 'Remember Herb?' She was crazy even to think of such a thing. And if the viking took her to the party, that would mean he brought her home. With everything that would entail.

*Oh Christ*, thought Julia, *what am I doing?*

But the viking could not be the Telephone Beast. And she would be with other people for a change; hear music, have a few drinks, maybe even meet somebody she liked.

If the party got raunchy she could always leave; she would take money for cab fare home.

And if the telephone rang, she would not be around to answer it . . .

In the end she decided to wear the denim jump-suit. Even though it had a zipper all the way down the front, it would be hell to take off. It was looser than before. She studied herself anxiously in the mirror. Her hair was longer than usual, she had not been to the hairdresser in months. Her eyes looked huge, and the hollows in her cheeks gave her an interestingly gaunt look. *No*, thought Julia, *with make-up she would look all right*. She smoothed on lilac-coloured eye shadow, rubbing brown wax pencil into the crease of the eyelid and drawing it out to the sides. She mascaraed her eyelashes and brows. Lipsticked her mouth pale moist pink and sprayed herself all over with Miss Dior cologne.

Then she was all ready and had only to wait for the viking.

He was late, as she had suspected he would be; he would not, in any case, have been able to reach her as she had left the phone off the hook again.

He did not apologize for being late. He glanced around the room and said: 'Nice pad. Ready? Let's go.' And then, taking in her face and figure, whistled and grinned. 'Hey, all *right*.'

The viking had an old MG which he drove very badly. It was in a dishevelled state of neglect, with crumpled fenders, and one headlight leaning out of its housing like a dislocated eyeball. The leather seats leaked stuffing, and the top had been slashed open and repaired clumsily with electrical tape. They shot down the hill towards the marina in lurching, nervous swoops, the viking driving one-handed, the other resting familiarly on Julia's thigh.

They swung forcefully on to the Marina Boulevard, picking up speed, roaring through a stop sign and coming to a last-minute, shuddering halt behind a sedate station wagon stopped at a red light. Julia, encased in her rape-proof jump-suit, shrank down in her seat, her right foot pressing the floor, her fingernails biting into the palms of her hands. 'Is it much farther?' she asked.

The viking gunned the motor and the MG roared, back-firing explosively, on to Doyle Drive and the approaches to the Golden Gate Bridge.

Julia asked: 'Where are we *going*?'

'Sausalito,' the viking sang cheerfully, squeezing her knee. 'Didn't I tell you?'

'No,' said Julia. 'You didn't.'

'Crazy guy, that Herb. Wild house. You'll see. Four floors, all covered in shag rug. Wild. And he has a sauna, and a hot tub, and a grope room. I'm telling you, it's far out.'

'A grope room? You mean – '

'You bet. Black fur on the walls, the floor . . . all over. Big water pillows. And lighting like a disco. You wouldn't believe it. Shit, what a circus. You'll flip.'

Julia hoped she had enough money for a cab from Sausalito.

## JOE

He had never had such a bad week.

She had been out every day, all day. And at night the relatives in town from Chicago, with dinners, parties, no privacy. Just one time he had managed to sneak away to his den to try to call her before they went to Trader Vic's to dine, and then the kid, who should have been in bed for God's sake, had sneaked in so quietly, had demanded just six inches from Joe's ear, 'Who're you calling, Dad?'

It had been a shock. He remembered he sat there, shaking with tremors while his heart pounded. He told the kid to get out, to leave him alone, and the child had departed, whining. *Jesus Christ.*

Now, he sat in his car across the street from her house. Her garage door was closed and locked. The Volkswagen, presumably, inside. The lights were on in her apartment. But the bitch was not answering her phone. He had tried three times. Six-thirty, no answer. Seven-thirty, busy. Seven-forty-five, busy. Then, at 9.30, when he was able to get to a phone again, no answer.

He tried to see in through her window, but the drapes were drawn inside. He pressed his ear against the glass, praying no neighbour would catch him, but he could hear nothing. No music. No talking. She had gone out.

And if she hadn't taken her car, she was in somebody else's.

He walked back to his own car feeling sick to his stomach, churning at the thoughts which crowded into his head about what she was doing and who she was with, at the same time as Officer Fein turned the corner, cruised gently down the block, noticed nothing amiss and drove away.

## JULIA

She could hear the party from the bottom of the hundred steps the viking said she must climb. They were rickety wooden steps, some of them missing, some hanging drunkenly. She climbed with caution, holding lightly to the rail, afraid of splinters and protruding nails. The viking followed her, cat-footed, not holding on to anything.

They climbed and climbed until they reached a cantilevered wooden deck, standing out above the cliffs on stilts. Then more steps, only this time of weathered redwood, climbing the outside of the house. On to another deck at the very top, and through a pair of massive carved oak doors which could have once belonged to a Mexican cathedral.

Entering, Julia began to be glad she had come. The house was beautiful, what she could see of it. The floor was of terra-cotta tiles with brilliant rugs scattered about; there was comfortable beige leather furniture, an antique brass chandelier hanging from the rafters, and a grand piano. There was a wall of oak shelving, filled with hi-fi and recording equipment – a much grander version of that on the boat – with a console of dials and switches like the flight deck of a jet. And ahead of Julia was the most magnificent view she had ever seen. The whole of San Francisco glittered across the bay, mirrored in the miraculously still water, while over to her left the lights of Berkeley and Oakland climbed up into the hills to merge with the stars.

Then, 'Well, hi babe. I'm Herb. Who're you?'

Herb's smile glittered. He held a drink in one hand, and the other rested loosely around the waist of an extraordinarily beautiful girl who wore a skimpy dress of flesh-coloured lace with nothing underneath. No; Julia risked another quick glance – nothing at all. She was taller than Julia; about 5ft 10 in., with long curling black hair and slightly slanted dark eyes. She had the largest breasts Julia had ever seen, standing out from her body firm as melons, the dark umber nipples showing clearly through the lace.

There was something vaguely familiar about her.

The viking pinched her on the behind; 'Hi Viv.' Then, turning, 'Herb, this is Julia.'

'Julia,' Herb said agreeably, 'nice to see you. Welcome to my orgy.'

'Uh – ' said Julia.

The viking asked what she was drinking. She said a Scotch and soda tall, with lots of ice please. The viking said: 'Gotcha,' and ambled towards a well-stocked bar presided over by a wild-eyed young man wearing jockey shorts and a yellow kapok life preserver.

Herb said: 'Julia, this is Viv.'

'Hi, Viv.'

'Hi, lover.' Viv flapped her eyelashes up and down, smiling enchantingly, and moved towards Julia with gentle purpose, slipped a slender tan arm around her neck and kissed her on the lips. Julia stepped sharply backwards, straight into billowing softness, and a cold voice from behind her said: 'Fuck off. You hear?'

'Scotch on the rocks, right?' said the viking.

'You heard me,' said the blonde from behind Julia, a striking sight in two panels of black rubber laced up the sides. And to the viking: 'Hey, you . . . this your chick? Well tell her to fuck off.'

It was Mrs Hall.

'Scotch and soda, actually,' said Julia, but the viking was

gone. She saw him join a group across the room. Husky young men all, ocean racers, animatedly talking shop together, saving the women for later.

Herb said to the blonde: 'Ronnie, take Viv away. She's stoned. She's a drag.'

'He's a piece of shit,' Viv told Ronnie disgustedly. 'A shit. I'm telling you.'

Herb said to Julia: 'What did you say your name was, babe?'

'Julia.' Wondering whether 10 dollars would be enough for her cab. *I must get out of here.*

'Then come with me, Julia. Let me show you some people.' Herb, the good host, caught her by the arm above the elbow. 'You're a gorgeous one. Where *did* Jim find you?'

A bell rang and there was a thunderous pounding at the door. A young man, unshaven, wearing a peaked cap, oily Levis, and a leather vest inscribed OAKLAND SADISTS! stood in the doorway holding a frizzy-haired, very young girl in front of him like a shield, who moved clumsily on six-inch wooden clogs. 'Hey,' Herb cried happily, 'it's the Snake. Howdy, Snake.'

'Howdy, Herb,' said the Snake. 'This here's Dub.'

The girl blinked up at Herb through fuzzy bangs, and clacked her clogs together like a Prussian soldier.

'See?' demanded the Snake, gesturing with one beefy, tattooed arm to Dub. 'Ain't this the craziest? Ain't it what I told ya? Huh?'

'Yeh,' said Dub.

Julia backed towards a staircase which curved away from her to a lower floor. More people were arriving; they included a man whose lips curved like an overripe Cupid's, with narrow predatory eyes which watched, measured, moved on. He wore tight suede pants, a ruffled white shirt, cut low enough to display the gold cross winking up from the mat of black chest hair. 'That's Vicente Colapietro,' somebody said beside her. 'The Colapietro brothers.'

'Oh,' said Julia. 'I don't know them. Who are they?'

'The Colapietro brothers? You're asking me who are the Colapietro brothers?'

'I guess I am.'

Her new companion, a short man, slightly balding, wearing

reassuringly normal clothes and looking rather like a successful doctor, lawyer, stockbroker, whatever, said with genuine
amazement, 'Where are you coming from?' Just as Vicente
Colapietro cried: 'Vivvie! Hey, Vivvie Baby! How ya doin'?'

'Christ,' said the short man, 'everybody's heard of the
Colapietro brothers. Don't you ever go to the movies?'

'Sure, but – '

'He's real big. Take Vivvie and Ronnie there; he made
them stars.'

'Oh,' said Julia. *'Those movies.'*

The man gave her an uneasy look and wandered away.
*I'm too square for this crowd*, Julia thought, and drained her
drink, thinking *My God, I could use another.* The bartender
bobbed and weaved in time to the rock music thundering
from the speakers. She suspected he was pretty high on something. Speed? Cocaine? But she reasoned she did not have
to do anything she did not want to, and at least she was safe
from the Telephone Beast.

She was standing next to Vicente Colapietro. The two
girls, Viv and Ronnie, clung together in a moist embrace,
moving their bodies slightly to the music. He said: 'Hi. I'm
Vic. Who're you? Why haven't I seen you before?'

'I've never been here before.'

'Ha.' He stepped back from her, eyes narrowed, apprais-
ing. He tilted her chin up towards him, caressing her jawbone
slightly. 'Beautiful. What's your name?'

'Julia.'

'Julia.' He savoured the sounds, his mouth rounding and
pursing, rolling the L and drawing out the final dipthong. He
poured her a drink, ignoring the bobbing bartender. He
rested his hand lightly on the side of her neck, playing with
her hair. 'Beautiful. Tell me, want to do a flick for me?'

'I don't think so. Thanks anyway.'

'I pay good. Hundred bucks a day.' His eyes raked her.
'We could sure use a new face.'

She thought involuntarily: *It'd sure beat working for Mr
Roblici*, and said: 'Who looks at the faces?'

Vic laughed. 'Jesus, a sense of humour yet. You and I, we
could get it on real good. You know it? Herb show you round
yet?'

She shook her head. 'No.'

'Who's your date? You gotta date?'

'The . . . uh . . . Jim. His name's Jim. Over there.' She could just hear, '. . . close-hauled, gusting maybe thirty-five knots and blowing a steady twenty-five to thirty, and the fucking main halyard goes and . . .'

'Oh him,' Vic said dismissively. 'Forget *him*. He'll find you later. Or you can find him. If you want him.'

She found herself then, held tightly in Vic's arms, walking down the thickly carpeted spiral staircase to a floor of bedrooms. The master bedroom – Julia assumed it was the master bedroom – overlooked the Bay and opened on to another redwood deck. There was a hard white moon rising, which threw a long finger of cold light across the calm water. She stopped to admire; Vic kissed her lightly on the neck. The bed was enormous, covered with a spread of soft fur, and the ceiling had mirror tiles in it. The light radiated from unseen sources around the room, low and gentle, but bright enough for Julia to see what the couples were doing on the bed. Vic laughed softly. He drew her onwards.

The bathroom was a masterpiece; there was a sunken tub, huge, in the centre of the room, surrounded by miniature palm trees. The walls were panelled in gleaming oiled wood, and hung with erotic Japanese prints featuring stern-faced Samurai, whose improbably gigantic organs spouted semen like geysers. There was a long, blue-tiled counter with three sinks set into it, upon which was arranged a selection of oils, colognes, and perfumes.

'Like it?' asked Vic.

Two naked people, male and female, splashed one another in the tub.

'It's amazing,' said Julia.

A young woman, also naked, strolled in from a door at the other side of the bathroom and used the toilet. Then she sat on the bidet to wash herself. Julia started for the door. 'Hey,' said Vic. 'Don't go. It's a turn-on.'

'Oh my God,' said Julia.

Vic followed her out through the master bedroom where the woman was now groaning in orgasm. 'I suppose this kind of thing is quite ordinary for you,' Julia said, 'but I'm afraid I'm not –'

'How's your drink?' They stood in a small lobby now,

entirely covered – floor, walls and ceiling – with red shag rug. Upon a glass table stood another array of bottles and glasses. 'How about a pit stop?' Vic said.

Julia allowed her glass to be refilled again. And herself to be led from room to room, past dozens of people in various stages of undress, and downstairs again, and through a doorway on to a gallery which overlooked what Vic called 'The playroom'. 'Here's where it all happens,' Vic said cheerfully. 'I've shot some good stuff in here. And Herb has some neat lighting – strobe, coloured spots, glitter – you name it.'

Julia looked down over the gallery rail, feeling quite unreal, at a sea of writhing bodies. They were male and female bodies, forming combinations of two, three, four, or more. 'I'll bet you move real nice,' Viv said, leaning against her from behind. Mysteriously, she found her jumpsuit had been opened all the way down. Vic was fondling her breasts.

And then, in a kind of doomed lethargy, she thought of fighting her way up through the house again, through all those bodies, swarming like bees. The dark murmurous weight of the house loomed above her, infinitely oppressive; she knew she could never get out by herself.

It was so much easier just to let Vic take her down there on to the pillows with the rest – what did it matter after all? Three strong Scotches on an empty stomach told her it did not matter at all. It was what everybody did; it was natural.

The music beat softly down here; the lights pulsed orange and red. Vic was above her, muscled and hairy, the gold chain swinging forward with his movement, over her face.

People arrived, stayed a while in the room, and departed. Pairs became threesomes, split up again like amoebae reproducing. Julia stopped thinking and lost track of time. Eventually Vic moved away from her, to seek fresh pastures or watch the action – she neither knew nor cared – and another man plumped himself down beside her, genitals swinging. She thought it might be the viking – he had a beard – but was not sure. They did not speak. It did not matter much, anyway. The lights flickered on and off, the strobe freezing all the participants in the grope room in instantaneous flashes of unearthly light. Around her people grunted, screamed, and moaned wild animal noises.

Later – God knows how long later or how many later – Julia forced herself upright. She had been one of a mindless, faceless group of warm sticky hands, moist organs, and sucking mouths. But now she was suddenly aware of nausea and a pressing need to go to the bathroom.

She tried to find the steps up to the gallery, staggering over bodies who did not heed her, while the glitter ball rotated slowly overhead, showering the room in spikes of light.

She climbed slowly upwards, the volume of the music increasing as she climbed. In one bedroom a tall slender man with a huge erection danced alone, eyes closed, while behind him on the bed a completely bald man grunted stertorously over the writhing body of a young girl whom Julia recognized vaguely as Dub, without her clogs.

In the bathroom, which she eventually found, two middle-aged, thick-bodied men sat on the edge of the tub, arguing in friendly fashion, holding drinks. One smoked a cigar; the other wore a thick leather strap around one beefy wrist which suddenly began to emit a loud bleeping. He said: 'Shit. Hey, Murph, where's the phone? I've got to get to a phone.' He departed grumbling, 'It's that damn Mrs Baumann delivering early. God*damn*. Why couldn't she have waited another day.'

Julia sat down on the toilet.

Afterwards she wandered foggily towards the bar, which was noisy and full of people seeking refreshment during their energetic evening. She noticed a tray of petit fours; somebody said: 'Sure as hell burn up a lot of calories, fucking.'

She found a glass. It was not clean, but that did not matter. She groped among the bottles for the Scotch, finding it hard to co-ordinate her eyes with her hand. She needed another drink. She would feel much better with another drink. Then another. Several people were smoking. She worried about cigarettes, being naked; whether somebody might not burn her. She moved gingerly. A sharp naked elbow jolted her arm from behind and she dropped her glass, bent over the table again, searching for it. The ice bucket was empty, but that did not matter. Julia found the Scotch bottle and splashed quite a lot, shakily, into her glass. Her nausea had subsided and her bladder felt comfortable again, but she felt sticky and used. She would have a drink, then take a cold shower. That would fix her up.

The red shag-carpeted room reminded her of an open mouth. The hot colour vibrated around her, and she found she was sweating. Most of the people here were naked; only a few standouts were left. She caught a glimpse here and there of a denim sleeve, a line of pants leg; otherwise it was a red-lit tangle of rounded buttocks, breasts, body hair, shoulders, and thighs. There was nobody here she knew. No Herb. No Vic. No viking, or Foxy Chicks. Just Dub on the bed in there.

Julia straightened up and raised her glass to her lips.

And found herself looking directly into the startled eyes of Wesley Bishop Fox III.

Fox moved towards her through the crowd as purposefully as a missile tracker. He ducked under an arm, a shoulder, around hips and backs and stomachs with fluid grace. Without stopping, he spun around her and moved her back into the bathroom where one man still sat on the edge of the tub and moodily stared at the glowing tip of his cigar.

Julia found herself backed up against the wall, her shoulder blades resting against one of the erotic prints, clasping her drink in front of her with both hands. Fox leaned threateningly over her, the palms of his hands resting flat on the panelling to either side of her head. He said: 'What the fuck are you doing in this zoo?'

'None of your fucking business,' said Julia. 'Someone brought me, if you want to know.'

The man on the tub said: 'Ah shit,' and flung his glass on the floor, where it bounced on the thick pile unbroken, and came to rest against the base of a palm tree.

'Who?'

'What does it matter?'

'Who brought you?'

'A guy called . . . a guy I met on a sailboat. His name's Jim.'

'Blond hair? With a beard?'

'Yes. You know him?'

'Sure I know him. He's a prick.'

'Oh,' said Julia weakly. Fox still leaned over her, his eyes

points of flame, his lips compressed. He did not look at all
like the gentle young art student she saw on Wednesday
mornings who drew so well and ate doughnuts with the old
Rumanian lady. He appeared to be completely sober, and
he was also one of the few people in the house with clothes
on. Fox wore tight-legged jeans with intricate detailing on
seams and pockets, and a blue work shirt with snap fastenings
down the front. A tuft of gingerish hair showed at his throat.
His sleeves were rolled up; his forearms showed long ridges
of muscle and tendon. The spareness of his body, which she
ha'd mistaken on Wednesday mornings for delicacy, now
spoke of lean, wiry fitness. And his body was not aroused.
Not in the slightest.

Julia said: 'Want to come on downstairs?'

Fox's eyes blazed and he slapped her across the face. The
man on the bathtub did not look up. He tossed the glowing
end of his cigar into the toilet, where it hissed viciously
for a moment on extinction, then moodily scratched around
his scrotum.

Fox caught Julia in a brutal, unbreakable hold by one wrist,
and dragged her after him across the bar, up the stairs, where
she stumbled and half fell, to be dragged back to her feet.
He hefted her across the living-room where the music was
loudest, the lights the brightest, where the bartender in the
life preserver had taken off his jockey shorts, where Vivvie
and Ronnie danced manically with the unshaven biker, where
Herb, looking sober, surveyed his circus with the contented
smile of the efficient ringmaster.

'My clothes,' Julia gasped, 'what about my clothes?'

'Fuck your clothes,' said Fox.

He threw open a closet close beside the front door, dragging out a black leather coat which had been hanging neatly
from a hanger. 'Put that on. It's mine.'

The coat was soft, smelled new, but the leather was cold
and slippery. Julia shivered.

'Put it on.'

'And my shoes . . .'

Fox said nothing. He flung open the front door, pushing
her ahead of him, into coldness and dampness of midnight
fog.

'But Fox –'

'Get up the steps and shut up.'

*These must be the front steps*, Julia's mind recorded automatically. In far better shape and better tended, made from railroad ties. Up through trees and bushes, to an upper road, where the Jaguar crouched blackly under budding magnolia.

'Fox, please –'

He opened the passenger door, and thrust her forward. 'Get in.' He did not speak again. Julia hunched down in the bucket seat while Fox flung himself in beside her. She heard his door close with a solid thunk. He reached across her and buckled her safety belt, and fastened his own.

Then she heard the deep-throated snarl of the throttle, twin blue-white streamers of light slashed through the darkness ahead of her like pointing fingers, and the Jaguar leaped forward.

They swung around several sharp corners, between parked cars and trees growing crazily in the centre of the road. Then Fox turned hard left, straight up, past the firehouse, and on to the approaches to the freeway. By the time he reached 101 North, he was travelling at 70 miles an hour.

'Please,' Julia said, 'Where –'

And as if in answer, she saw the winking green of the direction indicator, felt the surge of brakes as the car headed for the off ramp, involuntarily comparing Fox's driving with that of the viking.

They swept under a sign which said MILL VALLEY, STINSON BEACH.

*'I thought we'd go to the beach, Lisa.'*

*Fox is the Telephone Beast.* Julia knew it at once. *And now he's taking me – Lisa – to the beach.* There was nothing she could do about it, and now that it was happening, she felt curiously relaxed. *In fact, almost relieved*, thought Julia. *It just had to happen; I could never have stopped it and now I don't have to fight any more.*

Under the freeway. Past a Howard Johnson, lit up and cheerful. Over a creek, where a restaurant sign gleamed and the parking lot was full. To a Y junction where Fox swung left on to the Shoreline Highway and the car began to gather speed again until they were climbing in a series of looping hairpin bends, each tighter than the last, Fox playing with the gears, at one with the car. Julia caught a glimpse of his profile, now and then, etched sharply against the lights of his control panel and the dwindling yellow streetlights.

And then they were past all lights. They were up on the flank of Mt Tamalpais, fog swirling around them, and plunging down again, winding their way down a steep valley.

Held firmly in the moulded grip of the soft seat and the crossed-over safety harness, with the leather coat buttoned tightly and reaching below her knees, Julia's body barely moved as Fox flung the Jaguar around the tight bends. Down, down, past the ranches, the Zen centre, into the village of Muir Beach where Fox slowed momentarily, past livery stables, cottages, around a tight turn over another creek, up a barren hillside studded with half-seen futuristic houses dotted over the wind-blasted countryside apparently at random, and they had left civilization behind again. The road showed up ahead of them, straight and glaring white in the stabbing headlights, and the speedometer reached 90 m.p.h.

To their right lay the dark folds of valley and mountain; to the left a drop down hundreds of feet to the slashing Pacific waves and black snaggle-toothed rocks. They flew, the car soaring over bumps and hollows, Fox's hands light on the wheel, his face tense and abstracted, slowed sharply for the steepest series of curves yet.

Julia was not afraid. She realized dimly that he knew this road better than he knew his own skin. He was familiar with each bend, each curve, each towering rockface, each turnout. Sometimes they swung across the road and she could see far down to the creaming surf below and signs which said BEWARE FALLING ROCK. The Jaguar four wheel drifted in a howling right turn and Julia knew suddenly she was about to get very sick.

Above the growling of the throttle and the screech of tyres on asphalt she screamed: 'You've got to stop. I've got to – '

And almost at once Fox had pulled up amazingly smoothly into a gateway which had mysteriously appeared beside them as though on demand, leading upwards into a grassy meadow. The car idled, a gently breathing animal. Julia's stomach churned. Fox leaned across her, threw open her door, unbuckled her seat belt almost in the same motion and said: 'Get out. Quick.'

She stumbled out on to the dirt and gravel, teeth clenched shut, stomach heaving, throwing herself towards darkness, away from the harsh lights and the humiliation. There was no time to reach the bushes. Julia vomited long and noisily behind the Jaguar, then just sat on the ground, unable to get up or move. Fox sat in the car and waited patiently.

She leaned her head weakly against the rear fender of the car, then felt her body begin to shake, with long long sobs beginning deep down in her body and rising throbbingly into the back of her throat. Her mouth tasted foul and acid, of stale Scotch. Her teeth grated together and her ears prickled. After what seemed a long time she stumbled back to the car and fell back into her seat.

Fox gunned the motor, without saying a word, and away they flew again. Julia's eyes closed. The car swung and lifted, slowed and leaped until Fox braked again sharply, and she saw they had come into another little town, although she did not know what it was or where they were. Somewhere up the coast.

And then she saw a sign which said: 'Entrance to State Beach One-Half Mile.'

*The State Beach.*

*Yes . . .*

They drove decorously past, then, turned left, swung on to a private road and past a guard in a lit-up booth who said: 'Morning, Mr Fox.' A striped barrier lifted in front of them; Fox drove through.

The Jaguar whispered along a narrow causeway, sand-swept, and over several steep bumps in the road where Fox was forced each time almost to stop. And then left into a parking area behind a long dark house. He switched off the engine and shut off the lights. There was utter silence except for the distant pounding of the surf on the beach. The wild ride was over.

Julia waited to be let out, body slack, quite resigned.

She was at the beach at last.

With the Telephone Beast . . .

## PART THREE

## JOE

'Listen,' said the handsome man with the dark brown, curly hair. 'I really dig you. You're one terrific chick.'

Francine grinned and weaved her head, trying to keep him in focus. He was ever so handsome; he looked like one of her favourite TV daytime stars, just like the young doctor in 'The Way of the World'.

The man said again: 'I don't know when I had such a great time.'

Francine replied: 'Me neither.'

'We ought to do this again,' he invited.

Francine breathed heavier, shifted the gum to the other side of her mouth, and took a long pull of the drink her new friend had bought for her. Jeez, she felt zonked. And did she ever need to go. Shit, just when it was getting interesting she had to go to the toilet.

Francine said: 'I gotta go to the powder room. Be right back.'

'Take your time,' the man said. 'I'll be waiting.'

In the ladies' room she hurried; she fluffed up her hair at the sides where it was cut shorter and supposed to curl back but somehow never did, applied more dark red lipstick slightly crookedly, and sprayed herself all over once again with 'Love's Promise'. Then, ready for any joys the night might bring, tottered back to the bar on her towering platforms to join tonight's find.

He was the best ever, even though he kept calling her Lisa.

He greeted her with, 'Wow. If I hadn't seen it with my own eyes, I wouldn't have believed it. You look more terrific than you did before.'

Francine wasn't used to people talking to her like that. She bridled coyly; and the handsome young gentleman – you had to call him a gentleman, any other kid she knew would've had his hand up her skirt long ago – laid one strong-looking, shapely hand over her own pudgy one where it lay on the table, squeezed it, and said: 'Lisa, while you were out there I got to thinking: What would I do if you didn't come back? If you split and left me, and me sitting here like this, aching for you?'

Francine's eyes filled with tears. She began: '*Jeez*, I . . .' The bar blurred and tilted. 'Jeez, I wouldna done that.'

'I'd like to carry you out of here right now,' the man said softly. Francine's insides curdled with joy. 'Carry you away with me, back to my house. The bedroom looks out over the ocean. I'd throw you down on the bed, open up the windows, and make love to you for hours while the drapes blew gently in the ocean breeze.'

Francine's mouth dropped open and she forgot to chew her gum.

'Jeez – '

'Say yes, Lisa.'

'Well sure. Yeah, I mean . . .'

His eyes seemed to fill with tears of gratitude. He gripped her hand with passion (she noticed how strong his fingers were, and thrilled to it) and told her he didn't know how to say this but there was a problem. Francine's face fell; her mouth drooped. No, no, the man said, not that much of a problem. Did she see that odd-looking man at the bar? He was looking at them right now. No, not that one – yes, that was the one; the one with the sticking-out ears with the hat on. That was his wife's Uncle Lennie.

'But how can we go to your place, with the drapes blowing and all, when you're married?' Francine demanded.

Because his wife was away, the dark-haired man explained impatiently. And back to Uncle Lennie, he shouldn't see them leaving together. They shouldn't have risked talking this long.

'Listen,' he said urgently, 'we'll work it like this. I'll leave now and – '

Francine said, 'Leave?' Distressed.

'Wait. Listen. I'll leave now; you sit here and finish your drink. Wait ten minutes. See that clock there? When it says twelve-thirty, come on out. I'll be there waiting for you.'

*

'Jeez,' Francine said admiringly, 'This is sure a nice car. I never bin in a car like this before.'

And later, 'Where're we goin'? There ain't *nothing* out here.'

Then, 'Why're we stopping? I don't see no house.'

And, 'Now, look, mister, no funny stuff. I didn't mean for you to . . .'

And, 'Hey, that hurts. Hey, now lookit, mister, don't do that. I don't like that kind of stuff. I . . .'

And, 'Oh please no don't I don't want to I can't stand it it's hurting oh please please stop . . . don't . . . no . . . nooooo . . .'

Her final whimpers were unheard against the booming of the ocean.


## JULIA


She awoke slowly to a feeling of total disorientation. She lay alone in bed in a room she had never seen before. The light was a queer, flat white. Loose-weave white linen drapes blew gently around an enormous window, slightly opened. The bed she lay in was huge; there was a blue lacquered parson's table to either side of it, each table holding a stoneware lamp with plain linen shades. On her side there was, in addition, a white telephone, with a note propped against it. The note said: 'Gone to the store. Coffee in kitchen.' It was unsigned.

She read the note and lay back in the soft pillows, staring at the window. Fog billowed outside, huge wads of it, like soft cotton. Somewhere high above the fog the sun struggled, unsuccessfully; there was no light source and no shadows. The surf sound came to her muffled.

Julia began to remember. First the most recent things. She remembered Fox feeding her soup and putting her to bed as though she were a small child.

Before that was an ugly memory. Fox had pushed her into a bathroom, lit by a line of bulbs, brilliant, above the sink. 'You'd better look at yourself,' Fox had said, sounding angry.

She had, reluctantly. She did not look nice. Her face was blotched and drawn. Eye make-up had smeared around her eyelids so that she peered from out of messy dark holes. Her hair hung around her face in draggled, sweaty strings, and her mouth was swollen and pulped. 'Yes,' Fox said, 'You look godawful. Take a shower – a good hot shower – and clean yourself up.' He had said more – she was certain a great deal more – but she did not want to think about it.

When she stepped into the shower, she had been unable to stand against the jetting water, so she sat, hunched, while the water streamed around her, down on to her head, pounding, cleansing. She sat for quite a long time, hugging her knees, eyes closed; then she lathered her hair, rubbing and rubbing until her scalp ached, sitting among a nest of suds.

In the bathroom cabinet she found new toothbrushes, toothpaste, mouthwash, and aspirin. She used everything. Behind the bathroom door there had been a clean bathrobe of fluffy white terrycloth, slightly too short for her.

Would the Telephone Beast have done all that for her? Bullied her, fed her soup, put her to bed, and never once touched her?

She did not think so.

A chair stood against the wall with a small pile of clothes on it. A pair of boy's jeans, old, stained but clean. A man's wool shirt. A French cashmere sweater. A beautiful sheepskin jacket and a pair of decrepit thong sandals, size 7. Julia looked at the clothes for an instant, nonplussed, then put on the jeans, sandals, and cashmere sweater, with the man's shirt over the top. She found a Christian Dior silk scarf tucked into the pocket of the sheepskin coat which she knotted jauntily around her neck. Then off to the bathroom, where she cleaned her teeth again and combed her hair. Then to the kitchen, where, true to Fox's note, there was a Mr Coffee machine, half full, a mug, and a bowl of sugar. Fox was nowhere in the house, and a brief glance outside showed that the Jaguar was gone.

The clock above the breakfast nook said 11.45. She had slept for almost 11 hours.

Julia opened a screen door and climbed down two steps on to a red brick patio. Patio furniture was stacked under an awning to one side; purple and yellow iceplants grew luxuriantly around the edge, then dwindled before the dunes and seagrass. She looked inside a small, shingled structure to one side of the patio and found two empty garbage cans, newly lined with plastic. A summer home. Whose? Fox's sister's? His parents'? His own? She crossed the patio, climbed the dune, looking for the ocean. She could see it vaguely, a sluggish greyness. A few people and some dogs moved silently, like ghosts. A seagull mewed faintly somewhere away to her left. She stood still, holding the coffee mug, warm, in her hands, staring.

Fox could not be the Telephone Beast. Not now.

In the distance she could hear the deep growl of the Jaguar, approaching slowly. A crunch of gravel. Silence. And the clunk of the heavy door closing.

She returned to the kitchen as Fox entered from the other side carrying a grocery bag. He said: 'You were sleeping pretty well. Hope the clothes fit.' As though she were any ordinary weekend guest.

'They're fine,' Julia said. 'Thank you.'

She watched him arrange his purchases on the counter. A London broil – 'We can barbecue that, and it'll do for to-morrow, cold. We can cut bits off.' A head of lettuce, tomatoes, eggs, bacon, milk, butter, a loaf of French bread, orange juice, and two bottles of wine. And from another pack, a chunk of Monterey Jack cheese, and some peaches. 'If you think of anything I've forgotten,' Fox said seriously, 'we can run in again later.'

She could think of nothing, and told him so. And then she asked, 'Where are we? I don't even know where we are.'

'Stinson Beach,' Fox said, and added, 'I'm starved. Let's eat.'

Julia found herself to be very hungry. She cooked eggs and bacon while Fox made orange juice and set out plates, glasses, and silverwear on the butcherblock breakfast table. She did not know what to say to him; did not know where to begin. What could she say: By the way, thanks for taking me away from the orgy?

But breakfast was a pleasant, casual meal. They sat beside each other, facing the beach, and Julia found she was able to eat two eggs, three strips of bacon, and a large hunk of bread and cheese. She had three cups of coffee.

For the first time in months, she felt incredibly healthy.

They cleaned up. It was almost one o'clock and the sun had still not managed to break through the fog bank. People floated by, unreal, and the sea glinted silver. 'I like it in the fog, all still like this,' Fox said. 'That's the way I always remember it.'

Later, they walked along the beach. Above them, the sun began to burn through at last. It was 2.30 in the afternoon. Their shadows began to show ahead of them, pale on the brown sand, growing darker. The grey ocean deepened to slate, to indigo, to cobalt. The fog rolled away quite suddenly, a mile out to sea. They walked on.

Julia said: 'Thanks for last night.'

'You're welcome.'

'I must have been crazy.'

'Oh, well. Listen,' Fox said, 'get something straight. It's your life, know what I mean? For all I know, that kind of thing might turn you on. But what really burned me up was you going to a sleazy party like that one with some jerk you barely knew, when you wouldn't go out with me. I guess it was an ego thing. But I was mad as hell.'

'There was a reason why I wouldn't go out with you. A real reason.'

'Good.'

She said: 'I thought you were the Telephone Beast.'

Fox stood absolutely still, staring at her. 'You thought I was . . . *what*?'

'That you were the Telephone Beast.'

'Thanks a bunch.'

'I'm sorry. But it just fitted. You know? It started right after I met you, that same night. And you were the only person I could think of who knew where I lived. And there's another thing.'

'Jesus Christ.'

'He said . . . One of the things he said was, "I thought we'd go to the beach, Lisa." He calls me Lisa.'

'I remember.'

'So last night, when we turned off the freeway, for the beach – I saw the sign – I thought that was it. That you had to be him. Taking me to the beach.'

'Great.'

'But I wasn't frightend. It was odd. Maybe I had some kind of gut feeling I should trust you.'

'Then listen to your guts,' Fox said crossly. 'They're a hell of a lot smarter than your head.'

'Maybe they are. Listen, Fox, I'm sorry,'

'It's OK.'

'I'm really sorry.'

'And it's really OK.' Suddenly he grinned at her. 'Listen, we have some time to make up. That's all.'


## INTERLUDE


While Julia Naughton slowly struggled to full consciousness that morning at Stinson Beach, Gail and Dennis Patterson and their golden retriever Biff went jogging on another beach – Ocean Beach, in San Francisco. They jogged every morning, usually before going to work. But today was Saturday, and an unpleasant, cold, dank, foggy morning, too.

There were very few people out, but plenty of dogs. There was a pack of them – five at least, big dogs – snarling over something in a secluded steep pocket in the dunes. Biff took off to join the group with an excited growl.

'Shit,' said Dennis Patterson, 'a female in heat. We'll never get him away now.'

'So let him have some fun,' said Gail.

They jogged side by side, wearing identical royal blue warm-up suits with white stripes down the sides.

'Or it'll be something dead,' said Dennis. 'Remember that stinking awful seagull, how he rolled in it? They love it, something good and rotten. You don't want him bringing that stink into the house again, do you?'

'Well, call him then.'

'If he's rolled in it, it's your turn to give him a bath.'

'Dennis, call him. Hey, Biff. Biffie. C'mere.'

Dennis whistled on two fingers, shrill. Biff paid no attention at all. His plump rear end waved with enthusiasm.

'Oh shit,' Dennis said again, and whistled some more.

Biff ignored him.

Dennis sighed. 'We'll have to go and drag him off of it.' They approached the dogs.

But it was not a dead seagull the dogs were nosing so excitedly.

It was a dead woman.

'Jesus H. Christ,' said Dennis. 'Oh God!'

'Oh –' said Gail. 'Oh, Dennis, she . . . she's been –'

'Shut up,' said Dennis. 'Listen, go call the police. Run. I'll . . , I'll stay here and . . , and try to keep the dogs off her.'

A while later, a lone patrolman in a radio car arrived, having responded to an 802. An 802 means a dead person, by whatever circumstance, for whatever length of time. An 802 could be an accident, a suicide, a homicide – anything so long as the person is dead.

Gail and Dennis Patterson sat together among the iceplants, their faces an identical shade of putty.

Officer Solinsky took one look at the body, gagged, almost lost his breakfast, and radioed for a sergeant to come out with a backup unit. He amended the 802 to a 187 – Homicide.

In turn, the sergeant called for his Platoon Commander, for additional units to preserve the scene, always exceptionally difficult on a beach, and in this case almost impossible with the immediate environment having been torn up beyond recall by the dogs, and for help with crowd control.

By this time a large group had collected, comprising kids of all ages, joggers, passing motorists who were stopping and parking all along the Great Highway, and almost all of the officers from the Taraval Station, policemen having the greatest morbid curiosity of all. The crowd grew larger by the minute, and now a great many officials began to arrive.

The Homicide Unit, with two inspectors in plainclothes who took over everything from then on.

The Crime Lab Unit.

The Photo Lab.

The Coroner's wagon.

The media, with news photographers.

And the ambulance, and doctor, who finally and officially pronounced Francine Holub dead.

# JULIA

They lay together in the dunes on a blanket, drinking a bottle of Chablis and eating peaches. Julia wore an orange bikini which was too big for her. Each time she moved, the 36C cups which fitted Nancy moved away from the slope of her smaller breasts. Fox tried not to watch, at first.

Julia observed lazily, 'Nancy must have quite a big bust.'

'Yeah,' Fox said. 'I guess. But Nancy's heavy. Fat, actually.'

Julia turned on to her back, staring up at the glittering sky through half-closed eyes. Behind them a row of brown-green hills rose steeply; she could see large birds circling above them; buzzards? The other side the ocean lapped and whispered, with an occasional roar of a wave greater than usual. She wished this afternoon could go on forever. She felt glutted with sun, with food and wine.

Fox raised himself on one elbow and began to trace the light hairs on her forearm, gently, with one finger. He turned her wrist to stroke the soft white skin of the underside of her arm. He kissed the inside of her elbow. She moved to a half-sitting position, where she could look down at his thickly curling, reddish hair, at his freckled back and shoulders where the muscles bunched tensely under his skin, and at the creamy line of tender flesh exposed at the top of his bathing shorts. He said: 'I wanted to wait. Make all this last longer. I can't.'

'I . . .' Julia began, 'I . . . don't – '

But he was over her, his body solid black against the bright sky, rays of sunlight spilling out from around his head. His hands were planted now in the hot loose sand, supporting his half-raised body. He looked down at her, as she lay there under him, staring up at him, her face startled. Then he lowered himself gently until their bodies and faces touched, when he gripped her head with both hands, twisting his hard artist's fingers through her hair, and kissing her open mouthed with mounting ferocity, groaning her name in his throat while her hands clenched in his shoulders.

He moved away from her and sat up on his heels. He said: 'We'd better get on into the house. Someone might come by.'

She sprawled under him, the top of Nancy's bikini slipped under her left armpit. He swallowed. 'Jesus, Julia. Come on. Get up.'

He hated not to touch her. He wanted to swing her up into his arms, dive through the window and fling her on to the bed. The way it happened in the movies. But she was tall and well built, and the screen door was closed against the bugs. He dragged her body against his, hip to hip, and walked with her in step, his arm tight around her. Into the house. Through the kitchen. Down the passage to her bedroom, where she leaned against him, face pressed into the side of his neck, her breasts against his chest while he struggled to untie the bikini top. 'Goddamn,' Fox breathed, '*why* are these things so difficult? . . .'

He flung it across the room, and worked the pants off her, his hands caressing her buttocks, dragging her against him again.

She fell back under his weight, on to the bed, feeling the roughness of the coarse-woven spread under her, with numerous small worries crowding her mind. She had been expecting this to happen for hours – *Of course it was going to happen*, thought Julia, – *I wanted it too, didn't I?* – and now it was happening and she was not sure she did want it. She was self-conscious and nervous. She had never been with anyone, barely, save Gerry (last night meant nothing, and the memory would fade until it became no more than a bad dream) and now she was about to have sex with somebody else. To take a huge step into alien country. Fox's body was strange to her, all unknown – the touch of his tongue on her nipples; his hands on her thighs, opening; the touch of his skin against hers – all so different. And he was much, much larger than Gerry. She was half frightened. He was huge, and iron hard. It hurt, where it pressed like that against her groin.

Perhaps she should have stopped him, back there on the beach; now, his hands gripped her, tight; his eyes were slitted; face drawn in concentration. His breath came in ragged, open-mouthed gasps. She would never be able to stop him now . . .

She shrieked once, a bitten off cry of shock, at his moment

of entry; then control was gone, self-awareness was gone, all lost to a swirling darkness of pulsing movement, beginning gently, building to a jarring violence, with all the time the warmth and pressure of strong, enfolding arms, and hearing, later, someone crying out, wonderfully triumphant, happy sounds, and realizing they were her own sounds, and finding her face wet with tears but not knowing whether they were Fox's tears or her own.

They lay curled together under the spread, her body pressed into his. His face was buried in her neck. He mumbled happily: 'Haven't had a woman in six months. This is the first time in six months.'

'Me too.'

'First time in six months and the best time ever. We were made for each other,' Fox said comfortably. Then, 'I can give you presents, now.'

Julia muttered drowsily: 'Presents?'

His hand curled softly around her right breast. 'You can give your lover presents,' he said, sounding self-satisfied. 'People do. All the time.'

'Fox –'

'Know what your first present's going to be?'

'Tell me.'

'An answering service.'

'But Fox, I –'

'I know it's not romantic, but you gotta admit it's practical. I can leave you sexy messages, and it'll take care of the Telephone Beast.'

'The Tele – oh, Fox. Listen, you can't do that. You can't give me an ans –'

'Sure I can,' Fox said cheerfully. 'And anyway, you know, I feel kind of responsible for the Telephone Beast. With you thinking he was me. See?'

'Turn over . . .'

# ELLIOTT

Elliott Millner stared down at his hands as he drummed long fingers restlessly on the desk top in front of him, making a mental checklist of all he had accomplished that morning.

A highly productive day so far; one of his better days for quite a while; recently his attention had been slipping. But the correspondence was all cleared. A successful two-hour meeting with the President of Adflex Electronics. Personal business attended to. And now, a lunch with his stockbroker at Antonio's, a stately spot where the food was delicious, the cocktails huge, the ambience one of dimly lit, quiet dignity, and the tables, with pink tablecloths and red linen napkins, sufficiently spaced to allow the maximum of privacy for the forging of deals and discreet consummation of upper echelon business.

He had just two minutes now in which to skim the morning paper, which lay to one side of his desk. Not that there was much to interest him. There were crises in the Middle East, the Far East, and all over Africa, desperate as usual. Nothing changed; it bored him. And Page 2 carried the story of the latest murder – again routine.

A girl's mutilated body had been found by two joggers, out for a morning sprint on Ocean Beach. Elliott read on with idle curiosity. Twenty-three-year-old, blonde, blue-eyed Francine Holub had lived alone in a studio apartment on West Portal. She had been an intermittent student at San Francisco State, when she had hitched rides to and from class.

She had been a regular in several singles bars, in particular The Glass Slipper, where she spent her last evening. And although she had left the bar alone, she had been observed talking with several men during the course of the evening 'on very friendly terms'.

From the tone of the article, one would infer that Francine's demise, although brutal, should not have been too unexpected, considering her high risk lifestyle – with just the barest hint, prudishly, that she had perhaps got her just

T.C. – E

deserts. Elliott concurred — hitchhiking, for God's sake — and glanced at the photograph of Francine, years old and blurred. A chubby-faced teenage blonde gazed insipidly back at him.

*Well*, he thought, as he tidied his desk top preparatory to leaving, *so much for Francine.* He wondered whether the police would find the man who had killed her, who had dispatched her once and far all to the big bar up in the sky where all the men looked like Burt Reynolds and bought her drinks for eternity.

She had left the bar alone; but somebody had been out there, some sicko; perhaps somebody had called from the shadows: 'Hey, Lady, want a ride?' And stupid Francine, probably more than a little loaded, had come closer, had seen he looked like an all right guy, had said: 'Sure.'

Poor, stupid, easygoing Francine; so friendly with the men . . .

## JULIA

She shared a sofa with Fox at the Cliff House, watching the western sky, seeing the sun sink, become lozenge-shaped, spilling moltenly sideways across the horizon before sliding down behind the ocean until just one brilliantly golden crescent remained. And then that, too, was gone. The sky deepened in colour to purple, and the ocean darkened to gunmetal with just one wild crimson patch above to show where the sun had been.

They were silent. Julia, certainly, did not feel like talking yet. She had spent her day filing again, for the Savings and Loan Company. For lunch she had had a greasy hamburger and a glass of milk. She had felt her clothes become dirtier, her nails grimed, her armpits stiff with sweat as she dragged filthy boxes of last year's correspondence about to be sorted and filed somehow. And then the wait for the 41 bus; the fight to get in; and standing pressed against strangers until Washington Square when enough got out so that she could at last find a seat.

But then, coming home, she had called the answering service.

'This is Julia Naughton, No. 706. Any calls?'

And the comfortable voice of Darlene, her operator: '706. Sure. Hold on, hon.' Pause. Then: 'Miss Gilchrist called, from the Haldane Agency. You can start work at the Mercantile Bank tomorrow, starting eight a.m. Call her before four-thirty. Guess you missed out on that one.'

'Never mind,' said Julia.

'And Fox called. Said for you to call him the moment you get home.'

'Right. Did I get any hangups?'

'You sure did, hon. Five or six. Guess he didn't like the sound of my voice.'

'He didn't say anything?'

'Nope. You're the lady with the nut calling her, right?'

'Yes. That's me.'

'Well, listen hon. You got twenty-four-hour service here. Just don't answer your phone at *all*. It'll take a couple days, then he'll quit. He won't get *no* satisfaction. You'll see.'

'You're . . . you're sure?'

'Sure I'm sure. I been in the business twenty-five years. I heard some stuff would curl your hair. But don't you worry none. These freaks are all mouth.'

And then Fox had come for her in the Jaguar, to sweep her from the sour memories of dust, sweat, and old files into the mellow richness of walnut dash and leather seats, and the hard clean wind of the Cliff House, at the farthest westerly point of the city.

The transition was almost too abrupt.

But it was wonderful.

Later, Fox took her back to his apartment above the garage. It was quite early still. 'Probably not eleven yet,' Fox said. 'It looks like they're all still up, in the house.'

Lights flared across the courtyard. Behind the kitchen issued a flickering blue glow where Wong, with tortilla chips and can of Coors, sat happily watching 'The Curse of the Mummy's Tomb'.

In one of the smaller second floor bedrooms Miss Doyle had retired with a new issue of *Clairvoyance Today*, while in the mighty master suite, Hope Hartley paced the thick rug, glass in hand, mind wandering down long ago pathways.

'Wonder what Mother's up to,' said Fox. 'She's usually passed out by nine.'

And in the master bedroom, Hope paused suddenly in mid-flight, posing, throwing a gleaming smile over the shoulder, hand touching the flung back hair, the wine slopping on to the rug, while batteries of news cameras recorded for the world her entry into the theatre, on the arm of Samuel Goldberg, her studio head, for the première of 'The Scandals of Susan'. She posed, arm raised to blow a kiss, her wine-stained bathrobe and grubby nightdress now a floor-length sable caught casually back on her elbow to show off the daring white satin sheath and the flashing emerald choker given her by the Estonian prince. Hope smiled again, brilliantly, tossing her curls; and then the smile faded and she stood for a moment quietly in the middle of the rug, staring without recognition, with confusion, at the large carved bed with the turned-down rich brocade spread; at the little tray which Miss Doyle had brought her with the plate of melba toast, and the small bunch of purple grapes to tempt her failing appetite. *What am I doing here?* Hope wondered vaguely, with a dismal sense of loss, as the flash bulbs ceased to flash and the cheering screams of the crowd faded and finally died. All she heard now was the far-off sound of a motorcycle; the wailing of a siren; the foghorns on the bay. Hope hated the foghorns; they reminded her of death. Especially the deep-throated diaphone which she thought the most dismal sound in all the world. Shivering, she crossed to the window and drew the heavy drapes across the ruffled sunblinds in an attempt to muffle the sound, and turning, met, eye-to-eye, a drawing of a gaunt, ravaged old woman which she had seen somewhere, recently. The woman had sunken cheeks, pouchy eyes, lipstick smeared in the creases of her mouth and oddly misplaced rouge high up her face. Hope moved forward, hand outstretched, to touch the drawing. Only it was no drawing.

It was a mirror.

She drank some more wine, confused. And more. Until the image changed slowly in front of her and the gaunt cheeks filled out and pinked, the beautiful blue eyes sparkled

and the charming lips, which in their time had been kissed
by some of the most famous mouths in the world, drew back
in a provocative smile, showing the perfect, pearly little teeth.

Hope Hartley smiled with pleasure that she now and forever would always look her best.

'She has beautiful bones,' Julia said politely.

She sat on Fox's bed, looking through his sketch books.
'This is your mother, isn't it? She doesn't look much like
Hope Hartley the star any more though, does she, poor thing.
It must upset her terribly, getting old.'

Fox sighed. 'Of course. But if she drinks enough then she's
still eighteen.'

'She drinks a lot?'

'Wine. All day. I guess you'd call her a wino. But all the
wine in the world isn't going to keep the fantasy going forever. She works at it, though. Doyly says half the time she
doesn't know where she is. She thinks she's back in the good
old days, signing autographs and having her picture taken.'
He moved, restlessly. 'We're a self-indulgent family, I guess.
And we all need our particular crutch. Mother has her wine;
Nancy has food . . .'

'And you?'

'Me? I run. When the going gets tough, Wesley Fox gets
going. I suppose that's really why I bought the Jag.'

'I ran too,' said Julia. 'It didn't help much.'

Fox did not answer. She watched his face, half turned, lit
in profile by the refrigerator light as he searched for something to drink. She looked down again at the drawing of Hope.
She said: 'You know, you don't look much like your mother.'

'No,' Fox agreed. 'Nor like my father either. Maybe he
wasn't my father, though,' he said flippantly. 'Maybe it was
all a lie of mother's, saying I killed him.'

'She said you *killed* him? *How* did you kill him?'

Fox told her. 'Maybe she was pregnant by somebody else,
or maybe she told him she was pregnant by somebody else,
and that killed him. You never know with Mother. I'd ask
her if I thought she'd ever tell me the truth; but she finds lies
more fun.'

'Oh,' Julia said, not knowing what to say. She turned a
page of the sketch book. 'This is Miss Doyle. Right?'

'Right,' Fox said as he poured wine for her.

'She's got a great face.'

'Yeah. She's a great person.' He settled down beside her, and took the sketch book from her hand. She leaned against him; he held her close.

'It's amazing,' Fox said happily, after a moment, 'but I feel just incredibly sexy again. I had no sex for months and months, and before that hardly any for years, and now I need it all the time.' He took her glass from her and set it down on the floor.

Julia said: 'Couldn't we turn some of the lights off? It's so bright.'

'I like it this way,' Fox said. 'Do you mind? I don't like the dark. And I want to see what I'm doing.'

'Surely,' said Julia, 'you could still see if –' but his fingers were unbuttoning, unzipping, pulling the shirt from her shoulders. He did not answer.

They lay together then, panting, naked from the waist up and barefooted, unwilling to separate for the seconds it would take to get their jeans off. She felt him pressing ruthlessly into her. She said: 'Foxy, please.' His face was set; eyes closed. Hands gripping her convulsively. 'You're hurting. Let's get our pants off. Please, Fox. '

And after that, her own eyes closed, the light was only a red glow against her eyelids and she barely noticed it.


FOX


'You're looking very well today, Wesley.'

'Yes, Mother. I feel good.' And he did. He looked down on his mother with none of the usual distaste and confused emotion which made him stammer and in the old days had brought on the fears and the asthma. Today, she was just an old woman. A sad old woman who had once been beautiful, who drank herself into a stupor to cling to the remaining shreds of illusion. He could even feel a vague affection for her.

'Do you know what day it is, Wesley?'

Fox blinked. 'Tuesday?'

'The date, dear. The date. Doyly, please – '

Miss Doyle refilled the proffered glass.

'Mateus Rosé, dear,' Hope said. 'Such a pretty bottle. Don't you think it's a pretty bottle, Wesley?'

'Yes, Mother. It's a very pretty bottle.'

'When I was making "The Great Ghengis", with Harry Savage – such a long time ago – ' Hope gave a shrill little bark of laughter, remembering the Great Ghengis, and herself a captured Northern princess, in such cute gauzy costumes and jangling jewellery – 'Such fun then, dear, not at all like movie making nowadays – just business . . .'

Fox wondered what this had to do with Mateus Rosé, but looked at his mother with what he hoped was encouragement.

Hope raised the glass to her lips.

'Yes,' Fox said. 'It must have been a ball.'

'My birthday,' Hope said suddenly. 'A party on the set – such a party. Count Carvalho Do . . . something . . . the Portuguese Ambassador, you know . . . sent such beautiful presents.' A magnificent cross of heavy gold, set with sapphires; a case of Mateus Rosé wine in its graceful flat bottles; two dozen red roses delivered to her trailer every day in the Californian desert, where Hope Hartley, enslaved princess, fluttered her astonishing sapphire eyes and bared most of her remarkable bosom for Ghengis Khan during his conquest of Abyssinia. 'It was so hot,' Hope complained, draining the rest of the wine. 'So utterly hot. And the poor roses are . . . the roses died, poor things.'

'You looked so pretty, dear,' said Miss Doyle.

'We must have another party,' Hope said fretfully. 'I haven't had a party in years. And it's my birthday . . .'


## JOE


It did not last.

It had not lasted the first time, nor the next, the initial warm spread of release, although each time, right after, he had felt like singing, especially the last time when, resolutely, he had got rid of Lisa for good.

But he knew it had been wasted effort. Lisa was back. He had seen her, almost. For, three days afterwards, he had cruised down her block, drawn like a moth to flame, and the lights were on in her windows. Even as he watched, one was extinguished. And the Volkswagen was there in her garage; he could see its yellow rear end through the open door. She had company, too, for there was a dark blue, old-model Jaguar parked in her driveway, its nose up against the tail of the Volkswagen.

He sat there for a while, watching from across the street, staring with hatred at the Jaguar. Then he drove to a nearby bar, and called her.

But it was not Lisa who answered.

A quite different voice said: 'Ms Naughton's residence . . .'

He hung up, his head spinning with nauseating vertigo, and stuff rising in his throat, so he clenched his hand over his mouth.

*The bitch had got herself an answering service!*

## FOX

During the next few days, Hope drank less, wandered less in wistful re-enactment of the past, and busied herself with guest lists, harassing interviews with caterers, bartenders, and maids, although Miss Doyle pleaded uselessly against the rising tide of orders, counter orders, and muddle, 'Hope, dear, leave it to me, do.'

The invitations arrived from the printer's.

The society editors called from the newspapers, wanting interviews.

Miss Veronica, the owner of the Scented Garden, spent a morning with Hope to talk about the flowers. She was very enthusiastic. 'Just everything's blooming at this time of year, Mrs Fox, we can do something simply exquisite for you. I would suggest pinks and golds.'

Hope touched at her hair, smiling.

'. . . and I would suggest white wicker baskets, lots of them, with the blooms *trailing* . . .'

Fox was delighted about his mother's party. With so much on her mind, she did not miss him if he did not visit. 'Not that she likes having me around,' he told Julia. 'It just gripes her if I don't go.' He had far too much on his own mind, too, to spare the time.

He was in love, and had thoughts only for Julia.

They roamed the city together, eating in out-of-the-way restaurants which he enjoyed; at Mexican lunch counters in the Mission District; at Basque hotels in North Beach where course followed course in perplexing volume; at an old house miles up the coast, run by a health food commune. They packed picnics and drove to the wine country, eating sourdough bread and Camembert cheese, drinking a bottle of aged Pinot Noir on parched brown grass beside the Jaguar, or in the shade of a war memorial in a small adobe town.

Julia forgot all about finding a job; about her dwindling supply of money. And almost completely forgot the Telephone Beast, the frequency of whose hang-ups was apparently decreasing. 'Told you so,' said Darlene.

Day followed day, melting in a shifting blaze of colour, and those bucolic first weeks with Fox, looked upon later, seemed an endless picnic under the arcing sky punctuated by his love-making, so intense and so absorbing that she forgot Gerry too.

There was only Fox.

Gerry was a faraway memory, a fading glimpse of a life that had happened long ago to somebody else.

And when they were not driving somewhere, eating, drinking, or engaged in timeless, voluptuous sex, Fox was drawing Julia. He drew her standing, sitting, eating, drinking, clothed, naked. He drew her feet, one hand, a delicate study of an ear, jawbone, and line of neck. He was planning a one-man show, His life was focused at last.

Because of Julia.

It was not surprising his mother told him he looked well. The very ends of his hair vibrated with health and requited sex.

Julia lost her look of wan delicacy. She ate like a long-shoreman and slept like the dead. Her cheeks filled out and her skin tanned.

They moved through the days together, vaguely, existing for each other, blind to the world.

'In a fool's paradise,' said Miss Doyle.


## ELLIOTT


Elliott, on the other hand, was not looking good at all. Miss Doyle, who somehow was never far off when he visited Hope, remarked later: 'Elliott looks peaky, I must say,' and Hope could not help but agree with her.

She no longer looked forward so much to Elliott's visits, for after the briefest of conversations, his manner abstract and perfunctory, he would leave as though glad to go. And his appearance had altered. Sometimes he looked unkempt, even sloppy. Extraordinary for Elliott. There were deep umber pits under his eyes these days, his face was thinner, and so, appallingly, was his golden hair, which along the part was now even showing a half-inch of mousy brown.

'I never knew Elliott dyed his hair,' Hope remarked with disappointment to Nancy. 'Neither did I,' said Nancy.

But they both had too much on their minds to worry about Elliott's possible malaise. Hope had her party to look forward to; Nancy had domestic problems. Amparo had quit, with characteristic thoughtlessness, just two days before the party, and a week before they were supposed to leave for Tahoe for the July 4th weekend, with the children.

'Latin people are quite impossible,' Nancy sighed with frustration, searching for the phone number of Aunt Betty's Agency.

'I think the peach chiffon, Doyly. Don't you think the peach chiffon?' asked Hope. 'And you will remember Elizabeth Arden's, won't you.'

# JOE

It was impossible to sit at his desk, go through the motions of working, and make decisions over meaningless problems.

He continued to leave the house every morning at the same time as usual, but instead of going downtown he would park in Lisa's block and watch for her. Often he would see her, but never alone. Always with a lean-bodied young man with red-brown hair and untidy clothes – the owner of the Jaguar.

Often they would drive up the hill to a house on Pacific Avenue, where Joe would be forced to abandon them, for this was also his territory and he did not wish to be seen there, lurking and watching.

There was no pattern to their comings and goings.

Frustratingly, at no time was he able to predict where they would be. He had to follow them.

He followed them to restaurants, when he would sit outside and wait. To a discotheque on Fisherman's Wharf. To the theatre. To the Cliff House, one of their favourite haunts obviously, three times. And once to the Sausalito Ferry where, undaunted, he had watched them board, and then driven across the Golden Gate Bridge to watch them disembark and wander hand in hand into the Trident for lunch.

The night before he had sat outside Lisa's house after they had gone in, late. He had seen the lights go out, had still sat there, knowing what they were doing inside in the darkness – 'It's my house,' Julia said firmly, 'and I can't sleep with the lights on,' – feeling the blood pound mercilessly in his ears.

It was useless calling Lisa. He tried that endlessly; and endlessly. 'Ms Naughton's residence,' replied the answering service.

They never noticed him. Not once.

# MISS DOYLE

Miss Doyle ate no dinner the night before the party.

Wong asked: 'What's the matter? Not hungry?' They had chicken fried crisply in peanut oil, boiled rice, and baby mushrooms. He had cooked it himself. He faced Miss Doyle across the kitchen table, mouth drooping like a fat, disappointed baby.

'I'm sorry, Wong. No. No, I guess not.'

'You worry too much,' Wong said. He wagged his head. 'Tomorrow, all soon be over.'

'I don't know,' Miss Doyle said nervously. 'I just don't know.'

'Of course all over,' Wong said firmly. 'Then nothing more to worry.' This afternoon he had wasted more than two hours driving around the town looking for rancid sturgeon's eggs, and had a crumpled fender to show for it, for at the eleventh hour Hope had decided to serve Greek hors d'oeuvres. Now there would be stuffed olives, dolmas, and taramasalata – a yellowish curdled mixture of sturgeon's eggs and olive oil which Wong thought not only looked disgusting but also smelled bad.

*Enough is enough*, he thought determinedly; *forget it.* So his appetite remained good. He finished his own dinner, and Miss Doyle's too, washing it all down with beer while Miss Doyle sat there, still nervous, twisting her handkerchief into a moist ball in her lap and pushing her cup of tea around the table in circular patterns.

*Getting old*, Wong thought sagely. *The poor old thing must be over seventy; and working for that old bat all her life sure is no picnic.*

*I must talk to Foxy*, Miss Doyle thought wretchedly, the helpless thoughts skittering through her mind like ferrets in a cage. *I must warn him. Must tell him –*

*What?*

For although the messages were coming to her thick and fast, they were couched as a formless urgency and oppressiveness. There was nothing she could tell him. Nothing he could understand and believe. Not that he ever had believed.

And to add to her difficulties, Fox was desperately in love and totally self-centred. He would never listen to her. He never had, so why should he now, of all times?

'Have some cheesecake,' Wong said, munching. 'It's great. Cherry . . . your favourite.'

Miss Doyle looked down at the cheesecake, covered with bright red cherry topping, but it only made her feel sick. She said: 'Thanks, Wong, but I guess not. I need some rest. I think I'll be getting to bed.'

'OK. Well, sleep well.' And Wong reached happily for another slice.

'Tomorrow's going to be a long day,' said Miss Doyle.

## PART FOUR

## MISS DOYLE

The day of Hope's birthday party dawned hot. It was the first day of what was to be nearly a week of weather inversion, where the fog never rolled in to cool the San Francisco peninsula, where the motionless air lay heavy and breathless, in the nineties and climbing, and the smog built up over the city in layers of saffron.

Hope was delighted; now there could be little lanterns in the garden and her guests could drink their champagne outside in the dusk. It would be so romantic.

Wong was sent off to Chinatown in the increasingly battered Cadillac to buy little lanterns.

Miss Veronica from the Scented Garden arrived, with several exhausted-looking girls, sweating in the baby-blue nylon smocks. There followed a predictable period of acrimonious wrangling while Miss Veronica organized the flowers and Hope instantly moved them.

One of the girl assistants burst into tears, and even Miss Veronica reached a plateau of frustration and snapped, 'You must remember, Mrs Fox, that we flower people are creative artists too.'

By 2.00 p.m., after Hope had reduced the whole house to a quivering shambles, Miss Doyle was at last able to persuade her to go upstairs and lie down in her darkened, cool bedroom. Only then was she able to pacify Miss Veronica and her helpers, and redirect Wong. Wong had been interrupted several times in cleaning the silver, which he had now abandoned. He had hung a dozen hideous paper lanterns in the trees and taken them down again. He had moved furniture from place to place while Hope tried to decide what looked best, and he had begun to set up the buffet three times. Although so far he had borne all these trials with a shrugging impassivity, even Wong, as Miss Doyle knew, had a breaking point which would arrive unheralded and quite irrevocably, when he would retire to his room with his horror comics and never come out again.

As usual, it all fell to her. But her back was broad and she had stood up to 40 years, give or take a few, of Hope Hartley. What was one more party; she could do it on her head.

But her head was aching so badly.

*It must be the heat*, thought Miss Doyle, taking two aspirin after breakfast.

But they did no good, and as the day progressed and the headache grew steadily worse, she knew there was no medicinal remedy in the world that could help her.

There was pressure building, up and up, until she thought her skull would burst with it, and as soon as the beautician arrived from Elizabeth Arden's to wreak professional miracles on Hope's ageing face, Miss Doyle abandoned the kitchen, where everything was now set up for the caterers, arriving at four; abandoned Miss Veronica, who was returning all the flowers to where they had been before Hope moved them; left Wong to finish the silver at last.

And went to see Fox.

## JULIA

Julia went shopping, downtown. Tonight she would meet Fox's family for the first time; she was nervous, and amused at her nervousness. Today being so hot, none of her dresses would do for the party. She needed a new dress; she wanted to look her best.

She still resolutely refused to think through this relationship with Fox, still content to drift along in her bubble of happiness, not caring where she was going. But it would be nice if Hope Hartley, Nancy and Elliott Millner thought she looked attractive.

Fox did not count; he would think she looked beautiful in a gunny sack. She smiled, contented.

In Magnorama there was a lime green chiffon with a split seam which was marked down to $50 from an original staggering $250. It was a designer dress, and it fitted so perfectly it could even have been designed for her. The split seam was a matter of a moment with a needle and thread; no more.

It would be perfect for this hot evening, and the cool colour against her newly acquired tan would be striking.

*It's a perfect day*, thought Julia.

## JOE

Joe followed Lisa. For once she was alone. Soon, now . . .

He waited under Macy's awning across the street while she shopped in Magnorama. He knew there was only one entrance; he could not miss her.

She came out, swinging a black and white checkered shopping bag, looking happy. She crossed the street, passing within a yard of him, not seeing him. She went into Macy's.

She wandered into Sportswear, fingering blouses, looking at slacks. She disappeared upstairs, riding the escalator to the second floor, where, riding right behind her, he saw her heading for the Junior Miss Department. Joe was conspicuous on the second floor, which was all women's clothing, so he loitered outside Junior Miss while salesgirls seemed to pour on him from all directions – 'Can I help you, sir?' – 'Looking for something special, sir?' – until in frustration he entered Junior Miss himself. But Lisa was not there. Junior Miss led directly into Shoes, which – oh God! – led to a separate exit on to Union Square.

Joe ran. Pushing rudely past incoming shoppers, shouldering aside salesgirls, elderly ladies, wrathful matrons, he exploded on to the street in time to see her – he was certain it was she – just turning the corner left on to Powell Street.

He ran on to Powell, leaping in front of a heavily loaded cable car to cross in time, while whistles blew and people shouted; running up O'Farrell, turning left again, and right, on to Ellis. Catching glimpses, as he rounded each corner, of Lisa just a block away; of a fall of dark blonde hair; a black and white shopping bag.

Until he stopped, panting, knowing he had lost her finally. He felt blown and dazed; he needed a drink.

And providentially, there was a bar right beside him. A neon martini glass with a flashing green neon olive signalling welcome. Cool darkness inside.

Lisa sat at the bar, toying with a drink which stood in front of her. She looked very young; too young to drink, far too young to do it in a bar. Her hair was lighter than he thought he remembered, and it was tied back in a blue Alice band now. She had also changed her clothes. The black and white checkered bag was nowhere to be seen.

Joe slid on to the empty stool beside her. The bar was more than three quarters empty; lunch hour was long over; happy hour not yet begun. Office workers still toiled at their desks, shoppers still shopped, tourists and conventioneers were spending their afternoons at the pursuits for which they had come to the city.

But Lisa was here; Joe could not believe his luck.

He smiled at her; ordered a bourbon and water.

She returned his smile just slightly; a small shy twitch of the lips before looking away.

Joe studied her discreetly from close range. She wore very little make-up. In the subdued light, her cheeks looked smooth and fresh; her ears like small pink shells. His breath came faster.

He said: 'Hi.'

She did not answer. She turned to look at him briefly, smiled noncommittally, her eyes flicking away to the empty eye of the television set hanging in the corner.

'Get you another?'

'Another drink?' She faced him. Her eyes were wide; huge eyes. Green-grey, beautiful. 'That's nice of you. I don't suppose I ought – '

Joe said expansively: 'So be a devil. Have one anyway. Keep me company; I hate to drink alone.'

After much persuasion, Lisa agreed, prettily, to a Scotch and water, tall, lots of ice. And, as usual, began to tell Joe about herself, as though he needed telling.

Her name was Lucia.

'Lucia? That's pretty. I like it.' Lucia – Lisa. Close. She was catching on. 'But I like Lisa better.'

'Lisa? But that's not —'

'Yes,' said Joe, his lips tight, 'Lisa.' He'd taken a lot today.

The blonde girl looked at him, smiling slightly and said gently: 'All right. You want me to be Lisa, I'll be Lisa.'

'About time,' Joe said. 'Let's get out of here.'

Lisa kept a worn little room in a hotel half a block away. In the room was a large bed with a faded pink rayon spread, a fibreboard dresser, bare save for a tasselled lamp, a night stand, and underfoot a heavily travelled and stained imitation Turkish rug. It was a dreadful little room.

But he was alone here with Lisa.

Outside, people shouted, the traffic roared and a fire engine wailed down on Market Street. It was very hot.

He would do what he had to, and nobody would hear . . .

He turned to her, triumphant. 'All right now, Lisa —'

But Lucia/Lisa, her face hardened, mouth, eyes, voice all different, looking 10 years older, was holding open her wallet for him to see the I.D. card, and the badge pinned inside.

'OK, Buster,' Lisa said in her different voice. 'Lieutenant Lucia Ascolini, Vice.'

'What?' Joe said faintly. 'But you can't —' His stomach contents rose sickeningly in his throat and the room darkened until all he could see were those eyes, which were not green-grey at all but brown, and he had never before thought brown eyes could look cold.

Then his head cleared. 'Jesus, lady, you're making a mistake. I didn't want a hooker. I —'

'No?' Lisa asked coldly.

'Oh Jesus, you fucking little cunt,' Joe moaned, 'let me out of here.' He gripped her by the shoulders, pushing past her, and Lisa cried crisply, 'Angelo!'

The door must not have been closed properly, for now it was open, and a man stood there. A large man. Dimly, Joe remembered seeing him in the bar. His face was dark olive and pitted over the nose; the mouth was very small; the eyes close-set black holes. Behind him there was — oh God! — another man, this one light haired, wearing a cheap brown suit which did not hang well.

Plainclothes cops. He had stumbled into a stake out. *Jesus Christ!*

'Sergeant Angelo Taylor, Mister. Vice Squad,' another badge, 'and Officer Ellis. We been watching you.'

Oh God oh sweet Jesus what could he do? His voice falsely hearty, Joe said, 'Listen, officer, there really has been a mistake here; I was taking the lady home, you know—' thinking how dumb that sounded, and remembering vaguely that he had read somewhere about Vice Squad sweeps in the tenderloin; how a hooker's john was as guilty now as the hooker herself. And, desperately: 'Couldn't we make some arrangement? Surely there's something I could—'

'Arrangement?' Sergeant Taylor's voice was frigid.

And Joe found himself, to his disgust, pleading about his wife and children, and his job and the number of people who would suffer if he was busted.

'What do you mean,' demanded Officer Ellis, 'by an arrangement?'

'You mean money?' Lucia asked. She had seen the 50-dollar bill in his wallet when he had paid for her drink, and other bills behind it.

'Oh yes,' Joe begged. 'Please. Look, here. I have a hundred—'

With hands that trembled he tore the wallet from the inner pocket of his jacket. 'Please. Maybe the Police Widows and Orphans Fund—'

Sergeant Taylor said, 'Ellis? What do you think?'

Lucia said, 'Ah, he's probably a first timer. Give him a break.'

'Well,' Officer Ellis shrugged, 'well maybe.' He took the wallet from Joe's hand. 'Let's just see what we got here.'

'Hey,' Joe cried, 'wait. You give that back. I'll . . . don't . . .' and lunged. Which was a mistake.

Pain exploded in his groin, so sickening he did not even feel the follow-up blow on the bridge of his nose. He lay prone on his stomach on the Turkish rug, which smelled of dust and cat's pee, retching, hearing from some faraway place Lucia's voice, as soft and alluring now as a fingernail rasping on a chalk board, saying, 'Thought the motherfucker was holding back.'

'That ain't his driver's licence,' he heard Sergeant Taylor say. 'Hey, mister, are you in trouble. Stolen driver's licence – '

'No, that's him,' Lucia said. 'He's wearing a rug, is all. He's the type – puts on a rug when he wants to get away from the wife and get laid. Hey, mister, you wearing a rug?'

'Jesus, who cares if he's wearing a fucking rug,' Angelo said.

'Let's get out of here,' said Ellis.

Then there were ungentle hands on his head; those sweet little girl hands, so soft, with the nails cut short and enamelled pink.

'Yep,' Lucia said briskly, 'wearing a rug, all right. OK, fellas, let's go.'

She tossed the wig on the floor, beside the prone, humiliated body of Joe Capelli, and the wallet, empty of cash, on to his back.

'Better get on back to the wife and those cute kiddies,' Lucia said mockingly, 'Mister Elliott Millner.'


## MISS DOYLE


*Doyly must be getting old*, Fox thought casually. Nothing else could explain this peculiar visit. She must, finally, be letting things get away from her, for how else to explain her tension and querulous anxiety, her insistence that he 'take care'. 'Foxy, there's evil close to you; I can feel it. Foxy, please – '

'Oh Doyly. Come on. Now relax.' He wanted to start dressing, he wanted to go over to Julia's; he had lost his evening shoes. 'Come on, now, Doyly. Sit down. Nothing's wrong.' *How could anything be wrong? Everything was perfect.*

'Oh Foxy – ' Miss Doyle fumbled through her mind, through the roaring pain of headache for yesterday's messages, now confused and lost in all the extraneous clutter of the day. 'Foxy, *please* listen to me – '

*There's nothing like Hope during a crisis to upset everybody*, Fox thought; *she would drive Jesus, Mohammed, and the*

*Mahatma Ghandi himself into the screaming nuthouse.* 'Come on, Doyly, put your feet up for a minute. Rest your bones. Listen, I'll watch out. I promise. When's the evil supposed to come?'

'I don't know,' Miss Doyle wailed. 'I never know when things are supposed to happen. I told you that, Foxy; it's never clear.' He was an artist. Why, then, did he have to be so sceptical? Why had he never believed it? 'It could be any time,' she urged with desperation, 'but I think it will be soon. I've got this terrible headache —'

'Poor Doyly. That's rotten.' He pushed her gently down into the pillows. 'Listen, I'll make you a cup of tea and get some aspirin. You'll feel better. I know what it must be like over there.'

He was so solid and calm.

It made Miss Doyle want to scream.


## ELLIOTT


Elliott Millner whimpered into the smelly Turkish rug, lying face down in his own vomit, while the circle of grinning faces surrounded him, Lisa right there in front in her tight green sweater with the purple orchid corsage still pinned to it though the petals were broken now and streaked with brown. Her long green eyes were malicious, and peal after peal of cruel laughter issued from her wide red mouth so that he could see the double row of perfect teeth, and the moist pink gums down to the pulpy redness of throat from where the laughter was welling.

She had led him to this. She had betrayed him.

And he had thought she had liked him; had found him interesting. How could he have been such a fool?

'Egon, your mother's dead. Where are you going?'
'Out.'
'How come out? Where?'
'I've got a date with Lisa Kreitser.'
'A date with Lisa Kreitser?'

'Yes, Dad. That's what I said. A date. With Lisa.' *Jesus, Dad, do you think I'd let anything stop me? I'm talking about Lisa. The most beautiful girl in the school. You have to be really Somebody to get a date with Lisa Kreitser.*

His father, amazingly, had been crying. Even though his mother was lying right there, dead, in the casket, Egon found it difficult to remember why he was crying. For ever since Lisa's best friend Helen had sat down next to him in the cafeteria yesterday, and begun talking with him just like he was anyone else, happening to mention that she had heard Lisa say how she really liked him, he had thought about little else and the squalid facts of his mother's death had paled to total insignificance.

She lay not eight feet away from him, a sad diminished little yellow monkey with prune-coloured lipstick on. The room was clean now, and smelled of disinfectant. All she awaited was the arrival of Mr Keller from the funeral parlour, the drab little ceremony at the Lutheran Church, and then the long ride out to the cemetery and eternal rest.

Egon did not pretend to understand why Lisa, with the long blonde hair, tilted green eyes, and a magnificent pair of boobs, should prefer him, Egon the Freak, over Jack Miller, but Helen had said, 'She thinks you look so *interesting.* One of the most interesting boys she's met.'

It was like a miracle.

'You're not going no place,' said his father.

'Yes, I am, Dad. Let me out of here.'

He had spent the whole day getting ready. He had shined his cracked black shoes until they gleamed; rubbed at all the spots on his best suit with spot remover, steamed and pressed the pants, washed and ironed his white shirt (too tight, and too short in the arms, but nobody would notice if he did not take his jacket off).

He had spent almost five dollars on a purple orchid tied up so prettily with mauve ribbons and gauze. He had stolen 15 dollars from the box on his mother's bureau where she kept housekeeping money; her dead eyes were closed, and his father was not noticing anything. He felt no guilt. Erna had never given him anything, not even a quarter for a goddamn soda. She sure owed him. And now he could take Lisa to the new Cary Grant/Doris Day movie, with a hamburger and shake after.

But after the movie (which for Egon passed as a bright, noisy blur far too quickly, for Lisa let him hold her hand all through, and once actually touch her knee), she said she wasn't hungry. 'Jeez,' Lisa said, switching her gum provocatively into her other cheek, 'who needs food? Why don't we go over to my place and just . . . uh . . . talk. I could fix us a real drink. My mom's gone out, you know. It'll just be us.'

'Uh . . . sure,' said Egon, thinking of the two of them alone in Lisa's living-room. In just half an hour or so, he would kiss Lisa. *Surely, oh God surely, she was going to let him kiss her . . .*

Inexorably, the movie in his head rolled on to the second reel.

'Let's have some bourbon,' Lisa was saying. 'I know where my mother keeps it.'

The room was slovenly – a sofa with a cracked leg, a coffee table bearing a heap of magazines stained with coffee rings – *Silver Screen, True Confessions, Secrets of the Stars* – and lamps with soiled, pink-fringed shades. Lisa would not let him turn on the overhead light. 'Who needs that? We'll be cosy, huh? With the lamp. Romantic.' It had a pink bulb, yet. It was dim and hard to see, but Lisa managed to find the bourbon bottle all right – 'Mom always hides it here. Dumb, huh?' – and two jelly glasses.

Then, 'It's real warm in here,' Lisa cooed into his neck. 'Don't you think it's real warm? Whyn't you take your jacket off?'

He did not want her to see his shirt. But Egon said 'Sure,' with the unfamiliar heat of the bourbon coursing through his body to his fingers, his toes, his brain. 'Why not?'

Lisa took off his jacket, laid it neatly on a chair, and began to unbutton his shirt. In shivering joy he felt her light fingers caress his naked chest, her warm moist tongue lick circles around his nipples. He leaned his head against the greasy back of the couch, eyes closed, feeling Lisa deftly undo the ugly black belt around his waist, and then . . .

Her fingers, long, strong and sensitive, closed on little Peter.

In convulsion, his body leaped and bourbon splashed into his lap.

'Oh my,' Lisa said laughing, 'I guess we'll have to take them off, now.'

And then he heard the noise. A small creak, and a shifting rustle, quickly stilled.

Lisa heard nothing. 'Noise? I didn't hear no noise. Listen, Mom's out, I'm telling you. There's nobody here. Don't *worry*.' And she began to lick at his ear. He forgot the noise.

In a minute Egon found himself nude except for his shoes and socks. Little Peter strained upwards, stiff as a pointing finger, and Lisa said: 'Stand up a minute, lover. Let me look at you. And I want to take this junk off. Oh, lover, are you ever ready –'

'Lisa,' Egon said, 'I love you. Oh I love you . . . love you . . .'

Then an explosion of light. The room lit up like a movie set (later he realized Lisa must have put 200-watt bulbs in every light save the small pink lamp) and pulsated with bluish magnesium flashes. Egon was blinded. He stood helpless, hands automatically trying to cover himself, hearing a babble of senseless sound.

Somebody screamed, 'Surprise!' and a male voice cried, 'Hey, looka the Freak. He kept his shoes and socks on, yet.'

And other voices. 'Hey, man, lookit that pecker.'

'What pecker? I don't see no pecker.'

'Shit man, that what he's holding on to there.'

'That ain't no pecker. That's a peanut.' Jack Miller.

'Shit, man, that must be the tiniest goddam pecker in Milwaukee.'

'Milwaukee? Shit. Try the fucking country, man.'

And, 'Hey, Freak, wanna see yourself?'

Stiff slippery paper thrust into his hand. His eyes, just beginning to adjust, able to make out a Polaroid photograph, his face twisted against the glare, mouth open, scrawny hairless body. And peeping out between his fingers, the smallest cock in the country . . .

Almost a quarter century later, Elliott Millner struggled to his feet and stood clinging to the shoddy bureau; inside his head, where Joe Capelli and Egon Milhausen merged like horrible Siamese twins, a dark, echoing pain.

Voices sneered or screamed. Lisa howled with derision.

Julia said: 'You fucking leave me alone.' And, 'I'm calling the police. Right now. I'm calling the police, you hear me?'

Fox said: 'The N.P. Club? Why ever *there*?'

Jack Miller said: 'You better not go staring after her no more, you hear me? She was getting real pissed off, the way you was staring.' He looked different now, with slighter figure, pointed chin, red-brown shaggy hair; but he was still Jack Miller, who would always be Somebody, who, of all people, could stand proud in the public urinal.

Who had taken Lisa from him.

Who was doing so now, and would again and again, always . . .

## JULIA

Fox said, stunned, 'You look . . . terrific. Just sensational.' Thinking how fatuous that sounded, and what an understatement.

If he had tried for years he would never have thought of that shade of green. It reflected in her eyes, which glinted like emeralds, and made her tanned skin glow with a sheen of copper. He wanted her at once. Never before had he felt such a flood of sheer lust. 'Jesus, I want you so badly, Julia,' he said helplessly, hearing her say, 'Later,' just as he had known she would.

He glowed as he looked at her. She told herself proudly: *I guess I still have something going, to make somebody look at me like that; tonight I feel beautiful. Fox wants me. He loves me. And we make a fantastic-looking couple; we really do look well together.*

She studied their reflection in the mirror on the back of the door. Fox was wearing a summer tuxedo 'The first time in six years. Mine didn't fit, of course; I had to rent this.' Julia thought he looked taller and older, in the stark black and white. They could now be about the same age, the years between them vanished; *not that I'm that much older anyway*, she thought, *only five or six years – that's nothing*, allowing herself for the first time a flicker of anticipation, a fleeting dream of perhaps a future with Fox . . .

Julia said hello gaily to Miss Doyle at the door, who looked frail and exhausted, and then, for the first time, came face-to-face with Hope. Hope Hartley Fox, posed in front of a backdrop of cascading flowers, looked every inch the movie star. Her hair had been restored to its original strawberry blonde and fell in graceful waves about her face. Together, the hairdresser and beauticians had done a wonderful job; Hope's face had been deep massaged, deep cleansed, and mud packed, after which a great many layers of cosmetics had been applied with skill. For once the mascara was not beaded on the eyelashes, which tonight were artificial and laid correctly on the lids. The rouge on her cheekbones was discreet and rightfully placed, and her nails had suddenly blossomed into long, coppery talons. Hope looked 15 years younger, but for this there was a penalty. She must keep her face utterly still lest the work of art crack into fragments.

'Wesley darling,' Hope said now, seeing the two of them through a blur of champagne. She kissed the air an inch from Fox's ear, and as usual he was tempted, hearing the unfamiliar 'Wesley' to turn his head to see whether somebody stood immediately behind him. 'And your friend . . . how nice,' Hope greeted Julia. Julia took the limp hand offered her and held it a moment, wondering whether to shake it, kiss it, or let it go. She let it go. It fell loosely to Hope's thigh. 'So nice,' Hope said again. 'So good of you to come.'

'It's very exciting meeting you, Mrs Fox,' Julia said. 'I've been looking forward to it so much.'

'That's sweet, dear,' Hope said glassily, lips parted in a careful grimace, and turned to greet the next guests.

Fox took two glasses of champagne from the tray which Wong instantly thrust under his nose. 'Thanks, Wong. How are you doing?'

'Pretty good, Foxy. Pretty good.'

'I'd like you to meet Julia. Julia, this is Mr Wong.'

Julia smiled. 'Hello.'

Wong beamed approval. He would now, Fox knew, dog their footsteps; Wong always took care of the people he liked at parties, at the expense of others who would be forced to wait a long time for a drink. 'Champagne OK, Foxy? Or Scotch? Anything you want, I go get it right away.'

'That's OK,' Fox said quickly. 'Thanks anyway; champagne's fine.'

Wong eased away between the guests, holding his tray firmly to his chest, seeking out his favourites and cleverly and unobtrusively ignoring General Casey, who was almost certainly drunk already, and Senator Welch and his hard-faced ambitious wife who always gushed at him. He contrived to have his back turned to Elliott Millner, just arrived, whom he despised.

'It's all so beautiful,' Julia said. 'Fox, look – there's the *Mayor*. Isn't that the Mayor?'

'I guess,' Fox said, without turning.

'*And* Senator Welch. I'm not used to this kind of high-powered company.'

'They stick to Mother like glue,' Fox said disdainfully. 'Always. With their hands out. Let's go get something to eat.'


## ELLIOTT


'Don't just stand there like an idiot,' Nancy said. 'I want a drink, Elliott, for God's sake go and get me a drink. I'm parched. Elliott, what's the matter with you?'

Elliott looked at her as though he did not know who she was.

'A drink, Elliott,' Nancy repeated. 'Have you gone deaf?' It was really time that Elliott had a checkup. He was getting so vague. And today, Rita Greenfield had called from the office to ask whether he would be coming in later; there were some letters to sign that had to go out. 'Rita, you have to be joking. Elliott went to the office hours ago. He has to be there.' And she had listened, unbelievingly, while Miss Greenfield told her that Elliott had not been in today at all. Or yesterday. Or the day before.

*Perhaps*, thought Nancy, *Elliott ought to go and see Dr Love, who was such a help with her own depressive state after Courtney was born. Perhaps Elliott was entering the mysterious zone of the male menopause. She would call Dr Love tomorrow, first thing, because this was becoming ridiculous. Why, he even forgot Mother's party tonight*, Nancy thought crossly, too hot, and uncomfortable in her too-tight girdle.

And he had still not got her a drink. She turned, to find Elliott staring through the archway, into the dining-room, eyes empty. 'Elliott?' Nancy said, touching his arm. 'Elliott!'

'She laughed at me, Mother. It was just like I knew it would be. She laughed at me. They all laughed at me, because of how you've made me be . . . it was your fault, Mother.'

He was looking down at that sad little body, face made up with cosmetics for the first time, now that she was dead.

His father stared at him, eyes hollows of pain. He was much shorter than Egon now, the famous belly hanging loosely, inadequate to hold up the sagging pants. He was no longer threatening; no longer able to yell, to punch, to bruise. 'You went out with a girl,' he rasped, 'with a girl, and your mother not even buried,' glaring with distaste at the lipstick smears on Egon's glistening white face, all over his shirt. 'You're no good,' Herman whispered hoarsely, his body trembling with rage. 'No damn good.'

'Give it to me,' Egon demanded, strong white teeth clenched. 'Give me my money.'

'No good . . .'

'Give it to me. Now. Or I'll fucking hit you, Dad.'

'It's for her funeral. It's all there is for her funeral.'

'So who gives a shit! What does she care?' Egon said brutally. 'She's dead.'

'You're filth,' Herman said, backing away, hands clinging to the belt under his shirt. 'She always tried so hard. For nothing. Thank God she'll never know – '

'Give it to me. It's mine.'

'Filth – '

'*Give me my money*,' Egon screamed, his voice cracking, eyes mad. 'I've *got* to have money.'

Flaccid arms raised defensively, Herman backed against the wall, against the little shelf where Erna's personal treasures still sat. Family photographs in heavy frames. A glass snowstorm, from Germany. Two plaster reproductions of Dresden shepherdesses.

Egon hit his father in the mouth. He felt the flesh split against his teeth. He watched the trickle of blood ooze down his father's chin, and licked at his own grazed knuckles.

Erna lay silent, sharp yellow nose pointed at the ceiling.

'Give me my money.'

'All right,' Herman said painfully, 'all right. I'll give it to you. Take it. But don't you never come back no more. You hear me? I don't never want to see you again. Not never . . .'

'Suits me,' Egon said impatiently, watching his father tremblingly heave up the plaid shirt, catching the faint sour smell from the unwashed greying underwear.

The money was warm from his father's body. He handled it with distaste.

'Get out,' Herman said tiredly. 'You got it. Now take it and get out.'

Egon moved to the door. He paused for a last look at his mother's painted face. 'She laughed at me, Mother . . .'

The swirl of guests eddying through the hallway and formal drawing-room had momentarily parted, leaving a clear trail across the oriental rug to the opposite wall, where Jack Miller stood in front of a huge, dark oil painting of an elderly man in nineteenth-century clothes. Jack's head was bent; he was talking animatedly, lips curved in a smile of total absorption, with Lisa.

He moved towards them, slowly. The room was a zoo cage filled with creatures with huge screeching mouths. Mouths which screeched with laughter. He heard his name called. In some distant part of his brain this was noted, that someone was trying to attract his attention, just as, moments earlier, he had been dimly aware of Nancy's voice, although not what she was saying.

'Well, Elliott, hi there, old buddy. Haven't seen you in a — Elliott? Hey, Ell, you feeling OK?'

The words reached him in pulsing waves of sound, and all Elliott could see was Lisa, the overpainted lips writhing back from the perfect white teeth, the cavernous mouth opening, and laughing, laughing . . .

Lisa –

'Elliott, for Christ's sake, look where you're going!'

And for pure survival, so as not to ruin everything, he forced his mind back, forcing himself outside the screaming cage, acknowledging friends, acquaintances, and even said: 'Hey, Fox. Good to see you. Who's your beautiful friend –'

Staring down at Julia's face, seeing Lisa's long fall of blonde hair, Lisa's long green eyes, and red, red mouth.

'Julia, I think you met Elliott once before.'

'Weren't introduced properly, though,' said Julia, smiling. 'It's nice to see you.'

Elliott smiled back at Julia. At Lisa. And the soft lighting hid his mad eyes. He said something to her and she answered. It must have been something funny he said back to her, for she laughed, and so did Jack.

'Try the fritatta,' cried a woman's voice behind him. 'It's utterly delicious.' While the hired help skilfully made room for the two dressed whole salmons in hollandaise; the baby potatoes; the salads; the tiny crusty vol-au-vents stuffed with creamed shrimp.

And Wong served champagne to his favourite people and the hired butler covered those Wong ignored. And Hope spilled wine right down the front of her gold and peach dress. And the Senator advanced on her chivalrously with a napkin. And the Senator's wife flashed all her teeth and some which weren't her own at the national president of the computer conglomerate and was utterly, utterly charming.


## JULIA


They were separated.

The party swirled around and between them, carrying them away in different eddies towards different parts of different rooms. Julia found herself backed up against the wall by a heavyset man with a deep magenta face who appeared to be some relation of Fox's dead father. Having demanded she tell him all about herself, he instantly set out on a long rambling personal anecdote from the early forties involving Hope Hartley, himself, a confusion of cars, and a wrong hotel room in San Diego, where Hope was making a personal appearance at a Navy entertainment.

Julia managed to escape after what she at last understood was the denouement, when she laughed uproariously and made a hasty retreat to the ladies' room upstairs.

Fox was nowhere to be seen.

## ELLIOTT

'Hey, Fox. Wait. I want to talk with you.'

Fox turned, pausing in his meandering search for Julia, who had vanished.

'It's personal,' said Elliott. 'Is there some place we could go, somewhere private?'

Fox frowned. 'Can't it wait? Listen, Ell, I'm sorry, but I–'

'No, it can't.' Elliott moved closer and lowered his voice. 'I have to talk to you about Julia.'

'What about Julia? Jesus, Ell–'

'We can't talk here. What about your father's office?'

'I suppose, but–' *Where the hell was Julia, anyway?*

Elliott said impatiently: 'Let's go then. Fox, I wouldn't force this on you if I didn't think it was important. Believe me.'

'It had better be good,' said Fox.

'It is,' said Elliott.

Down a passage, immediately before the swing doors to the kitchen, was Wesley Fox, Jr's old den. Elliott followed Fox down the passage, away from the clamour of the party save for the rushed journeyings of maids in black and white starched uniforms carrying platters of food.

Miss Doyle watched them leave from her station at the front door, and something pounded heavily inside her ribs. *Foxy*, she cried soundlessly, *don't. You mustn't go with him –*

Mrs Sydney Margolis had just passed her a white mink wrap. She held it in her hands a moment, sweat beading her forehead, before dropping it to the floor and turning to run.

'Well, I must say, really –' said Mrs Margolis.

Upstairs, Julia used the gleaming white and pink bathroom, sprayed more perfume behind her ears and between her breasts, retouched her make-up, which was still faultless. Then she wandered down the gracefully curving staircase, fingers trailing on the polished mahogany rail, wondering how it would be, living in a house like this.

Miss Doyle was moving through the hallway fast, her face grey and glistening. *My God*, Julia thought, *she must be ill. She's having another attack. Poor thing. She's old and she works so hard. She's probably exhausted.*

She followed Miss Doyle towards the kitchen, wondering whether she could help.


FOX


His father's den was more or less in the same state in which it had been on his death. Except for the pile of correspondence and general litter, the room was almost untouched. 'Like a museum,' Miss Doyle once said, 'Make that a shrine,' Hope snapped.

The beige and white wallpaper remained, as did the sensible mottled brown rug, the massive rolltop desk, and the leather-covered swivel chair and footrest. There was the same gold pen and pencil set, with the blotter and cut glass ink pot. The same photographs hung or stood in place, the same display of golf trophies, even the property department's Marine Corps dagger, presented to him by Hope's co-star after 'The Last of the Mighty', in 1941.

In the corner there was even the wicker dog's basket, with the same worn hairy bedding inside, where once Ghengis the black labrador had slept. Ghengis had died about the same time as his master, but Miss Doyle had never had the heart to dispose of the basket.

Nobody ever came in here. Certainly Fox never did. Never. Involuntarily, Elliott wrinkled his nose at the smell of musty neglect; but it was a very good room for his purpose. He closed the door quietly behind them. Nobody would come here to disturb him while he killed Jack . . .

'Christ, it's hot in here,' Fox said, leaning across the roll-top desk, trying to open a window which had not been opened for years. 'It's goddamn stifling in here.' Then, 'OK, Ell. What's on your mind? What's this about Julia?'

'Not Julia,' Elliot said. 'Her name's Lisa. Lisa Kreitser. She's a filthy little tramp. She – '

Lisa. 'Oh my *God!*' Fox spun around quickly, but not quickly enough because the gold-plated golf trophy still hit him a glancing blow across the neck and shoulder. He dropped, stunned, and lay spreadeagled awkwardly across the desk while the overhead light pulsated and wavered in his eyes, and he could do nothing, nothing at all. He watched Elliott's face looming over his, watched the trophy in his hand. *He's going to smash my head in,* Fox thought helplessly, willing his limbs to move, his voice to scream, anything but lie there useless, sliding slowly down the slope of the rolltop, feeling each curved slat moving under his shoulder blades. The harsh light looked like the sun through smog, with a dark ring around it.

'I've been waiting a long time for this, Jack,' Elliott said. 'A long, long time.'

Fox tried to concentrate, to will the dark circle from around the sun, but it was no good. The sun was fading, Elliott's voice came from farther and farther away, and at any moment another blow would smash him away forever.

'She's got to die,' Elliott said gently. 'She's got to learn.' The time lag between Elliott's fading voice and his own brain was enormous, whole moments before Fox realized that Elliott was talking about killing Julia. *Oh God. Julia –*

But then, disturbance. Another voice. Miss Doyle's voice. 'Elliott? Foxy? Elliott, what have you done? Elliott, are you *mad?* Now give that to me at once. I won't allow it, do you hear?' Speaking to Elliott as once she had spoken to him and Nancy as children, so long ago. 'You'll give that to me right this instant. I won't be having it, do you hear me?'

'Doyly – ' Fox croaked, 'Doyly, watch out – ' hearing a

T.C. – F

scuffle and a thin scream and Elliott's voice saying, 'Fuck
you, you old witch,' and a greyish blur in front of his eyes
which slowly resolved itself – far too slowly – into Miss Doyle's
thin figure slumped on the rug with threads of blood trickling
across her unconscious face. Elliott was gone.

Forcing his eyes to stay open, his mind to clear, Fox was
just able to move his body into his father's leather seat, where
he sat, quite still, his pounding head leaning against the head-
rest until, miraculously, he was able to move his hands. Both
of them, with his teeth clamped shut on his lip, unable to stop
a moaning whistle of pain. But the shoulder was not broken;
could not be broken, because he could move his fingers. He
sat blinking, eyes watering, forcing himself fully conscious.
He had to think. He had to help Doyly. And Julia – Elliott
was going to kill Julia.

He staggered for the door, stepping awkwardly over Miss
Doyle's prone body. She was alive, she was breathing, but
her colour was ghastly.

He leaned against the doorjamb, breathing hard, feeling
desperately sick, telling himself that all that was wrong with
him was a slight concussion; he'd be all right. He *had* to be
all right. And on into the hall, where he crashed full tilt
into one of the maids carrying a tray of glasses.

She snapped, 'For God's sake, look what you made me do,
you klutz.'

Their feet crunched on broken glass. Fox felt himself falling again and clasped her around the waist. He felt her
struggle against him as she tried to push him away. 'You
drunk idiot. Let me go.'

He sat down heavily among the smashed glasses, hearing
himself tell her from far away, 'I'm sorry. Hurt. Get Wong.'

'Get –' She stood quite still, staring at him. 'You're hurt?'

'Get Wong,' Fox said through his teeth. 'Jesus, woman,
do as I say. I'm Wesley Fox. Get Wong.'

'Oh,' said the maid, backing away, 'S – sorry, Mr Fox. I
didn't know . . . I . . .'

His head fell forward. The maid stood quite still, holding
her empty tray aslant, which dipped spilled champagne on to
her shoes, while the young man who called himself Wesley
Fox slumped at her feet among the mess. He was hurt. She
could see that now. There was blood on his face. It felt as

though somebody had punched her in the stomach. She could not breathe, suddenly. She dropped the tray on top of Fox and the glasses, and stumbled for the kitchen, trying to scream, but only making thin sounds – 'Ee – ee – ee – '

Hope Hartley, 21 and beautiful, wandered through Hearst's Castle at San Simeon. It was midnight. W. R. himself and Marion Davies had retired upstairs to the Gothic Library, and the guests were free to amuse themselves. Clark and Carole Lombard splashed in the gold-leaf indoor swimming pool; Hope smiled and waved to them, and saluted them with her champagne glass, but declined their invitation to join them. She passed on down long misty corridors; between phalanxes of marble pillars with gold-leaf capitals; through the mighty Casa Grande, where other guests chatted in smiling groups; past the longest refectory table in the world, flanked with suits of armour from the days of Agincourt. It had been – still was – a wonderful evening, with 'Wings of Glory' shown after dinner in the private projection theatre. Everyone had loved her in it. And now, dreamily beautiful, a poem in rose and gold, sipping champagne, reflected on all sides by Versailles mirrors, so lovely, so happy, she was suddenly assailed by unwelcome agitation.

An amazingly ugly woman tapped her arm, saying: 'Really, Hopey dear, I thought I had to say *something*. Just dropped it on the floor, my dear. I mean, *really* . . .' And from the other side, a small dumpy creature in a black and white uniform, half hysterical, was tugging at her, crying: 'Mrs Fox! Oh Mrs Fox! There's been an accident. Please, come quick.'

'Who the hell are you?' demanded Hope Hartley Fox, staring down at the maid nonplussed, while the magnificence of William Randolph Hearst's 'ranch' swirled and vaporized around her into dim confusion. 'What in hell's going on around here?'

The maid had not been able to find Wong. Instead, being hired for the evening and knowing no better, she returned with Hope, still disoriented, with the Senator trailing behind.

Hope stared petulantly down at the blurred outlines of Fox, lying in a heap of broken glass, and, as the Senator pushed open the door of the den, at Miss Doyle just inside. She said: 'Doyly. You dropped Mrs Margolis's fur.'

Miss Doyle stirred, very slightly. Fox crawled over to her, touched her face. She moaned and her eyelids twitched, then opened. She stared up at him, eyes unfocused. Hope said irritably: 'Doyly, for God's sake get up. What do you think you're doing, lying there? Are you drunk?'

Fox said: 'Please, Mother –'

The Senator, realizing belatedly through a fog of alcohol that something was wrong, said: 'Hopey, dear, I think –'

Miss Doyle said: 'Foxy. Come closer. Got to tell you. Waiting. Waiting for it to happen. You wouldn't listen –'

And then, mercifully, Wong was there. He took control decisively, having lived through it all, albeit vicariously, so many times. He dispersed the staff on errands – to call the police, the ambulance, the doctor, to get a blanket for Miss Doyle, who should not be moved, and snatching a bottle of Courvoisier from the reserve liquor cabinet in the pantry, forced the neck of the bottle between Fox's lips. Fox choked, swallowed, and gagged. 'It was Elliott,' he gasped. 'Wong, go find Julia. Bring her here. Please. Very important. And check Elliott's car. Check if it's gone. Hurry.'

'They went already,' Wong said.

'What do you mean? They went?'

'They left, out front. Elliott was holding on to Miss Julia like she'd had too much – like she wasn't feeling too good. I opened the door for them.'

Fox stared at him. 'You goddamn fool. She wasn't drunk. Oh my God, he must've – must've hit her, or –'

'Foxy. You mean Elliott –' Wong's eyes opened wide, bulging with horror and shame that he, of all people, should have made so gross a mistake. 'You mean *Elliott* did this? But he seemed . . . *normal*. You know. Kind of laughing. Said they were going out for a breath of air on the beach.'

'On the *beach*?' Of course – *I thought we'd go to the beach, Lisa*. 'You're *sure*?'

'What it sounded like.'

Fox's shoulders slumped. 'Now we just have to find out which beach.'

'Foxy, you've got to go after them,' Miss Doyle whispered.

'How? There're dozens of beaches –'

'Stinson,' Miss Doyle said faintly. 'Elliott always loved the beach house. He said once it reminded him of a . . . place. A . . . special place. It'll be where he'd take her.' Tears trickled across her temples, into her ears and the disarrayed grey hair. 'Foxy, go after them. You'll catch them. Nobody can drive like you, son.'

'No,' agreed Fox.

Behind him, Hope hissed in her breath.

Fox began to struggle to his feet. 'Doyly. You said "son". You mean, you're my –' Knowing at once, even through his pain and dizziness, how right it was. Realizing he had known since the day in art class, when Mrs Pospicil had asked, 'That your mother?'

'Of course she's your mother,' Hope snarled. 'The sneaking bitch. After him for years, just as though she could ever hope to get him. The lying slut.' She weaved on her feet.

The Senator looked confused.

Wong said: 'Foxy, get going.'

'. . . always after him, couldn't leave him alone. Then getting him so drunk he put it in her. Killing him.'

Fox stared down at Miss Doyle, his mind churning.

Wong looked from Hope, to Miss Doyle, to Fox. 'He's been gone already almost ten minutes. Foxy, take another pull of this brandy here. You not bleeding bad; you'll be OK. You get on after them. Foxy, this isn't the time –'

'No,' Fox said slowly, 'you're right. I'll think about it later.' He felt the resolution and strength sweep through his body with the brandy, and with the resolution came a dreadful anger. Elliott had taken Julia. Had tried to kill his mother. 'I'll get him,' said Fox.

'. . . said my husband, my Wesley, who had only ever loved me, had loved her. The goddamn liar. Just because he'd had a drink too many and it was too hot. And then he died . . . with her.' Hope's eyes filled, and tears coursed down her cheeks in murky black trails.

The Senator said: 'Now, Hopey dear . . .'

Fox said: 'Wong, call the Marin County Sheriff. Tell him you think Elliott might be headed for Stinson. Tell him a maroon Mercedes. Give him the licence number.'

'I loved him,' Miss Doyle said with defiance, 'which is

more than you ever did.'

Fox threaded his way out almost unnoticed to the court yard, where the Jaguar now stood alone.

'Mother, what's going on? Mother, I saw – Oh God! Wha a mess!' screamed Nancy, pink faced and flustered. 'Let m go and find Elliott. He'll take care of – What was it? A burglar? Has someone called the *police*?'

'. . . of course he never loved her. But she would have his *brat* . . . I offered to pay, to . . . she wouldn't listen , Goddamn Catholics.'

'Whose brat, Mother? What are you talking about?'

Miss Doyle's eyes closed.

'Get that woman out of here,' Hope snapped. 'I hate her.'

'Ambulance coming,' said Wong.

Limousines were double parked all down the block. He coul see a cluster of chauffeurs under a tree, smoking and gossip ing.

'Did anyone see – ' Fox stumbled towards the group. 'Di you see anyone leave from there?' He gestured towards the courtyard. 'They came out the front. A man, and a woman in green. In a maroon Mercedes – '

The drivers looked dispassionately at Fox, who stoo swaying in front of them, white ruffly shirt torn open, grip ping a bottle of cognac by the neck.

One man said: 'Must be one hell of a party in there.'

But another said: 'Couple came out. Sure. Looked lik the lady'd had too much. Gets to you, hot nights like this.'

'Oh Jesus,' Fox said 'Did you see which way they went?'

He took a long pull at the cognac and wiped his mouth on his sleeve. The drivers looked at one another.

One shook his head, sneezed, and reached for a large white handkerchief from his pocket. 'Goddamn acacias.'

'Ed's allergic to all kinds of trees,' another man said help fully. 'Round about this time of year. You should hear hin when he – '

'Did you see which way they *went*?' Fox was almost scream ing.

'Listen,' Ed said placidly, 'you settle down, buddy. You

take a cab on home and – '

'For God's sake,' Fox begged, 'you had to see where they went!'

The first driver shrugged. 'Downhill, I guess. Turned down Laguna.'

Ed sneezed again. 'That's right. Down Laguna.'

Hearing a sinister ringing sound start in his ears, Fox said: 'Thanks,' and weaved towards the Jaguar, still clutching his bottle.

He heard one of the drivers call, 'Hey, for Christ's sake, you can't *drive*! You'll fucking kill yourself, shape you're in,' but he did not look around.

And as he had expected and hoped, once seated in the Jaguar, with the familiar dials and levers around him, and his body enfolded and strapped into the bucket seat, his head miraculously cleared. He was at home.

The Jaguar's engine roared into life. Twin headlight beams raked through the soft lavender dusk. The chauffeurs gloomily watched Fox back precipitously out of his mother's courtyard, turn, and plunge away down Laguna Street 10 minutes after Elliott.

'He'll fucking kill himself,' muttered Ed.

At the bottom of Laguna ran Lombard Street, a glaring neon thoroughfare lined with motels, bars, restaurants and gas stations. The light hurt Fox's eyes with a jarring stab and momentary aching blindness, but he held the Jaguar steadily on its course, took the turn on the yellow, and cruised gently with the traffic at 25 m.p.h. through timed lights until reaching the beginning of the Golden Gate Bridge Freeway at Doyle Drive, where he began to open the car up.


## JULIA


'No, Lisa,' Elliott said calmly. 'He won't be coming after us. I hit him much too hard. Jack's dead.'

'Why?' Julia whispered. Her throat was aching and swollen where Elliott's fingers had reached around under her hair and squeezed the side of her neck at so precise a lethal point that she had blacked out in his arms. 'What are you doing this for? I never saw you before in my life –'

'Sitting in that car,' Elliott said, 'outside Hope's house. Waiting for him. I knew, then, he'd always take you away from me.'

*He's crazy*, Julia thought; *absolutely crazy*. Gently she massaged the side of her neck and swallowed, wondering what to do now. There had been no time for fear; she only felt a great numbing unreality, a conviction that this was not really happening.

But it was happening. And to her.

*Fox will get me out of this*, Julia thought trustingly; *Fox won't let him hurt me.*

The traffic was still heavy coming across the Golden Gate Bridge into the city. It was nine o'clock. The steady line of traffic to their left boomed past them with a rhythmic whap, whap, whap, but northbound traffic was light and Elliott held the Mercedes to a steady 55 m.p.h. Once across the bridge it was suddenly much darker, the highway opening out to four lanes, and the sparse traffic dispersing across them. The darkness was enhanced by the steep black cuttings culminating in the Waldo Grade tunnel. Elliott increased his speed slightly. Julia wondered whether there was some way she could attract attention. Surely there must be something she could do. She was recovered and able-bodied now, surely . . . They swept through the tunnel, and as though reading her mind, Elliott braked sharply and pulled into a turn-out, reaching for her with brutal, skilled hands as she flung herself at the door.

Her head fell forward; she felt light-headed and nauseated, temporarily paralysed while Elliott pulled the glove compartment open, dragged out a length of white cord and bound her wrists together. He was saying in a neutral voice, 'Can't have you jumping out at the first stop light, can we?'

Passing cars flashed by, picking out intermittent details in the Mercedes with each stab of light. The side of Elliott's head, his hair silvered; one ear; the clock on the dash; maps in the glove compartment; one long-fingered, powerful hand. 'I was in the Service you know,' Elliott continued, 'for four years. You didn't know that, did you, Lisa? I did real well; learned a lot. I could have been an unarmed combat instructor, you know. They said I had real talent.'

He doubled her over and bound her wrists to her ankles. 'Good with ropes, too. Came in useful, huh?' He examined his work critically, checking his knots.

He sat back and stared at her, then leaned over her, stroked her exposed right breast, pinched the nipple. 'I'd sure like to stop and play with you right now, Lisa,' he said with regret, 'but we'd better push on, you know. There'll be plenty of time . . . Don't worry about a thing, Lisa. I'm going to play with you real good. Like you never been played with before, not like you played with me – '

'Oh God, God,' Julia cried. 'Elliott, I'm not Lisa. My name is Julia Naughton. I've never played with you in my life. I don't know what you're talking about. Now, please, for God's sake, stop all this crazy stuff and let me go. You take me back right now, I won't say anything. Elliott, please. I've never done anything to you. Elliott!'

'I can't go back,' Elliott said reasonably. 'I killed Jack.'

Julia cried: 'And who in hell is Jack? D'you mean Fox? You killed Fox – '

'They're the same,' said Elliott, excitement rising as he looked at her as she lay there so awkwardly across the seat, bent knees under the dash, face against the door. Her dress had ridden up over her hips, almost to her waist. He stroked her naked flank, insinuating one hand between her thighs, fingers probing, pressing. Julia struggled helplessly, gagging in her revulsion, while cars sped by, indifferent.

'They'll think we're making out,' Elliott said, panting. 'And we are. Aren't we, Lisa? Making out. But it's going to be better, much better, later on. I promise.'

He withdrew his hand. They swung back on to the freeway, picked up speed, then slowed into a turn, passed through deeper darkness and reverberation, and Julia guessed Elliott had taken the Mill Valley Stinson Beach turn-off, driving under 101 North.

He drove decorously for a while then, not touching her. She felt the Mercedes climbing, up and up, and realized they were swinging up out of the Tamalpais Valley, around the same steep curving bends she had once travelled (it seemed so long ago now) with Fox. She had been a helpless prisoner then too.

Elliott swung over the top of the ridge then, passed the exit to Mt Tamalpais and the Panoramic Highway, and began the long swooping descent for Muir Beach.

*If he touches me just one more time I'll throw up*, Julia thought miserably.

## FOX

Far behind, Fox roared up the Waldo Grade at 100 m.p.h., slowing sharply into the tunnel in obedience to his instincts which had never failed him yet. Sure enough, the other side of the tunnel two Highway Patrol cars were pulled over to the side with two Corvettes between them, both with vivid racing stripes down their glossy sides. The policemen did not look up as Fox cruised decorously by at 60 m.p.h., and a quarter of a mile farther on he let the Jaguar out again, hearing the momentary flung-back echo as he shot under the freeway, weaving in and out of indignant motorists at high speed, and shooting the red light at the Tam Valley junction, cutting across the nose of a camper whose driver screamed obscenities at him and leaned on his horn. Then Fox was up and away, looping up the hillside as Elliott had done minutes earlier, pleading to God and any other deity there might be, in a continuous droning plea, 'Help me, God. Don't let me be too late, God. Please, God, let me catch him.' Not knowing that God had already paid a little attention, Elliott having wasted three precious minutes fondling Julia on the Waldo Grade.

The Jaguar, obedient to his urgings for more speed, held the road beautifully, hugging the shoulders and leaping forward on the rare stretches of straightaway. Fox drove by instinct, alert and strained, his concussion forced far back under the power of his will, adrenalin surging through his body along with the cognac.

As he flashed across the entrance to the Panoramic Highway, he could see twin paths of light ahead of him, twisting down the road perhaps two miles ahead, across the valley. 'Let it be Elliott,' breathed Fox aloud. 'Oh God, please let that be Elliott,' and gunned the Jaguar into a screeching, nerve-wrenching descent.

# ELLIOTT

He was not quite sure at what point he saw the headlights in his mirror, and was never quite sure how he knew it was Fox. For Fox (or Jack?) was dead. He had killed him. Had seen him lying there at his feet, dead for sure.

But those lights in the mirror were growing steadily, inexorably, brighter, and although Elliott told himself they could belong to any car in the Bay area, he knew, just the same, that they were on the Jaguar.

Julia heard him curse and mutter under his breath. Elliott stepped on the gas; the big car lurched, and she was flung painfully against the door.

'You'll kill us, you know,' she said calmly. 'How are you going to play with Lisa then?'

'You cockteasing bitch,' Elliott snapped as the Mercedes screeched around the next bend; there was a sudden sharp smell of scorched rubber. Julia said hopefully: 'What's the matter, Elliott? Someone after you? Seen something?'

'Shut your fucking mouth,' cried Elliott savagely, hunched forward, both hands gripping convulsively at the wheel. He could feel the sweat popping out down his spine. As he swung left and far too near the edge of the cliff, past the Green Gulch Ranch, he could see nothing behind him but darkness, but then, screaming into the next turn, the headlights were back, far closer than they had been before.

*It had to be Fox. No one else could drive like that. Christ, he was driving like a maniac. And if he was taking the turns that fast – and God only knew, the Jag, being so low slung could hold the road better than the Mercedes – what the fuck would he do when the road opened up and straightened as it would any minute now through Muir Beach, and then up the cliffside on to the ridge where it ran in a gentle switch-back for over a mile?*

Julia struggled in her seat, trying to raise her head above the level of the window, arching to see, hardly daring to hope. With a monumental heave of thighs and knees, helped as the Mercedes skidded around the final turn before the yellow streetlights of Muir Beach, she was able to get her hips and buttocks under her so that she crouched in a curled, half-sitting position, head resting against the window.

She saw people in the street, scattering, leaping for safety, as Elliott, instead of slowing, gunned the motor and charged at lunatic speed through the settlement. The sign marking the entrance to the state beach passed by her in a blur, then white picket fences around a livery stable. She could hear angry shouts and a scream fading behind them, and then, surely, above the noises of fury another noise; a deep throated echo of their own motor, fading periodically, then gathering again, louder surely, each time. *It's not true*, she told herself. *It can't be. Nobody could have caught us so quickly.* But then, faintly but quite definitely, she heard the remembered note of a powerful horn, an endless note – blurrp – blurrrp –

'It's Fox,' she told Elliott with satisfaction. 'He's not dead. He's going to catch you. You'll never get away from him now.'


## FOX


People stood thronged across the street, staring after the Mercedes through the layer of dust which swirled in the stifling air.

Fox leaned on his horn, praying nobody would be idiot enough to try to stop him, watching the people leap away from him, listening to angry shouts, only conscious of abstract relief as he swerved left across the creek that he had driven through Muir Beach without killing somebody.

He had lost sight of the car ahead. There were steep banks on each side of the road now, covered with bushes and spring flowers. It was a beautiful spot, particularly on a hot spring ight, but Fox did not notice the flowers or the shrubbery, ntent on the road ahead, waiting for the headlights in front of him to reappear. It must be Elliott, who would know by now that Fox was after him.

He took the final quarter-mile of the hill's flank, and oared up on to the ridge, screaming by a white Cadillac which rested half-in, half-out of the ditch. For a second, an elderly man wearing a narrow-brimmed hat was clearly caught in Fox's lights, turning, to mouth something through the closed window. He drove the poor old guy off the road. Fox thought, *I'm almost on him.* He saw the tail-lights of the Mercedes disappear around the rocky headland half a mile in front of him.

Fox drove like a demon, thanking everything that it was dark and he'd be able to see anything coming for miles. He was gaining on the Mercedes steadily now as Elliott's driving grew more erratic. He estimated perhaps another five or six turns.

Then he'd have him ...

## ELLIOTT

Elliott's hands were slippery; his knuckles white on the wheel, The car behind him was much closer. Only about four turns behind him now, but the road at this particular stretch was wilder with more and sharper bends than at any other spot. Steep grass-grown pasture sloped down on the right, ending 20 feet or so above the road in a rocky cliff face. To the left there was nothing ... nothing for several hundred feet in most places, and below, black snaggle-toothed rocks and the swirling, sucking boom of the Pacific breakers.

And then, just before the next turn, light was actually shining into the car from behind him. Elliott raised one arm across his eyes; the Jaguar's headlights on his rear-view mirror blinded him. For an instant he relaxed his foot on the gas. And then the Jaguar was only a yard behind him, its great lights glaring devil's eyes. Elliott screamed. He swung out to block Fox in his sudden forward surge, but Fox hung

on his tail, waiting his moment, cool, and as Elliott took the
next turn, badly, wheels scrabbling and burning, howling
for purchase on loose gravel, Fox was alongside.

The Jaguar had been built back in the early fifties when
cars were made to last. The heavy steel body, manoeuvred
by Fox like a weapon, forced the Mercedes off the pavement
on to the verge of loose shale and broken rock, and ground
it up against the cliff face with a dreadful rending of tor-
tured metal. Fox heard a muffled explosion as Elliott's front
right tyre burst; then both cars were at rest, the Mercedes
locked between the Jaguar and the cliff.

*If Julia hadn't been in the car*, Fox thought savagely, *he'd
have taken the Mercedes from the inside, forced Elliott over
the cliff and into the ocean*; now, trying not to injure or kill
Julia, he'd had to leave the Mercedes relatively undamaged
which meant that, presumably, unless there had been an incredibly lucky break, Elliott also was relatively undamaged
inside.

Although he would be trapped, of course; he would never
be able to get out. All four doors would be jammed . . .

But not the sun roof.

Elliott, unhurt and mad-eyed, came through the sun roof
with the speed of a pilot from an ejection seat. He held Fox's
father's Marine Corps dagger.

*Oh Jesus God*, thought Fox, and tilted the Courvoisier
down his throat for the last time, taking a final pull while
Elliott danced across the interlocking paths of headlights.

Fox flicked his lights off as Elliott hurled himself around
the left front fender of the Jaguar. Then on again. The flashing lights threw Elliott into momentary confusion to give
Fox a chance to brace his legs against his car door. As
Elliott leaped forward he thrust it violently open. The heavy
steel door caught Elliott square centre, knocking him backwards in a staggering, off-balance ran, feet scrambling, to fall
flat on his back among the rocks on the other side of the
highway.

In the passenger seat of the Mercedes, Julia writhed and
twisted, attempting to place a foot to either side of a piece
of sharp, buckled metal under the dash which could have
been Elliott's radio casing. The passenger door had twisted in-
wards upon her, the glove compartment was sprung, and a

shower of maps, a flashlight, a pair of gloves, a screwdriver, and other small objects littered the seat and the floor. She heard a rending of cloth as more of her skirt tore, unable to see what was happening outside but able to make guesses from the horrible sounds. Elliott's knots had been tied very professionally; her struggles only served to tighten them. The rope must be cut – she prayed that the twisted edge of metal would be sharp enough. She began an agonizingly slow, awkward, sawing motion with her feet.

Quite off balance, Elliott fell heavily; but once landed, rolled nimbly enough to one side as Fox leaped upon him to kick the knife from his hand. Fox's foot never connected. Elliott caught at him and twisted, using Fox's own momentum to lift his body from the ground. Fox was flung backwards, cracking his head again on the macadam surface of Highway 1.

He dragged himself up, trying to concentrate, attempting to draw on the memories of various bar-room tricks he had picked up himself in various sleazy backwaters of the world.

Elliott used his body well, but was stabbing badly with the knife. He was not a knife fighter; Fox could see he even held it wrong, with the blade sticking downwards. *Go for the knife*, Fox told himself; *go for the knife and he will think only of that; he will forget to protect his body* . . .

Elliott rushed him, stabbing. Fox ducked under his arm, nimble as light, feeling heat thread across his back but guessing the wound to be only a shallow scoring. Fox grabbed for Elliott's wrist, and as Elliott stabbed again, punched him brutally across the windpipe with a backhand swipe of his left hand, following it up, being too poorly positioned for a crotch kick, with a solid meaty blow into Elliott's gut. It sounded to Julia, still sawing, like a sack of wet cement falling on a stone floor.

Elliott was down, gagging, but still conscious and still gripping the knife. Fox knew this was his chance; he must go in after Elliott now; kick his face in; the advantage was all his; but he stood there, head lowered, feet as immobile as lead while the singing darkness closed upon him. It must have been that last blow to his head on the blacktop. He felt so dizzy and so exhausted . . .

In the Mercedes, Julia kicked one foot free. Surely she

could now get the other foot free too. She wrestled with knots and loops, unable to see what she did, cursing and crying in frustration.

Elliott was on his feet again, and coming for him. Fox rubbed at his face, trying to clear his brain, forcing himself to move, to act, to do something, and felt his foot hit something on the ground – a rock – and a useful size, too.

He stooped and picked it up, feeling as though he moved through water, as Elliott fell upon him again, lungs wheezing, grunting with pain, but too big, too strong, not nearly so badly hurt as Fox, who now saw him in double vision. Fox smashed the rock against Elliott's face. It gouged a bloody furrow across his forehead, which threw Elliott enough off balance so that the knife slashed Fox's right arm instead of his belly. But Fox knew then that he was finished.

His arm felt very hot, and suddenly his fingers were dead; he could not move them. Elliott's hand was across his throat, pressing his thumb and forefinger to either side under his ears, forcing him backwards across the hood of the Jaguar, in the same position as he had been less than an hour before lying over his father's rolltop desk.

Fox had time to think how unbelievably stupid he had been, seeing with a sudden chilling clarity that unless he had killed Elliott immediately with the car he had never had a chance. He had not even brought a weapon.

Now he was lost.

And Julia too . . .

Elliott's double face swam above him. It did not look mad at all; Elliott smiled at him and said: 'You shouldn't have taken Lisa away. You knew Lisa was mine . . .'

Fox felt almost comfortable. The pain had retreated into a blurry distance. His arm lay limply beside him, incapable, feeling nothing, as remote as somebody else's arm. Fox thought with detachment, *I'll never be able to draw again*; then, seeing the knife point above him – *How dumb. I'll never do anything again . . .*

Julia kicked her other foot free.

She could move. She could see. And even with no hands, she could do something with her legs.

And when she saw what was happening, she knew she

had all of two seconds in which to do it.

'Fox!' Julia screamed crazily, 'get up off your ass!' And leaned on the horn with all her might.

The sudden jarring noise was shocking.

Elliott jerked up his head, momentarily loosening his grip on Fox's throat.

Fox, in a last-ditch convulsive reflex, doubled his knees to his chest, and with a final reserve of strength dragged from beyond will-power, drove both feet into Elliott's crotch, thinking, in a detached corner of his mind, how lucky it was that he had not been able to find his proper evening shoes. Instead he wore a good pair of black Florsheims, with re-inforced toes . . . Elliott flailed backwards, with a shrill scream, and in the same fluid movement as the kick, Fox was off the hood of the Jaguar. He drove his left knee under Elliott's chin with a force which lifted him almost clear of the ground, snapping his head back, carrying him staggering backwards across the narrow highway to the rocks, and over, in apparent slow motion, slithering down on to a crumbling slope where there was nothing to hold him, nothing for 200 vertical feet, down to the ocean.

Fox crawled to the edge and peered over, half expecting to see Elliott's bleeding face appear once again, but he could see nothing. He could only hear a heavy sodden thudding as Elliott's body bounced from spur to rocky spur in a rattle of shale and stones, down to the black rocks and the boom-ing surf boiling palely below.

Julia freed her hands at last. She hoisted herself clumsily through the roof of the ruined Mercedes, crawled over the Jaguar, dropped to the ground where her knees instantly gave way underneath her.

*Oh come on now, come on, get moving*, she railed at her-self weakly. She forced herself to her feet, leaning against the Jaguar, bracing herself with her hands, taking long deep breaths, before she went to Fox.

He lay in a huddled heap, face down. Julia turned him over gently, supporting his head, cradling him in her arms like a child. His back was sodden with blood, and the white ruffly shirt was not white any more. It clung to Fox's ribs in wet tatters, stained dark, the stain spreading.

'Cold,' Fox said plaintively. 'I'm so cold.'

Then he said nothing else. He lay in her arms as still as death.

She did not know where or how badly he was hurt. She tried to find out without moving him too much. She had seen the back of his jacket, ripped from armpit to armpit, was soaking. The side of his head was matted with blood from a wicked lump and contusion behind his ear. Blood dripped from the ends of the fingers of his right hand. She did not know where to begin; what to do.

He might even be dying.

*Hell no*, Julia told herself, the dreadful idea bringing her strength, *he's not going to die.*

His back wound, she decided, was probably superficial. He had been slashed high across the shoulder blades; anything vital would have been protected by a shield of bone. His head was battered; he could have a fracture, even, but the blood was already clotting in his hair. There was little, anyway, that she could do about it.

But she could do something about his arm.

She searched, in sudden panic, for something to use as a tourniquet, remembering the cords Elliott had bound her with, running back to the car with a burst of desperation. She tied one of the cords around his upper arm, twisting it tight and tighter with Elliott's screwdriver for leverage, and was rewarded. The blood flow eased and no longer trickled between Fox's fingers.

He moaned very softly, his face a greasy white in the glare of the headlights.

And far away, so far as to be only a dim suggestion of sound, Julia thought she heard the wail of sirens.

It was Fox's first day for visitors.

Hope did not come because, under the supervision of Dr Birdwell and the staff on the third floor of the Home, she wandered continually through Hearst's Castle now, nodding her unkempt head, giggling to her friends, champagne glass in hand raised in an endless toast. She was 21 years old forever. Beautiful. Famous. With every man in the world in love with her. 'Such lovely flowers,' she told Nurse Gundry. 'Doyly, we'd better send Count do Carvalho a thank-you note. Would you see to it?' Then, 'Twelve dozen red roses! Bless the man,' Hope said, nodding her head like a mechanical doll, smiling with her withered lips.

Miss Doyle did not come because she was still immobilized, mending slowly from the heavy concussion and skull fracture.

Nancy did not come because she blamed Fox for everything. 'Why did he have to come home?' she demanded uselessly, time and again. 'Everything was fine before he came back. He just seemed to trigger something off.' And Wong, all his fantasies realized, was buying every newspaper in town to read the gory details and leaving them around so that Nancy too would see the screaming headlines: SOCIETY SEX MANIAC SLAIN.

'I don't understand,' Nancy said plaintively time and again, while the young detective tried patiently to align the dates of Elliott's absences from home on 'business dinners' with the strange allegations of rape and molestation which were now coming in, so far from half a dozen young women, all approximately 5 ft. 7 in., all with long, dark blonde hair, all of whom said, without exception: 'Yes, he called me Lisa. All the time.'

'It's not true,' Nancy moaned. 'It can't be true. It couldn't have been Elliott. Why would he do such dreadful things? Elliott had everything . . .'

And then there was that murdered girl – a disgustingly common little tramp called Francine Holub. She had been noticed in the bar talking for some time with a man with dark curly hair; Elliott's photograph, with dark curls added, was positively identified by the bartender. And in the back of Elliott's closet, tossed haphazardly among his tennis things after his confrontation with Lucia Ascolini, Vice, was the dark brown curly wig. Nancy stared at it with astonishment. 'I . . . that isn't – can't be Elliott's. I've never seen it before in my life. Unless he kept it at the office. But why ever should he do that?

'No,' Nancy reiterated once more, 'I didn't notice anything different about his behaviour. Only in the last few days he seemed to be growing a little vague and forgetful. I remember I thought he should have a checkup. I just thought he'd been working too hard. I just didn't know . . .'

And over and over again: 'Why did Fox have to come home?'

Mrs Pospicil was Fox's first visitor. She had besieged the nurses' station almost hourly for progress reports, and as soon as the ban was lifted for visitors other than close relatives, none of whom came, she burst into his room carrying gifts: a bunch of overripe purple grapes, a sticky bag of pastries, and a dark bottle of Hungarian Bulls Blood wine. 'That'll put the hair back on your chest,' Mrs Pospicil said with satisfaction. 'It used to be Mr Pospicil's favourite.'

Five minutes later, Julia arrived; and then Mr Brucker and Mr Bottarini.

Fox did not want to see anybody yet; not even Julia. He said listlessly: 'Oh my God, a party,' and closed his eyes, exhausted.

He understood he had been there almost a week, five and a half days, to be precise, floating in and out of consciousness, a barrier of anaesthetics and drugs guarding him, after the concussion had safely gone, from the pain of the reconstruction surgery on his arm, while darkness merged into light into dark, into soft meanderings and whirling dimness, punctuated by flashes of sick nightmare, when he screamed, silently impotent, at Elliott's bleeding face rising towards him over the rocks.

He lost track of time totally; the only measure of time was the frequency of the blurred face above the white uniform, and the clean-fingered hand holding the needle . . .

His right arm, his drawing arm, was a huge, immobile white slug. It lay beside him, stretched out on a board. It throbbed jarringly, and was supposed to be healing quite well. 'You can expect seventy-five per cent efficiency eventually,' the surgeon said, twinkling with cheerfulness. 'You're a very lucky boy.'

'That's great,' Fox muttered, indifferent.

Now he heard Julia say, 'I guess we'll never know who Lisa was.'

Fox said listlessly, 'Does it matter? Do you mind?'

Mrs Pospicil began to rummage in the bottom of her capacious purse for a corkscrew, while Julia answered, 'No. No, I guess not. Poor, sick man. But whoever she was, she must have looked like me. And like those other girls. He saw me when you took me to your house that time . . . that Wednesday I first went to class. He followed us back to my apartment. And then he followed me to the bar that night, wearing his wig. That was the night the calls started, late.'

Mrs Pospicil drew the cork from the Hungarian Bulls Blood with a sharp pop, and poured wine into five paper cups. She said to Julia, 'Stop that now, dear. Stop even thinking about it. It's over. You have things to look forward to now.'

She passed the wine around. It was solid and potent. *Too heavy*, thought Julia, *to drink in the morning.*

'And you, Foxy,' said Mrs Pospicil. 'A bottle of that every day will have you kicking at the ground. Then you can come on back to class. Even Ms Mendoza wants you back, Foxy. After all, you're a hero now. And everyone misses you. Even these crazy old men, here. Don't you, fellas?'

Mr Brucker and Mr Bottarini, a pair of ancient caryatids flanking her on the slippery naugahyde sofa, nodded their heads in unison.

'They haven't even thrown things at each other since you've been gone,' Mrs Pospicil said. 'It's been real dull, you might say. So you hurry on back, Foxy.'

Fox stared apathetically at his useless right arm, and said, 'Whatever for?'

'He just lies there,' Julia said later, 'like a zombie. He doesn't react to anything. He doesn't want anything. He doesn't even complain.'

'Quite normal,' said the doctor. 'Give him a chance.'

'But he's so passive. It's been a week now; surely, by now –'

'Now, Ms Naughton, listen to me. He lost a lot of blood. Suffered serious trauma. Has had some painful surgery. Believe me, this is all for the best. His mind doesn't want to handle it right now, so he's switched off, so to speak. It's Mother Nature's cure –'

'But he's not even trying!' Julia was close to tears. 'And he doesn't even really want to see me.' It had been a brutal week for her, of unsparing interviews and interrogation from police and news media, anguished phone calls from home, and frustrating dialogue with Fox's doctors and the hospital staff, all apparently in league with one another to keep her as much in the dark as possible.

'Yes, Mr Fox is doing as well as can be expected.'

'Mr Fox is resting comfortably.'

'Are you a relative? Then I'm sorry, Mr Fox cannot receive visitors yet, except for blood relatives.'

And now, Mother Nature's cure.

*Jesus God.*

Fox even greeted the news that his right arm might be permanently damaged with the composure of utter indifference, lying patiently in his hospital bed while the news wires buzzed like angry bees all across the country, for there was everything involved in the case that the media loved. Rape. Murder. Money. Movie stars. A spectacular car chase. And to top it all off, the heir to the Wesley Fox Empire was illegitimate.

'So I won't have any money after all,' Fox told Julia passively. 'Will you mind? I mean, now, I can't inherit –'

'No,' said Julia. 'No, I won't mind.'

'There'll be something, though,' Fox said. 'I mean, half the beach house is mine, free and clear. And Nancy won't dare take any action yet. Think of what people would say.' His mouth twisted wryly. 'I mean, me being a hero and all.'

'Don't worry about it,' said Julia.

'All right,' said Fox. 'If you say so. But I want to have something to offer you.'

Days before, as, very late, she finally climbed into bed exhausted, Julia's phone had rung. Her first thought was: 'Fox has died.' She did not wait for the answering service, and snatched the receiver off the cradle with hands that shook.

But it was not the hospital with news of Fox's death.

It was her husband. Gerry Naughton.

'Julie, love,' said Gerry.

'Oh,' said Julia, body melting with relief, 'hi, Gerry. How are you? And . . . Sarah?' Fox was alive. He was still alive . . . making it.

Sarah, it seemed, had gone. 'It was quite a mistake,' Gerry said. 'The second worst I ever made. The worst was leaving you in the first place.'

'Oh,' said Julia. 'It didn't turn out well, then. I'm sorry.'

'I want you to come back, Julie.'

Julia found herself saying: 'That's . . . uh . . . very thoughtful of you.'

'Reading about all of it . . . seeing you in that interview . . . God you're beautiful, Julie . . . made me realize how I'd have felt if he'd . . . I mean, if you'd been . . . Oh God, Julie, it made me feel sick. All of it.'

'Yes,' said Julia. 'Well, thank you. I appreciate it.' She wanted him to get off the phone so she could get to sleep.

'I guess I just found out too late how much I really love you. I mean, sometimes it takes something like this to make you understand.'

'I suppose,' said Julia.

'You know, Julie, for a while we had something so special going there.'

'For a while,' agreed Julia.

'I'll get on the first plane out in the morning. I can be in San Francisco by eleven in the morning. God, I miss you, Julie.'

'I don't think you ought to do that, Gerry,' Julia said evenly. 'I mean, coming out here. Fox is going into surgery tomorrow morning. I'll probably be at the hospital all day.'

'Well, later then. I'll make it an afternoon flight —'

'No, Gerry. Not even then.'

'But Julie, love, you don't understand. I love you. I want us to get back together again. To be married again.'

'I'm going to marry Fox.'

'It's been a nightmare without you. I want to . . . you're going to what?'

'Marry Wesley Fox. As soon as our divorce is final.'

Gerry began to bluster. 'But you can't do that. Jesus, Julie – you can't be serious. Wesley Fox is just a kid.'

'I'm serious,' said Julia.

'But Julie. I must see you.'

And Julie yawned, wondering whether Gerry could hear it in New York. She thought: *I'm damned if I'll see you.* And cynically: *And you won't get that exclusive interview out of me you want so badly, either.*

She said: 'Gerry, thanks for calling. But there's really no point in your coming to San Francisco.' She yawned again, a real jawcracker – he must have heard that one – and added: 'Sorry, but I guess I'm really tired. You know, it's been a very long day. Goodbye, Gerry.'

'Julie! Please –'

She hung up on him. It did not give her any particular pleasure. She had long ago stopped caring.


'Doyly . . . uh . . . I'm so glad. I'm really so glad. But it's going to be a little while, I'm afraid, before I get used to calling you Mother.'

'That's all right, dear.' Miss Doyle, bandaged still but ambulatory now, sat on the chair beside his bed, holding his left hand. 'Of course it's going to take some getting used to.'

Fox asked distantly, 'How . . . how are you feeling?'

'I've felt better,' Miss Doyle admitted, 'but I'm a tough old bird. I'll get by all right.'

'I wish it hadn't happened,' Fox said, 'you getting hurt. Doyly, I'm sorry. If I'd listened to you, maybe I'd have taken more care. It just seemed so –'

'Crazy,' said Miss Doyle. 'Sure, I understand. Seemed crazy to me, too.'

'Messages,' said Fox. 'If you hadn't come along then, I'd be –'

'But I did,' said Miss Doyle. 'I knew. Just in time.'

'Well, thanks,' Fox grinned wanly. 'Thanks . . . uh . . . Mother. And I'll always believe you from now on.'

'No need,' said Miss Doyle. 'There won't be any more messages. I don't need to protect you any more. You'll be OK now.'

'But I don't feel OK, Doyly. I keep thinking about him—about Elliott—and how I screwed everything up. I keep thinking how he's coming back up the cliff after me . . . and going to kill Julia . . . and I can't stop him.'

Miss Doyle said: 'He's gone. He'll never come back. I promise you, Foxy, you'll get over this.'

'I don't know how.'

'Because you have to,' said Miss Doyle. 'You're not a child any more, Foxy. You must.'

Fox leaned back against the pillows, exhausted. There was a silence between them.

Then, 'Is Mother . . . uh . . . Doyly . . . What am I supposed to call her now? Hope? What happened, afterwards? She hasn't been in to see me. Not that I want—'

'She won't be coming, either.'

Fox looked relieved.

'You won't have to see her again. Unless you want to.'

'I don't?'

'No point,' Miss Doyle said matter-of-factly. 'She's gone, Foxy. She'd never know you. But she's being very well looked after.'

'Oh,' said Fox, digesting the news slowly. Miss Doyle could see his tired brain struggling to understand. 'You mean, she's—'

'Yes.' Miss Doyle nodded. 'She's in the Leith-Hampton Home.'

'That's good.' Then, 'What I don't understand, Doyly—why did she say I was her son in the first place? It doesn't make any sense.'

'No, I guess it wouldn't,' Miss Doyle said slowly. 'Not to you. Not now. But it made sense then. Those were different times, then. You see, I wouldn't give you up. I wouldn't have an abortion, no matter how much money she offered me. I . . . I wanted the baby so badly. I loved your father, you see. I really loved him. For years—'

'But I still don't see why she—'

'Because she didn't dare have me go. She didn't trust me.
I knew everything about her, quite a lot of – well, rather
unsavoury things. I'd never have said anything, of course,
but she'd never believe that. And if I stayed, and said it was
your father's child, there would have been all the gossip
and the mud-slinging scandal. She wouldn't have that, either.'

'But . . . surely – '

'Those were different times, like I said. So she fixed everything. And everyone thought the baby was hers, except at the
hospital. All it took was money . . .'

'Oh,' said Fox.

In fact, nobody had thought it at all strange that Hope
should retire into seclusion after her husband's death, and
her reappearance 10 months later with a new baby was greeted
with a wave of sentimental approval. The baby had, of course,
been born to Miss Doyle in a highly discreet Santa Monica
nursing home, Hope restlessly occupying the room next
door, where the staff were accustomed to handling far more
bizarre situations. Not even Nancy guessed, although 'Nancy
never does notice anything about people,' Miss Doyle added
drily, 'apart from herself, that is. And after you were born,
of course, I stayed on. Business as usual.'

'Why?' Fox asked wearily.

'Hope needed me too badly. She never could take care of
herself. And she still didn't trust me.'

'It must have been hard.'

'It was hard,' Miss Doyle said, calm. 'We hated each other.
But there didn't seem much else to do.'

'No,' Fox said. 'I guess not – ' His hand slipped out of
hers; his eyelids drooped.

She sat still beside him, watching him, seeing his whole
body tense in a sharp, momentary spasm.

His eyes flicked open, wide and staring. 'Doyly! Doyly!
Elliott – '

She took his hand again. 'It's all right, Foxy. Elliott's gone.
You'll never see him again; he can never come back. Foxy,
promise you. I *know*. Now go to sleep.'

'I don't know,' Julia said fretfully. 'I just don't know. He
doesn't seem to care about anything.'

Miss Doyle was back in bed, flowers stacked around her

Many people had sent flowers and gifts; she too was a hero. She said: 'Pour me some lemon, would you, dear?'

'I know the doctors say it's normal,' Julia went on, 'but they don't know him. He was so strong and vital. It's not right. He doesn't seem to be getting any better.'

'No,' agreed Miss Doyle, and then, 'tell him about the car.'

'Doyly! No, I can't. I can't do that. It'd kill him, knowing about the car.'

'Rubbish,' said Miss Doyle. 'It'll be a shock for him, but he could use a shock, to bring him back to life. He's afraid —'

'You're serious? You really think I should?'

'Yes,' said Miss Doyle. 'Tell him.'

'I found us a house,' Julia said. 'It's on a hilltop in Berkeley. It's everything you said you wanted. Glass walls, view all round, and on stormy days the lady said the clouds are down below you.'

'Sounds all right,' said Fox. 'Buy it, if you like it.'

'And there's a little unit downstairs, separate, which I thought Miss D — your mother — might like.'

'Sounds great.'

'And then, Fox , , , there's a bit of bad news.' Julia swallowed.

'Oh?' said Fox, plucking listlessly at the sheet. 'What is it?' Yet again, last night, Elliott's battered face had risen from behind the rocks, and once again his crushed fingers settled on Fox's neck at strategic points of blood vessel and nerve. Fox was beyond worrying about mere bad news.

Julia said: 'The Jaguar's totalled.'

Fox blinked at her once, only half comprehending. Then, '*What?* What did you say?' He leaped convulsively in his bed, falling back with a grunt of frustration as pain coursed through his body. 'Fucking hell! Where is it?'

'Impounded right now,' Julia said. 'There'll have to be insurance claims when you're well enough. I don't know how you'll want to sort it all out. But I had the guy from British Motors look at it. Oh Fox, I'm so sorry. But you can get another one —'

'Another one! I can get another one —' Fox stared up at her from the bed, eyes flame-coloured in his white face.

'That car saved your goddamn life, you ungrateful bitch.'

'Fox, I know. I wish I didn't have to tell you.' And she thought warily: *It's working. He's certainly reacting. Doyly was right.*

Fox glared at her. 'All right,' he said dangerously, sitting up again, breathing heavily. 'Allgoddamnright. I'll show them who's totalled.' He dialled British Motor Cars with his left hand, then tucked the receiver under his chin, drumming hard fingers impatiently on his bed tray. 'Let me talk to Lenny,' he snapped.

Julia could hear whining sounds, screaming machinery. It seemed a long time before the voice of Lenny could be heard on the other end of the line.

Fox said accusingly: 'Was it *you* said my car was totalled?'

A muffled explanation; excuses.

'Now you listen good,' Fox said, voice quiet enough, but body vibrating with fury. 'I want that car back on the road in two weeks. Two weeks, no more. You hear me? Sure I'll be able to drive. What? Well, have them fly the fucking parts out. I don't care how much it costs. I want *that* car. Not another one. That one.'

He hung up with a crash and lay back among the pillows, breathing hard, triumphant.

Julia took his good hand in both of hers and held it tight. She said, 'Well, I guess you're feeling better. It won't take long now.'

Fox looked at her, eyes still fierce. 'You sure know how to lay it on a guy, don't you?'

'If that's what it takes.'

'Yes. Well . . .' The corners of his mouth lifted. 'You know, back there on the road, with . . . with Elliott . . .' Suddenly, for the first time, he was able to think about it; to talk about it – 'You shouted something at me.'

'Yes.'

'What was it?'

'I said something like: "Fox, get up off your ass." '

He grinned, for the first time in more than a week. 'OK. I guess I didn't need telling twice. You should try it some time, having someone battering your guts out and the lady you're supposed to be protecting yelling at you to get up off of your ass.'

Then, 'Julia, why don't you close that door. And it's awfully bright in here. Could you turn off the overhead light? Do you mind?'

'Of course I don't mind,' said Julia. 'Not at all.'

He was looking at her, flushed now, eyes bright. His left hand reached for the cord of the hospital pyjamas. 'And touch me. I want to feel you touching me. Get your little hand in here under the sheet, and touch me. Like that. Yes.' His eyes closed; his breathing quickened. 'I'm going to be all right, Julia. Oh my God, am I ever. That's great. That feels really good . . .'

'I can do better than that,' said Julia.

'Then do it,' said Fox.

She nestled her face into his lap.

He stroked gently at her hair. The pain in his arm was gone; everything was gone . . .

He lay in bed alone. It was late. Julia had turned out all the lights when she left, but the darkness did not trouble him any more. And he knew he could sleep now without seeing Elliott's face.

Fox smiled to himself in the darkness. He felt replete, his body happily and splendidly tired, and deep inside him stirred the beginnings of returning strength.

Before going to sleep, he drowsily summed up the profit and loss aspect of his new life, feeling the satisfaction of a child in maths class whose equation has suddenly, miraculously balanced. There was no escaping, of course, that it was Elliott's madness and death which had been the instrument of Fox's new beginning, although – *I would have worked things out eventually; I'm a survivor*, thought Fox. *Yes, I am.* Feeling now, seeping into the horror and guilt of having actually killed somebody deliberately, a slow pride that, driven as he had been to the final extremity of pain and exhaustion, he had still beaten Elliott.

Yet, without Elliott, Miss Doyle would not have called him 'son', the word which at one stroke had trimmed away all that was distasteful or unwanted from his life.

Now, he had no more responsibility towards Hope or Nancy beyond, hopefully, a disinterested kindness. They had lost all power to hurt him; Hope was now just sad and prematurely senile; Nancy, a shallow-minded, overweight, very ordinary woman of whom Fox did not expect to see a great deal in the future.

That gloomy great house was no longer his, either. Nor was the bulk of the Fox money. *Thank God, too,* thought Fox, who had dreaded the smothering idea of 10 million dollars. *Money isn't freedom; it's a goddamn millstone around the neck.*

*I am free,* he thought, slipping away at last into untroubled sleep, feeling so light he could imagine he floated, listing contentedly all the things he did have now; things which, little more than a month ago, he barely dared to dream about:

He had Julia.

He had a mother who loved him.

He had a house on a hilltop in Berkeley which he had never seen, where one looked out over clouds during a storm.

And when his arm recovered, which he would goddamn make sure it did, and soon, he had the beginnings of a career, for he was free to prove his own talent now, with nobody to say he had bought success.

And then, finally:

*He still had the Jaguar.*

# Ross Macdonald

'Classify him how you will, he is one of the best American novelists now operating . . . all he does is to keep on getting better.' *New York Times Book Review*. 'Ross Macdonald must be ranked high among American thriller-writers. His evocations of scenes and people are as sharp as those of Raymond Chandler.' *Times Literary Supplement*. 'Lew Archer is, by a long chalk, the best private eye in the business.' *Sunday Times*

THE BLUE HAMMER  80p
THE GOODBYE LOOK  75p
THE INSTANT ENEMY  70p
THE MOVING TARGET  70p
THE NAME IS ARCHER  70p
THE WAY SOME PEOPLE DIE  75p
THE WYCHERLY WOMAN  80p
THE ZEBRA-STRIPED HEARSE  80p

Fontana Paperbacks

# Fontana Paperbacks

Fontana is a leading paperback publisher of fiction and non-fiction, with authors ranging from Alistair MacLean, Agatha Christie and Desmond Bagley to Solzhenitsyn and Pasternak, from Gerald Durrell and Joy Adamson to the famous Modern Masters series.

In addition to a wide-ranging collection of internationally popular writers of fiction, Fontana also has an outstanding reputation for history, natural history, military history, psychology, psychiatry, politics, economics, religion and the social sciences.

All Fontana books are available at your bookshop or newsagent; or can be ordered direct. Just fill in the form and list the titles you want.

FONTANA BOOKS, Cash Sales Department, G.P.O. Box 29, Douglas, Isle of Man, British Isles. Please send purchase price, plus 8p per book. Customers outside the U.K. send purchase price, plus 10p per book. Cheque, postal or money order. No currency.

NAME (Block letters)

ADDRESS

37